THE NEW SON

IAIN MAITLAND

INKUBATOR
BOOKS

Published by Inkubator Books
www.inkubatorbooks.com

Copyright © 2024 by Iain Maitland

ISBN (eBook) 978-1-83756-356-2
ISBN (Paperback) 978-1-83756-357-9
ISBN (Hardback) 978-1-83756-358-6

For Tracey, Sophie, Georgia and Sophie.

PROLOGUE

Hi everyone! I'm Nina. 35. I live in Trimley St Martin with my partner, Gary, and his daughter, Chloe! I work in insurance administration in Ipswich.

I don't mention I lost my baby six weeks ago and am signed off work indefinitely, at least through this long, hot summer.

I sit looking at what I've written on my computer screen. I'm not certain what to put or how to phrase it. I want to sound happy and friendly. I've used exclamation marks, but wonder if maybe they seem a bit forced.

It's a Facebook page for mums and families in Felixstowe, the nearest local town here in Suffolk. I want to be part of the group. It's a sort of Mumsnet, I suppose, offering help and support to each other, possibly get-togethers too. I hope so. That would be nice.

I wanted a baby. So, so much. I think, at some stage, we will try again. But I feel so old. I know thirty-five is not, really. It gets harder to conceive though as you get towards forty.

My friends from school all seemed to have children in their early twenties. And, what with one thing and another, I have lost touch with them, even though most of us still live locally. We sometimes smile when passing each other in town. That's about it.

I do have friends, of course. At work. We go out now and then, for something to eat, and there is always a big do in early December. I should be back at work well before then. I don't have a best friend, though. Someone to talk to. I wish I did.

I remove the two exclamation marks and look again at what I've written, wondering how it might read to a stranger. Better, I think.

There is a knock at the front door. A simple tap-tap with the knocker. I am at the computer in a front bedroom – the box room – of my four-bed detached house and can stand up and lean forward at the window to see who it is.

I do it carefully, though – downstairs, the living room has horizontal blinds and thick curtains, so it's easier to look out without being seen. Up here, we just have curtains, so I can be seen by anyone looking upwards.

The porch roof obscures a full view. All I can really see are long legs in a pair of jeans and two feet in white trainers. An Amazon delivery driver, I'm guessing. He can leave whatever it is on the doorstep and take a photo as proof of delivery.

Gary, my partner, is my best friend, of course. He is what my parents would have called 'a man's man'. He was, still is, my window cleaner. We got talking one day six months or so ago when I was off work with anxiety. One thing led to another. We had not been together long when I fell pregnant. He then moved in with Chloe, from his previous marriage to Gemma. We are planning to marry next year. And to try for another baby after that. Gary wants to be a father to a boy. A 'mini-me', he says.

I have had a chequered love life, to be honest, going right back to my first boyfriend, Ryan, when I was fifteen. My parents, who were religious, did not approve of him and all that happened between us. I have had some tough times since. I don't want to think about them now. Or Ryan. I've never got over him, truth be told. The love of my life.

It is strange to think that Gary's daughter, Chloe, my stepdaughter I suppose, is not much older now, at sixteen, than I was when I was with Ryan. She seems much more grown-up than I was at that age. She is feisty. She misses her mum, who lives with a car sales executive over in Ipswich. Gary hates him, but tries to disguise it. He says I must cut Chloe some slack, and I do as far as I can. She hates me, though, because I am not her mother.

There is another tap-tap at the front door. I stand up and look down again and can see the same legs and feet of whoever it is waiting there.

I look around the close of eight houses, almost identical detached homes, and note there is no Amazon van, nor the postwoman's red trolley. I don't know who it is.

It's probably a teenager going door-to-door, selling tea towels and dusters and polish. I have had them here before. At the start of every summer, really. I will ignore him, and he will leave soon enough.

Going back to my computer screen, I am happy with what I have written so far. I think I will add another paragraph, though, and I sit back, thinking what to put. I want to sound nice and jolly more than anything else. I haven't been on social media for ever such a while. I must get back into the swing of things.

I don't want to appear sad or desperate, going back over my life and everything that has happened. I'm not a victim. I've always been able to keep the bad stuff deep down inside me. I'm my own worst enemy sometimes.

Hesitating for ever such a while, I then write:

It would be lovely to make new friends.

I read it three times and then press 'send' before I change my mind. I turn off the computer and head downstairs.

As I get to the bottom of the stairs, turning into the hallway, I jump in surprise. Through the frosted glass of the front door, I can see the outline of the teenager still standing there.

I had thought he had gone. I am irritated by his persistence. But then I think, maybe he needs to sell something to earn himself enough to eat and drink today. I will buy something. A tea towel or two.

I open the door and see him standing there, this slim boy in a black tee shirt, faded blue jeans and white trainers. He has fine, brown hair. There is something about this handsome, blue-eyed boy that ...

"Nina Bolitho?" he asks, in a clear and distinctive voice. He's from Essex, I can tell.

"Ye–" I answer, my voice cracking as I know in that instant. I just know.

"I'm Alex," he says. "Your son." He steps forward to catch me as I feel myself falling backwards.

PART I

THE RECKONING

1

MONDAY, 3 JULY, EARLY AFTERNOON

I lie here dazed on the sofa in the living room. I feel as though I have had some sort of funny turn. I am disoriented and dizzy.

It all comes rushing back. The teenager at my door. Alex. My beautiful son.

I struggle and sit up. He is in an armchair opposite, just sitting and watching me. He is a nice-looking boy – young man, really. I burst into tears and sit here shaking.

It's not like me, this. I am usually such a strong person. Try to be, anyway. I have carried the weight of the world on my shoulders for so long.

My parents forced me to give up my son for adoption just after he was born. I was sixteen. I have hated myself – and them – ever since. It has been my agonising secret all these years.

I wrote to him via social services – letters into the void – every year on his birthday and at Christmas in the hope that one day he'd somehow read them and come and find me. I don't know if that's how it happened. Or whether, when he turned eighteen, he accessed his birth and adoption records and tracked me down that way. No matter which, really – here he is.

I snuffle, wiping my eyes, nose and mouth with a handkerchief from the sleeve of my cardigan. I'm embarrassed that I can't pull myself together.

I look at him, a glance really, and he sits patiently, his face neither encouraging or discouraging. I expect he's feeling awkward, too. I want to speak, but the words won't yet come.

I'd like to get up and make a pot of tea, the fussing about with tea bags and cups and saucers and milk and sugar helping to calm my nerves. But the truth is, I don't think I could stand up without falling straight back down at the moment.

So we sit here, him seeming calm, me a complete and utter emotional wreck. And I am trying to think of what to say.

I don't know whether to be mundane – asking how he is, whether he has come far – or profound – *I'm so, so, sorry. I've been in torment every day and night since I was forced to give you up.* I calm myself, eventually preparing to speak. I blow my nose.

We then look at each other, properly this time, and he smiles and says, "Hello, you."

I laugh through my tears and reply, "Hello, you, too." He sits there, inclining his head slightly from side to side, as though umming and aahing, not sure whether to speak first, I think, or wait for me. I'm still dabbing my eyes, though. So he clears his throat, ready to say something.

I have imagined this reunion so many times in my head over the years that I am almost certain how it will go. A plaintive speech by him. A loving response by me. And then a long and tender embrace. Mother and son reunited at last – and for ever.

"My name's Alex ..." He stops, seeming uncertain, and then goes on. "Liam ... call me Liam." He hesitates, as though he's not sure what to call himself. "It was changed from Alex when I was adopted," he says matter-of-factly. "Liam Riley. I live with my parents in a village near Chelmsford ... Springham." I wince at the word 'parents' and then wonder, when I have driven by Chelmsford on the A12 to and from London now and then, how close he has been to me. A few minutes off the A12, that's all. I had imagined him far away up north. I don't know why.

I nod, struggling to keep more tears at bay. "That's good," I say, a silly response. I go to ask what his parents do, as my parents would have asked every young person, but decide not to. Other questions, 'What do you do?' and 'Are you at university?' seem equally unimportant in this momentous moment.

I have so many proper questions, so much I want to say. *What happened to you? Are you happy? Have you had a good life? I never wanted to give you up. I have thought about you every day. I love you.*

But, somehow, as we sit opposite each other, I cannot bring myself to ask either polite questions or more heartfelt ones. And so I sit here, calmer now, on and on, just looking at him with a silly expression on my face. I cannot take my eyes off him. I am transfixed. And frightened in a way. It's my dream come true. But I have no idea what's going to happen from here.

I WANT him to say more. I think he is waiting for me to offer a few words in response. I want to hear all about his life. Part of me – a huge part – wants him to have been happy. Idyllically so.

Yet a tiny part, deep down inside, tapping away quietly but persistently, wants there to have been sadness, too. I want to hear that he has missed me as much as I have yearned for him. So, finally, I say, "Tell me more."

He swallows, a dry mouth, and I realise I should have offered him a drink, at least a glass of water. No matter now. He begins to talk, in rehearsed, well-practised words.

"I was born ... Alexander James Bolitho and was adopted just after I was born. The birth mother was not able to look after me. My parents, Peter and Tracey, changed my name to Liam Peter Riley. They were not able to have children of their own."

I feel a sudden surge of unexpected anger that he talks of me – 'the birth mother' – as though I am not here, now, in front of him. And the comment that I was not able to look after him cuts deep. I think he has said these words many times before, perhaps to a therapist. His sentences sound coached.

"I was raised by loving parents in a caring home, and I had a happy childhood. I could not have asked for more. My dad works for the government, and Mum is a housewife. They love me," he adds, in an almost defiant voice. Another stab to my heart, with these well-rehearsed words

It is as if what he says – every phrase and word – is weighed and measured to hurt me the most. These are not the sentences of a teenager; it is as if he has been told to say these things.

"I did well at school and got top grades in all my GCSEs

and A-levels. I'm on a gap year. I have been offered a place to study at Oxford University from October. I've been spending this past year hitchhiking around Europe, and then back to this country, visiting different archaeological sites. I've just arrived in Felixstowe, and I'm at a bed and breakfast down near the amusements."

I have more questions. *What are they like, your adopted parents? Do you have other adopted brothers and sisters?* They swirl around my head. *What does your father do for the government? Do you know I love you too? That you have always been on my mind?* I do not ask any of them, not yet. He carries on speaking.

"My parents are wonderful; I could not have wished for a better childhood. It was perfect." He smiles, but does not look my way. "They have always been completely honest with me."

I cannot help but feel that, somehow, this is another dig at me. It makes no sense – I have never had the chance to be honest or otherwise with him! I believe, a growing realisation, that he perceives everything about them as perfect and everything about me as the opposite. *So why are you here!* I think angrily, but do not say anything.

"When I was eighteen, last year, they encouraged me to find my birth mother. 'To make peace'. I got a copy of my birth certificate showing me as Alexander James Bolitho. And you, Nina Jane Bolitho, as my birth mother."

The words 'to make peace' make me feel as though this is the end of a journey, that he can see me and move on, rather than the beginning of a journey, the two of us getting to know each other and being together for ever.

"It took a while to find you! But here I am. Mother!" He opens his arms wide, another rehearsed gesture, as if to beckon me across. But I stay put, something about it making me feel uncomfortable.

I look down, battling my emotions. I had expected something grand, almost melodramatic, at our first meeting. Words of love. Warm embraces. A lifelong bond. But his robotic sentences disappoint me, and his silly gesture makes me feel awkward. More than that, really. Much more. It feels like a physical blow has floored me. My hopes and dreams scattered far and wide, then stomped into the ground.

AND SO IT comes to me to speak, to tell him all about his conception, his birth, and how I was forced to give him up. And, somehow, I have to turn this situation around. Despite all the years in between, I have to tell him how much I have always loved him. And do so now. And always will.

I have had this speech in my mind these past nineteen years. I have said it out loud many times. And reworked it over time as he was getting older. I last said it aloud on his eighteenth birthday last year, the seventh of May at 6.23am, the time of his birth, sobbing out the words as I sat in the conservatory, doubled over in anguish.

Just as I am now, sitting in front of him, feeling broken and unable to speak, my head bowed, tears dripping onto the carpet. This should be the most joyous moment of my life, but my shaking body betrays me. I feel I am about to choke, unable to breathe, and I will slump forward and fall onto the carpet.

I glance up at a sudden movement. Alex – Liam, I must think of him as Liam – is getting up, ready to leave because I did not welcome his open arms. I search for the words to beg him to stay.

But he is not leaving, he is coming across the room, turning and sitting down next to me on the sofa, putting his arm around my shoulders.

And I lean into him, breathing in the clean, fresh scent of his aftershave, my head on his shoulder, and I am lost, totally lost forever, as he holds me tight.

Eventually, after endless minutes have passed and he has murmured so many times if I am okay, I ask him to fetch me a glass of water from the kitchen. And he does, handing it to me before sitting back in the armchair opposite. I take three long gulps before putting the glass on the coffee table. I wipe my eyes with my handkerchief and steady myself. I then say the words I have prepared these past nineteen years.

"I had you when I was sixteen. My ... my first boyfriend at school, Ryan ... he lived down the road in Trimley St Mary, towards Felixstowe. We were both fifteen and ..." I stumble to a halt before adding, "I lived here in the village of Trimley St Martin, but down a lane on the other side of the fields. My parents were very strict, just so religious. They died eighteen months or so ago, in a house fire, such a tragic accident ... they made me give you up for adoption."

Despite my years of preparation and rehearsing, the words tumble out of me haphazardly, the sentences in the wrong order, my brain now betraying me as much as my body. I stop and try to calm myself, gathering my breath to go on. I want to say how I hugged him and kissed his head and cheeks when he was born, and then he was gone so soon after, almost torn from my arms. I cannot say any of that without breaking down.

In my rehearsals and imaginings, my beautiful boy sits

invisible but adoring as I make my speech. I never imagined him as a living, breathing person.

Alex – Liam – is here in front of me again, his arms and legs crossed, his face calm. But odd movements, the slight twist of his head, the jerking of a foot, betray his true emotions.

I expect him to ask so many questions: *What was my father like? ... Did he look like me? ... What did his parents do? ... What were they like?* But he sits there watching me as I go on.

"I ..." And I wonder suddenly if I should mention how it was in the years that followed, my unyielding parents, the self-harm and, later, the attempts to take my own life.

I choose not to. I must be strong. "We stayed friends, Ryan and I, through GCSEs and A-levels, and then we went our separate ways." My little white lie, a kindness to my boy. Truth is, when I told Ryan I was pregnant, we talked first of running away together, but, as time passed, he kind of pulled away from me. Not turning up for dates. Not answering my calls. Ignoring me. Shattering my heart. I blamed his parents. They did not want him to be involved at all. As if it were just my fault.

My parents sent to me to an aunt's, my mother's sister in North Wales, to have my baby. She was even more devoutly religious, stricter, more intense, than my parents. I recall spending so much time on my knees on stone floors, praying for salvation.

By the time I returned, to my cold loveless home, Ryan was gone from the school. His family moved to Ipswich, and he did his GCSEs and A-levels there. I've seen him over the years in the streets when I am in Ipswich – so often that it is as though fate were pulling us together, or at least giving us the opportunity – but we never acknowledge each other let alone speak. I have tried to find out about him on social media, Instagram and so on over the years. But he is not there. I imagine he has a wife and children, though. Whilst I was on my own for so long, still missing him.

I summarise this briefly and superficially, making my last comments as upbeat as I can, not mentioning how I have suffered from anxiety and depression for years and have gone through boyfriends and jobs and friends searching for happiness. "I work in insurance ... boring! ... and I'm living with my partner, Gary, and his daughter, Chloe, and we're very happy," I lie. I reach out my arms. "Having you back makes my life complete."

As I get to my feet, he stands up with me, and we hug each other, and I sob into his neck, and it is such a precious moment.

I pull back, slightly and carefully, and look at him. He has Ryan's brown hair; that's about it. The rest of him, his features, his shape, is from me, I guess. I cannot see myself in him. I'm not sure parents really can. I breathe deeply and say, in a strong voice, "I love you."

And my heart breaks with joy as he leans forward and kisses me on the cheek and – at last – says the words I've longed to hear all these years: "I love you too."

2

MONDAY, 3 JULY, MID-AFTERNOON

I love my four-bed detached home. It's my sanctuary. Although it sounds big, it seems small and cosy to me. Downstairs, there is a little entrance hall, a cloakroom to the right side, leading to a living room to the left that goes all the way from the front to the back. I have a biggish kitchen and a dining area and a utilities section to the right.

Upstairs, there are two bedrooms at the front, the one Gary and I share, and the box room, my computer room. There is a bathroom with a bath and shower kind of in between the two front and the two back bedrooms. Chloe has a back bedroom. The other is a spare – it was going to be the baby's room. I don't like to go in there.

These bedrooms overlook a patio, a nice rectangular garden surrounded by fences and trees and a garage. Best of all – my favourite place – is the conservatory that's attached to the living room. It's rather grand and is my pride and joy. I love sitting there during the day when it's sunny, and sometimes at night I lean back, looking at the stars.

We are sitting, Liam and I, at the little table for two at the shady end of the conservatory. It is sometimes too hot to sit in here during the height of summer, but it is a cooler day today, and I prefer it to the kitchen. It's just that much nicer, calmer, really.

We have been relaxing and becoming more at ease with each other. We share a bottle of Coke Zero and bags of crisps and sweet and salty popcorn and Twiglets, too (which we both love). We're like a couple of teenage best mates bonding over likes and dislikes.

We go over all sorts of things, trying to discover what we have in common. We are finding we have more than I might have expected. We keep things light and jolly. It's best, I think, at this stage. Our conversation gets sillier and sillier.

"So." He has a sweet, soft voice. "Your favourite television programme is *Doctor Who*?"

I smile at him. It's not, really. I'm more your *Strictly Come Dancing* and *Dancing On Ice* type of person. But I have watched it with Gary, who is a big fan – although he loathes the new Doctor – and I like it well enough.

"Who are your favourite Doctors?" He laughs and goes straight on without hesitating. "Mine are ... one, David Tennant ... Ncuti ... and Jodie Whittaker. I liked Matt Smith, too. I didn't like Peter Capaldi. Too old, and he reminded me of someone at the ..." He stops, and his face clouds over, mentioning his school I guess, and then clears quickly back to his untroubled self. He smiles reassuringly at me.

"Um," I say, thinking that Gary would be going on at this point about the merits of what he'd call 'Classic Who' and 'New Who' and the differences between Tom Baker and David Tennant. And how two of the original Doctors, in his opinion, were simply 'awful'. I reply, "Jodie ... Ncuti ... David

Tennant." We smile, and he raises his glass, and I do too; we chink them together. We are so happy now.

Even so, as we chat on and on about this and that, time passes, and I start to feel a growing sense of tension inside me. The clock on the wall ticks further beyond 3.00pm.

Alex – Liam – has always been my secret. Gary and Chloe know nothing of him. Nobody does. Except Ryan. And Chloe will be leaving school shortly and back home in twenty minutes.

I know that Liam has to be gone by then. That they cannot meet. Not yet. I need to tell Gary at the right moment, when he is in a good mood, the very best of moods. Liam shows no sign of leaving. I have to say something now.

"I, ah ..." I reach out and hold Liam's hands across the table. "Gary, my partner, won't be home until after five o'clock ... I'd invite you to stay for tea at six, but, ah, not today ... he doesn't ... I haven't ..." My words tail away.

Liam smiles at me, this sensitive soul, my kindred spirit, and seems to know what I am telling him. "What will you say?" he asks gently. I think, somehow, he senses I am not happy in some way.

I want to reply that I have lost a baby recently, things aren't so good with Gary, not really, and I don't know what to say to him. We're not soulmates. Gary would despise me for having a secret son – and he would hate Liam and be so consumed with jealousy that it would destroy everything.

Instead, I sidestep this conversation by saying, "His daughter, Chloe, will be in from school soon, and she'll be, ah, well, she'll like you ... quite a bit ... but I'm not sure how I'll explain you."

He pulls a face, suggesting he'd not be interested in her,

girls at all, really. I get that vibe. And I am cool with it. Then, suddenly, he says it's time to go.

I look at him uncertainly, worried for a moment that he has taken offence. Gary would be livid if I ever made him feel he was less than the most important thing in the world to me. But Liam is not like that. He hugs me again, so, so warmly, and asks for my phone and the passcode to get into it, which I give him. He sends a text to himself, so he has my number, and puts his phone number into my contacts list so I have his. "I've just put 'L'," he says, smiling wryly at me. I smile back. We both know what's what, without saying.

"Oh, I almost forgot ..." He rummages in his pocket and takes out a knife with a wooden handle and unfolds a longish blade. He notices that I step back involuntarily, and laughs, saying, "It's my whittling knife ... here, this is for you."

He hands me a little piece of wood. Twisting and turning it, I can see it is a bird. I'm not sure what, maybe a sparrow or a robin, but it's pretty; he must be clever to have made it.

I will put it on the windowsill behind the computer in the box room later – where I will see it, but nobody else will, and I won't be asked awkward questions about where I got it.

I tell Liam I love it, but that he should put the knife away and keep it out of sight, as it may get him in trouble. He nods, folding it over and tucking it out of sight. I lean forward and kiss him on the cheek.

And so, a minute or two later, I watch Liam walking across the close and up towards the main road, his rucksack on his back. He is as slight as Ryan. His hair is similar to how Ryan's was but has a kind of pudding-basin cut. I like it. Gary has a short haircut, too short for his round, red face and almost horizontal ears.

I am calmer now, happier, almost bursting with joy, actually, knowing that Liam is in my life. I hope that Gary will welcome him into our family and home, perhaps even to live. I will have to explain things carefully to him. I don't know how, to be honest. Gary is a powder keg at the best of times. He's never exploded yet. Not with me, anyway. I've been careful to avoid it happening. It would be the end of us if he hit me; I know that for a fact.

As Liam gets to the top of the close, ready to turn on to the main road, Chloe walks by in her school uniform. With her bleached hair and hard face and shorter-than-it-should-be skirt, she looks too old to be dressed like this. She is a sad, middle-aged man's daydream. And as often as not, a nightmare for me, to be honest. Her moods change with the breeze. I wonder how she will be with me today. I suspect I will have to bite my tongue, as I always have to do.

———————

I sit on the sofa, pretending to read a glossy magazine, as Chloe opens the front door and comes in. I feel exhausted – it has been such a rollercoaster of emotions – but I also have a sense of peace and deep joy. I'd like to hug myself.

Chloe kicks off her shoes in the hallway and walks into the living room, dumping her rucksack at the bottom of the stairs. I look at her, smiling, as she walks on into the kitchen. She barely glances at me.

I hear a cupboard being opened, a tap running, and then the clink of a glass being put on the draining board. She comes back into the living room. I sit up and smile, hoping we might, for once, have an agreeable conversation.

"The trip." She looks at me as if I am supposed to know

what she is talking about. "Next week. Mrs Taylor was on at me at break time. I told her we were on benefits. Thanks a lot."

She stares at me with such a mix of ignorance and anger that I have, as ever, to swallow a sharp retort. I don't know what she is talking about. And we're certainly not on benefits. I look back at her blankly. It seems to annoy her even more. She shouts at me, "The trip! To London. You didn't pay it."

I don't think she's ever mentioned any trip to me. To say that though would just enrage her more. And I am damned well not going to apologise to her – to grovel – which is what she wants. I smile and shrug. It makes matters worse, as whatever I said and did would do.

"Fuck's sake," she spits, turning to go up the stairs. "I'll have to ask Dad to do it ... properly," she adds for good measure, and then she is gone, storming up the staircase, opening and slamming doors. Her bedroom had new carpet fitted last month, and Gary has yet to sand off the bottom of the door so that it doesn't jam into the carpet when being opened and closed. I laugh to myself, imagining Chloe trying to slam it shut a centimetre at a time.

Gary works as a window cleaner, which he believes is beneath him, and does not earn as much money as he thinks he should do. He has issues with self-esteem, and I work hard to make him feel good about himself. Money – his earnings – has also been an ongoing issue since we got together. I suspect that many of his financial issues come from his past, when he drank and gambled heavily when he was married to Chloe's mother. He's promised he's put that behind him. I doubt it, though.

I wonder sometimes, in truth, if Gary and Chloe are with

me because I am, if not rich, at least comfortably off. The death of my parents has meant that I have bought and own my house and have money put by and can afford, if not to stop work, to at least not have to be a slave to working Monday to Friday, nine to five, as I was doing. I could live off my savings for a year or two if I had to. Before their tragic deaths, I had rooms in an old Victorian house in Felixstowe town centre. I resent the fact I am now expected to pay for almost everything, including school trips! Gary needs to at least pay his way.

Then Chloe is clumping her way down the stairs again. I dip my head, flicking through the magazine, wanting to avoid an argument that will send my mood plummeting. Hopefully, she's just on her way to the kitchen to grab some crisps and bread, as she often does for a crisps sandwich.

During the early days of her living here, I said, in a jolly, friendly way, "Don't eat too much; you'll spoil your appetite for tea!"

She muttered, "Fuck's sake," (something of a catch-phrase) under her breath. I have not commented on what-ever she does since.

Gary said I should not take any notice of it – the swearing – unless she's swearing at me. And that there is a difference between swearing in conversation and swearing at someone. Also, everyone swears these days – except me – and I should not be so prudish.

Chloe now stands opposite me, a bag of crisps in her hand, at the foot of the stairs. She picks up her rucksack, which she left there. I look at her, expecting her to stare at me ('Wha-a-a-at?') before heading back up the staircase. But she looks back almost amicably.

"What's for tea?" she asks. I tell her it's spaghetti, which she likes, and she grunts agreeably enough before turning to go.

"If you message me the details, I'll pay for your trip before your dad gets in."

She grunts again, which I take to mean 'okay', and off she goes. I get the sense that, for now at least, we are at peace. It may all change by teatime.

———————

JUST AFTER SIX, the three of us, Gary, Chloe and I, are sitting around the table in the kitchen, eating spaghetti Bolognese, which was quick and easy to make even with my mind on Alex. Liam, I must think of him as Liam. I served up on the dot of six, the two of them waiting impatiently. Both are out of sorts. Neither said anything, but I could tell from the way they were sitting and holding their cutlery. They were both edgy.

Gary has had a bad day at work – as he came through the front door, he said one of his customers had not paid him, and another cannot afford him anymore. He made it sound as though it was my fault, and that I should do something about it. I made sympathetic noises, but did not ask him anything about them. I didn't want to anger him even more. He now has his head dipped, shovelling spaghetti, and barely speaks beyond, "Pass the salt," followed, when neither of us respond, by, "Please." In a tense voice.

Chloe, ever unpredictable, is hardly speaking either. She alternates between huffing and throwing back her hair with cutting her spaghetti into ever smaller pieces before putting them into her mouth. When she first moved in with Gary and ate spaghetti here for tea that first day, a mouthful of it hung down to her chin as she tried to suck it all up. It was as though she had never eaten spaghetti before. I laughed, not in an unkind way, but she took offence, as she does with so many things. It set the tone for our relationship ever since.

I am happy to sit quietly, eating spaghetti and drinking orange squash and daydreaming about Liam. I don't want to think about Gary and Chloe much right now. They cast shadows on my sunlight.

The start of our meeting was not as perfect as I had imagined – I was in such a state of shock – but it ended so well, and I have such high hopes for the future.

And I am excited, thinking of the text I will write to him later this evening, suggesting lunch soon, perhaps even tomorrow. I just need to put things on track with Gary.

"Well?" says Gary suddenly, in a slightly raised voice. Chloe glances at him, at me, and then carries on eating, her head down. I smile sweetly at him, gesturing that my mouth is full and I will reply in a moment. He waits impatiently. Truth is, I did not catch what he said. I am thinking what to say when he repeats the question: "How was your day?" As simple as that.

I know, of course, that I need to tell Gary about Liam; the sooner, the better. The longer I wait, the harder it will be. But now is not the time to say, almost in passing, "Oh, by the way, I met my nineteen-year-old son today; I've not seen him since he was born. I'm sorry I never mentioned him to you." Gary likes to know about everything that's going on. He shares his opinions. He will be so horribly upset about this – I need to do it carefully, both in terms of timing and how I put it to him.

"Good," I answer, patting my tummy gently. "I've been taking it easy."

He nods and smiles at last and reaches across to pat my tummy, too. "That's my girl," he says, and then, noticing Chloe's sulky look, he pats her on the shoulder and adds, "My girls." He makes it sound creepy. Chloe smiles warmly enough. I wonder if I am too old, at thirty-five, to be 'a girl,' but do not say anything. Gary is an old-fashioned man and set in his ways and views. "You've got to be careful ... take good care of yourself so we can, you know ... soon." Try for another baby is what he means. I keep my face as neutral as I can.

As I eat and drink, I wonder what I will text to Liam later, when I am lying in my lovely, warm bath, having half an hour to myself.

'Nice to see you, Liam! Would you like to have lunch tomorrow? My treat!' Too many exclamation marks. I won't use them. They make me sound like an overexcited schoolgirl.

I wonder what I should call myself. I'd love him to call me 'Mum' one day. I must be careful. For now, I will sign off with 'N x'.

Chloe is talking as I focus again on the here and now. She is asking Gary if she can stay with her mum and her mum's new man over in Ipswich this weekend. There's something on in a club in town on Saturday night. I can sense Gary growing tense. He is so angry with Gemma, his ex, who said some shocking things about him when they split up. Gary also loathes this new man, this 'shiny-suited salesman' as he calls him. I think he earns a lot of money. There is so much suppressed anger, so close to the surface.

Gary tries his best not to say anything negative about either of them to Chloe. He wants to be a good father, the best that he can be. I know he does not wish her to go there, though, with Gemma's poison dripping in Chloe's ear. The truth is that Chloe is here with her dad because Gemma does not really want her getting in the way of her 'out and about' lifestyle. So I try to help, saying that the event is 'for over eighteens only and will be full of drugs'. There is a silence. Gary looks furious. I should not have interrupted what he was about to say.

Chloe shoots me such a look. She does not say anything, but I can see it all written in her face, *Mind your own business, you stupid fat cow.* She has said much the same to me, early on, just between the two of us. I have always been conscious of my weight. Once, Chloe said it as Gary came into the house, and he overheard her. He gave her such a telling-off that she is not so verbally nasty to me now. Instead, she just gives me the looks and the mutterings, and we both know what she is thinking.

But then her expression changes, and she smiles and speaks: "Who was that guy I saw leaving the house when I came back from school?"

I almost gasp; I did not think she had seen Liam. I do not react as quickly as I should do. I swallow and then take a sip of orange squash. I can sense Gary looking at me; I don't even need to glance his way.

"You seemed really upset when I got in."

I swallow again, thinking I had acted normally when she arrived. I shake my head, not sure what to say. I need to tell them about Liam now, but how can I, like this? I dare not. The fallout would be immediate and far-reaching. I have to make something up. A huge white lie.

Yet I realise that when I talk about Liam at a later time, they will remember this denial now. It will make matters worse. Gary will be unforgiving.

"He" – I stumble over my uncertainty – "was selling tea towels, and I bought one, and ... I gave him £10 instead of £5 by mistake ... I should have gone after him."

Gary has a big thing about money, always being careful, counting out coins to pay for something rather than using a banknote, and he will not buy anything from cashless-only places. My words – that I gave away an extra £5 – are enough to distract him. He launches into a lecture about being 'on a budget ... watching every penny ... it will have to come out of housekeeping' (even though I pay for half of everything and a good deal more). I nod and smile and placate him and feel angry that I have to account for myself and every single penny.

I sense Chloe looking at me, and I glance at her and notice she has the strangest expression on her face. It is one of smugness. A moment of triumph. A look of malicious delight. She does not believe a word I have said, of course. I don't know how or why, but it is as if she sees right through me. She has never liked me. Has always resented me. She hates me, really, I can tell. But I have always felt I have had the upper hand. Just about. Somehow, in this moment, I feel the balance of power shifting.

As Gary's lecture – something closer to a rant – comes to an end, and I sit here trying to look contrite whilst screaming my resentment at him inside, Chloe clears her throat. She gives Gary a big *love you, Daddy!* smile and then turns to me with a butter-wouldn't-melt expression, for Gary's benefit. I know she is going to say something malicious; I just don't know what. "Bless, you're so sweet ... what sort of tea towel was it ... can I see it, please?"

I hesitate, knowing I should smile and simply say, "No." But that would arouse suspicions. And I don't want to be at odds with Chloe. I never want Gary to have to choose between us.

I look back at her and say, "Sure, does this mean you're going to dry up?" I smile again at her hard, blank face and am pleased with my little joke. Gary may take it that I mean drying the dishes, but the two of us know I am telling her to shut up.

I get up and go the kitchen and come back with an unopened pack of three tea towels I bought from a supermarket a week or two ago. A stroke of good fortune. She looks at me sourly, knowing I've got one over on her. Gary touches them, comments they are good quality, and seems happy enough. The moment passes, at least for now. I don't doubt we will come here again sometime soon.

———

I SPEND much of the evening on my own, cleaning and tidying around. I find housework soothing. After our dinner, Gary pats me on my tummy and kisses me on the cheek as I fill the dishwasher. He goes for a shower and heads straight off to the pub for a darts match. He is in a team. They play every week.

Chloe brings her plates and cutlery into the kitchen, leaving them on the side for me to load. She used to put them in the dishwasher, but left any sticky food on the plate and also placed the cutlery upside down – all to annoy me. Now I do it myself.

She then goes to her room. It is quiet for a while as she does some homework. The rest of the evening is a mix of on-off shouts and laughter as she is on her phone to friends. Then her music goes on, boom, boom, boom, the bass loud enough to be irritating, but not so loud that it's worth an argument.

Now I am relaxing in my bath as I always do for half an hour or so before going to bed. I like to be asleep before Gary returns home.

I have my phone in my hand, checking messages, hoping that I may receive one from Liam at any moment.

I stare at my phone long and hard, as if that will somehow pull a message from him. I shake my head at my silliness.

I wish, in this instant, that my parents were still alive to see this happiness unfolding. I would want them to meet Liam, see what a fine young man he is and know how he has done with his qualifications, so well that he is going to the best university in the world this autumn. I've played no part in any of this, of course. But I am still proud of him. I am his mother, after all. Somewhere deep down inside him, there is a part of me.

I always hated my parents, long before my baby was taken away from me so soon after his birth. I knew it would happen like that. I had, when I was pregnant, planned to run away, but my nerve failed me. I had no one to turn to, nowhere to go, so I stayed, waiting for the horror of losing him. I begged over and again, down on my knees once with my mother, my hands on her hips, pleading with her to let me keep my baby. She recoiled as she always did to physical touch, pushing me away, embarrassed by my raw emotions, my utter desperation and heartbreak.

So I was sent to Wales, to that cold aunt, and I can see now that I sank into a deep depression. I recall constantly imagining myself on Mount Snowdon one dark night, ending it all with a jump off a ledge onto the rocks so far below. I could not do it with my baby kicking inside. And I could not do it when I came back to my parents, nor even after I had my baby, in case he returned one day.

I just hated them all my life, going through the motions of being a dutiful daughter. I did not mourn their deaths in that house fire. Faulty electrical rewiring by a handyman. No smoke alarms. Both of them taking sleeping tablets. I just took my inheritance, from the sale of the land, although it was scant compensation for all I had lost. I would smile if they were here now. It would not, in truth, be a nice smile.

The sound on my phone is muted, as Gary gets irritated if it beeps and trills over and again. I have joined various online support groups lately, and I am notified of messages as they come in. The endless noises can be annoying.

So I check my phone, and I am thrilled that a message from Liam has popped up whilst I've been daydreaming.

'Chips! Pier? Noon? Chips on me! L x'

I text him back.

'Yes!'

I really mean *'YES!!!'* I am so excited at the thought of seeing Liam again. We can get bags of chips from Felixstowe pier and wander along the promenade. Gary will be out on his round out of town. And Chloe and her gossipy friends will all be at school. I will be safe.

I think, as I lie here, about Ryan, my first boyfriend – and, if I am honest, my one true love. We first met in the school library one lunchtime when we were both doing homework. We did not speak for ages, just glances and looks at each other. I then forgot my packed lunch one day, and he shared his with me. Boiled eggs, which I hate – the smell of them – but I took one anyway, swallowing it down in two bites without breathing. He was nice and kind and gentle and shy and – I think, to be honest – so was I at that time. We were a perfect match.

We walked to school and back, hand in hand, to Trimley St Mary, where he lived, and on to the top of my lane in Trimley St Martin, where he'd watch me walking to my home. He'd then turn back to his on Trimley St Mary's big housing estate. We made love in the fields near my home, just once, and it hurt so much but was over quickly, and I fell pregnant straightaway. It never occurred to me about being most fertile in the middle of my cycle. I was so young and naive.

Once I returned from Wales and learned Ryan and his family had moved to Ipswich, I was bereft. In the holidays, I would go and sit for hours in Ipswich town centre, hoping to see him. I never did. I messed up my GCSEs. I got five in all, including English and maths. Scraped a couple of A-levels too. I then went to work in offices in Ipswich, living my ordinary life. Dreary jobs. Boyfriends on and off. Happy now and then, but mostly sad. My mental health has been rocky. I then met Gary, got pregnant, and here we are. I still love Ryan, though. I'd like to somehow tell him about Liam. I've looked for him online, Instagram and so on, but he's not there. I don't know why.

Liam texts back a happy face emoji. I want to send him a heart or even a bulging heart emoji, but I reply with the same happy face he sent to me. I must be careful not to rush this.

I lie here a while longer in the bath, turning on the hot tap with my big toe and looking at my body. It is as though I was never pregnant. I don't know why I should be envious of mums with veiny boobs and stretch marks, but I am.

I am hoping Liam will text again so that I can go and curl

up in bed and we can just text each other all night. But he does not. I feel disappointed, cheated somehow, as I eventually turn off my phone.

I am in bed by the time Gary returns from his night at the pub. I pretend to be asleep. He is breathing heavily and clearing his throat repeatedly as he stands by the end of the bed, removing his shirt and pulling his trousers off and trying to step out of them without falling over. He is drunk, and I wonder, not for the first time, how he will manage not to fall off his ladder when window cleaning tomorrow.

He slumps forward onto the bed, on top of the duvet, in his tee shirt, pants and smelly old socks. I wait for a moment to see if he reaches out to paw at me as he sometimes does, whether he knows I am awake or not, but he doesn't. Instead, he is asleep almost immediately. I lie here listening to a cacophony of sounds. An orchestra of trumpets.

Beyond that, I can also hear whoop-whoop noises, some infantile music from Chloe's room – turned down a little, but still loud enough for me to hear. And I remember my life before all of this and wonder really if I am actually any happier than I was. I don't think I am.

But, of course, I am happy now, and excited too, that I have Liam in my life. I switch my phone back on, and as the screen lights up, I turn and look at Gary to check he is asleep. He is and is now making blubbery wet noises with his lips. I have a photo of Liam on my phone, taken to the side, in profile, as he was walking away from the house. I gaze at it, realising suddenly that all my hopes of true happiness rely on him.

LYING IN BED, before sleep, I try not to think about the baby and what happened. I missed a period. And I knew, straightaway, that I was pregnant. I did a test that confirmed it. Showed Gary the thin blue line on the stick. He was so excited. I let him and Chloe move in. We bought baby clothes and soft toys. Silly, really.

And then, weeks later, I had a period. The baby was gone. I tucked the stick away at the back of my jewellery box and tried not to think about it. Gary was so confused and angry. Chloe seemed indifferent. I did not grieve. I think, even then, I knew it was for the best. Gary being Gary.

And yet, somehow, even with Liam here, the son I've yearned for all these years, I mourn the loss of my baby. I can manage my thoughts in the day, but not at night. The baby comes to me sometimes in my dreams, breaking my heart. I lie here, recalling my last dream about my baby, going into it again as I sleep ...

I am in a maze, a dusty path at my feet and high hedges rising up to either side. It is dusk, and I am on my own. No one else is in the maze.

I am filled with a sense of urgency. I am looking for something, and I know I have to find it, whatever it is, before a terrible thing happens.

I want to run hard, but don't want anyone to see how desperate I feel, even though I know nobody else is in the maze. I hurry along, faster and faster.

I go up one dead end and around and up another. Then there is a long stretch that loops and returns me to where I was before.

I need to stop and somehow make sense of the maze. I think if I go left at every possible turning, it will bring me to where I want to go; the middle, I suppose.

To and fro, I go left-left-left-left, and I am certain I am back where I started again. Then right-right-right-right. I give up trying to be logical, and rush headlong every which way.

Eventually, soaked in sweat and stumbling with exhaustion, I come to the middle of the maze, a rectangular patch of grass, larger than I would have expected, with an old-fashioned street lamp in the middle.

Below, in the light of the lamp, there is a basket of some kind, made of wicker, and I can see blankets, soft white blankets, filling it to the top. Inside, I hear a baby gurgling.

I run forward, falling to my knees, my hands outstretched, ready to scoop the baby – my baby – up into my arms and to my breast.

But there is nothing, no baby, there. The basket is old and dirty and full of torn-up newspapers, like you'd put at the bottom of a cage for an animal.

I push the newspapers aside, tearing at them, to see what is at the bottom of the basket. There is just a deep, dark hole going down into the earth.

I reel back, a mix of disappointment and disgust – more than that, though. Much more. It is gut-wrenching. And I am inconsolable. The baby is not here because I was not good enough to save him.

And so I run, back the way I came, along the dark and dusty path, sobbing uncontrollably, stumbling and falling and going round and round, lost forever.

Beside myself with grief, and close to collapse, I push myself into the hedges that line the path, again and again, trying to force my way through.

And then I rest there, my face and arms and legs scratched and torn and bleeding, and the hedge kind of holds me up, my arms outstretched as though I am being crucified.

I awake into tears, as I do whenever I have this dream,

turning away from Gary so that he does not see me weeping. I get up, go downstairs, make a cup of tea, trying to be practical.

Gary heard me once, when I was in the middle of the dream – this nightmare – as I must have been making a noise. He shook me awake, saying I was breathing badly, as though I were choking. So loudly that it had woken him up.

I feel utterly sad and broken whenever I have this dream. It's partly because of the baby I lost, of course. It is not just that, though. It's Gary's reaction – it's as if only he counts and nobody else. Not me. I'm nothing.

3

TUESDAY, 18 JULY, NOON

I am sitting on a bench close to the pier, my phone on my lap, with the sound on, in case Liam messages me to say he's late or cannot come. I feel as though I am holding my breath, hoping it does not beep. I keep checking just in case I've somehow missed a message.

It is a sunny day with a gentler breeze than usual. There is often a strong breeze here on this coast, even at this time of year. It is busy on the promenade, with people walking along the main stretch from the theatre to the pier and back again.

Once Liam arrives and we have our chips, we can sit on the beach and look out to sea, talking and getting to know each other better. It is relatively quiet on the beach itself, as the schools don't break up for another week or two. There are just a few families with preschool children running about. I have earmarked a spot where we can sit.

I check the time on my phone, 11.53am, and then my appearance, wiping the corner of my right eye and pushing a stray strand of hair back into place. There, I am ready.

I fight the urge to look up and down the promenade,

searching for Liam. I want him to see me looking calm and relaxed. I do not want to appear anxious or desperate. I feel so needy, and it is not a nice feeling.

Whilst I am worrying, I feel a presence, someone sitting down next to me, and smile as I see it is Liam, the hood of his fleece pulled over his head. He looks much the same as yesterday, but a little sweaty as though he has been running. I fight the urge to hug him. But then he leans forward and embraces me, and I am thrilled by the gesture.

"Hi, you," I say, smiling widely at him. He has a smudge of dirt on his cheek, and it takes all my willpower not to take my handkerchief from a pocket and wipe it away. But I could not bear the thought of him recoiling from me.

He replies, "Hi, too."

I signal towards the fish and chip unit by the pier. He gets up and strides ahead of me, full of confidence. I hurry to keep up.

There is a short queue, and I try to think of something to say, more profound than, "Do you want a piece of cod? Or a pasty? Battered sausages, maybe?" But before I can form a question in my mind, he is already buying chips and two bottles of water. He turns to me when the large middle-aged woman behind the counter asks if we want salt and vinegar on the chips, and I nod, and then again when he asks me if I want ketchup. He gives both bags of chips a good squirting.

I thank him, and he gives me such a warm smile that I could almost hug him again. I don't. Just in case. Too much, too soon. Instead, I take his arm – he is happy with that – and lead the way to that quiet part of the beach, halfway between the promenade and the sea. He takes a small hand towel from his rucksack and lays it on the sand for me to sit on. Then he takes his hoodie off and puts it down next to the towel. And we sit beside each other, and I am bubbling over with joy. We talk, chatting away about nothing in particular – the weather, the pier, and other nonsense – as if we have always been together.

I ask him to tell me more about what he will study at Oxford in the autumn. He hesitates for a while, then answers, "Archaeology and anthropology."

I say, "That's good," not being sure what else to say, and not being 100 per cent certain what anthropology is.

He talks a little about archaeology and this and that and says he has always been interested since "Mum and Dad" – I wince, but say nothing – took him to Stonehenge on the way to a holiday in Cornwall when he was ten years old. He talks more about Stonehenge and other places he has visited. Mounds and humps and lumps and things.

I really want to hear all about the adoptive parents, but do not ask anything, not yet. I know myself well enough to realise I am jealous of them and that it would be better if I feign indifference, or something close to it. So I ask instead why he took a year out, and he talks about his A-levels and the hard work he put in and then adds that he wanted to travel and "see the sights."

I laugh and say, "What, Felixstowe Pier?"

And he answers with such wonderful words, "And, most of all, to find you." He then adds, "And to be with you."

We pick at our chips, and I ask him more questions, not about his childhood, but about the here and now and what he will do with his life. He says he is happy – "could not be happier" – and then, taking my breath away again, "Now that I have found you ... everything is complete." And I put my arm around him, and we have a little cuddle. I try not to cry, but I do not succeed!

He pulls away slightly, looks at me snuffling, and takes a cloth from his pocket. We both hesitate over who is going to wipe my eyes. I do. We both laugh. He then wants to know more about me, probing more than yesterday. I talk, meandering again, about my life to date, still making it sound as nice as possible. I mention Gary and Chloe briefly, but not that I lost a baby. He rests his hand gently on my arm. He has soft hands, long and slender, with clean nails. He's not grubby, like many teenage boys.

He asks, if he may, to know more about the 'other biological parent'. I hate the way he puts it, as though Ryan and I were no more than sperm and egg and a test tube. But I do not react. Instead, I talk a little more about Ryan, that it was first love, and what happened. I do not say Ryan is still round and about, and that I see him in passing now and then. I don't know why. Liam glances at me, at what must be the wistful look on my face, and goes to say something, but stops himself. *You still love him* is what he was going to say, I'm sure of it. He is correct.

"What's your happy-ever-after?" he asks, an unexpected question. I hesitate, formulating the words in my head, the order, the nuance of each sentence. In this moment, I want to say that, even though I am living with Gary and Chloe, I don't want to be – there, I have thought it clearly at last – and I would love so much to be a family with Ryan and Liam. Madness, of course. I mumble something about Liam being my happy-ever-after. We laugh cheerfully enough.

Liam, having finished his chips, puts the empty packet to one side next to the bottle of water, and then lies down on the sand. He smiles up at me, and, in the moment, he has a look of Ryan about him. The same sort of smile.

I take his chips packet and put it in my own empty one

and tuck them into my handbag. When I was young, my parents and I used to litter-pick the beach every Sunday morning. Old habits die hard. I still can't bear seeing rubbish everywhere. I then lie down next to Liam, and partly to stop my hair getting sandy, I rest my head on his shoulder. I wish I hadn't.

Suddenly, I see a shadow, a face, a body, leaning in above us. It is Chloe, who should really be in school, smirking at me. In the distance, on the promenade, I hear her friends calling, wanting her to go into the amusements with them, a magnet for teenagers for miles around. Instead, she says, "Hell-ooo, Nina, what are you doing here ... with?" And she looks at Liam, expecting an introduction.

IN THIS DREADFUL MOMENT, Liam sits up oh so casually and smiles at Chloe as she moves around and crouches on the beach, facing us, the sea behind her. He has no idea what this means. But, already, I sense he is my co-conspirator.

I sit up too, unsure what to do or to say. Chloe must recognise Liam from yesterday, and she will know I lied at dinner last night. He is not a stranger. She will make the most of this.

The three of us look at each other. Liam, open and welcoming. Me – tense and scared of what Chloe will say, and where this conversation will go. Chloe, smug and ready to bring everything crashing down around me. "This is Chloe," I say. I hesitate, but do not add, 'my stepdaughter' in case the implied closeness angers her. She triggers so easily.

"I'm Liam," he says, holding out his hand in a polite, old-fashioned gesture. Chloe responds by raising her hand in a high-five motion, even though she's not close enough for Liam to respond in kind. Liam continues speaking, "I'm from ... Nina's family ... just passing through."

"It was Liam who came round yesterday," I continue. "I think you saw each other as you were leaving? I bought some tea towels from him." I pray Liam will realise my predicament and help me. He does. My partner-in-crime.

"Yes," he says, laughing and picking up on my discomfort. "If you want tea towels, I'm your man. Red ... blue ... yellow." He stops and smiles. I wait to see if Chloe says something to push and pull at the flimsy lie. She does.

"Have you got any on you now, tea towels?" She gestures towards his rucksack. I am angered by the absurd question – as though she wants to buy one! – but stay quiet. I am fearful. He pulls a face and shrugs his shoulders as if to say, 'I'm all out, sorry.'

She nods. I don't know what to make of it.

"So," she goes on, still talking to him and ignoring me, "are you Nina's ..." She pauses for dramatic effect.

I think she is going to say 'niece' – she is stupid enough – and that would make me laugh out loud, even in this awful moment. But she might say 'son', and that horrifies me.

"Cousin?" She smiles sweetly.

"Something like that," he replies nonchalantly.

"You must come to tea tonight," she says, smiling back at him. "Meet my dad." And I feel I should say something at this point. To intervene. But I can't think what to say, which way to go. Then Chloe's friends are calling again – five of them, including Chloe, all bunking off school early, as it is getting so close to the end of term. I am distracted by their shouts and yells as Liam says something like, "We'll see," and she is up and away without a backwards glance.

Liam and I look at each other when Chloe's back up on the promenade and away to the amusements with her friends. He says, "So that's Chloe," and pulls a 'rather you than me' sort of face. We both laugh, and he then adds, more seriously, "You've not been able to tell Gary ... or Chloe ... about me ... just yet ... I'd best not come for tea, then."

I nod and then shake my head, feeling suddenly that he must be offended, so terribly hurt, that I have not revealed his existence to them – to anyone, really, over his lifetime. Like he means nothing to me. I feel ashamed of that, and scared, too. I also keep imagining Gary's face when or if I tell him the truth. He does have a horrible temper. "I'm sorry," I say to Liam.

Liam moves closer and puts his arm around my shoulders, saying in a quiet voice that he understands. I rest my head on his shoulder once more, and as I do, I feel that Chloe is watching. I turn around, but she has already gone into the amusements. I relax a little, for now, but I have the sense that this – Liam and me being together – is going to escalate oh so fast into dangerous territory.

———

It does, later this evening, as we sit around the table having chili con carne for our tea. Gary is tired and irritable after a long day's window cleaning. Chloe sits there, upright and smiling, waiting for her moment. I am tense and nervous, feeling trapped, dropping knives and forks more than once, and annoying Gary although he does not say anything. I am a mouse in the corner, waiting for the cat to strike.

I had a lovely afternoon with Liam. We walked all the way along the promenade, by the theatre, down to a place called The Dip, where we sat and ate ice cream and watched the boats go in and out of Felixstowe Docks. We chatted about 101 things. We really do have so much in common. Music. Books. Fashion, even. We then walked back and parted company at the pier with a long hug and promises to see each other again, same time tomorrow. Liam went to his bed and breakfast further along the promenade. I returned home to start doing the tea. I sat down for a while first, tired out, and worrying about Chloe.

Gary and Chloe came in together just before six. I wondered if Chloe had waited outside for Gary so she could tell him about Liam before they entered the house. But I think the timing was just coincidence. He was hot and edgy. She just kept smirking. I could see she was bursting to say something, to drop me in it with Gary, who would never let the matter lie until he knew everything. And so, as I sipped at a glass of fizzy water, I braced myself for Chloe's opening words.

She looks at me and smiles brightly. I gaze back, blank-faced. Gary has his face in his plate, shovelling away, one forkful of chili con carne after the other. Like it's his last-ever meal.

"How's Liam?" she asks, her face full of innocence. "Is he not coming for tea, then?"

I ignore her and start eating, as though I have not really heard the questions.

"Who's Liam?" Gary says, looking at Chloe and then at me. The moment of truth. I could lie and hope it never comes out. God help me if it does. Gary will be furious.

Or I could tell the truth. I cannot do that here and now. If ever. It would change everything between Gary and me in a flash. I want to stay in control of my relationship with Liam.

"I'll tell you later," I reply, answering him, giving myself time to think more, to decide what to say, when Chloe is not sitting here, taking it all in. Gary pulls a 'whatever' face.

Chloe won't let it go, though. I know what she is going to say next even before she speaks. And it is going to turn everything nasty regardless of what I say.

"Liam ..." she says, her voice raised and breathless excitement on her face, "was here in the house yesterday, and Nina was with him on the beach this afternoon."

I hope that is that. It's bad enough. But there is more, a sharp twist of the knife. "Nina had her head on his shoulder. He had his arms around her."

There is such a silence. Gary has a forkful of food halfway between his plate and mouth. It stays there, his hand trembling ever so slightly.

Chloe tosses her hair back, taking an elastic band from her pocket and tying her hair in a ponytail. She does not look at me, but her face is shiny and smug. I hate her for this.

I know I should shout out, *He's my son, Liam. My long-lost son. And I love him with all of my heart!* But it will make matters so much worse. And so I wait.

Gary puts his fork back on the plate, sits for a moment and then speaks with his head bowed. "Who is he?" His voice sounds calm, but underneath I can tell he is bristling with tension.

I understand why. Gary has had a hard life. He had a difficult childhood as an only child with a violent father and a drunken mother. He is estranged from his family. His wife cheated on him with different men before she left. He has a job he hates and little money. He does not feel good about himself. He takes it out on those around him with his anger and aggression. I can say Liam is my son, but Gary will rant and rave, saying I have lied to him all this time (which I have) and that it is horrible to find out like this (true) and I think more of this Liam than I do of him (which is correct). And then what?

I have seen him lose control once. It was when he discovered his ex-wife was planning to remarry, to the man she's currently living with. He came back from dropping Chloe there, and was in such a filthy mood, barely able to get the words out. He then went to mow the lawn, but the lawnmower did not work properly, so he trashed it, smashing it repeatedly against the back wall of the garage. It was funny in a way, but frightening, too; he could easily have come at me. The lawnmower was completely wrecked, and that seemed to satisfy him. I have that image in my mind as I answer him.

"He's, ah, what is it, my cousin's son. Liam ... second cousin? I met him for the first time in years yesterday. Out of the blue. When he came to the house. Then, when I was walking on the prom, I saw him again." I glance at them. He believes it. She doesn't. Not a word. "We got talking. He's, ah, troubled. He's, ah, bipolar, poor boy. Nervy. And so I talked to him."

"Bipolar?" Gary asks, and I kind of sense that he's thinking that doesn't sound good, that maybe I – we – should be careful, not really understanding what it means. So I pull back a little, saying that he's a sweet boy, very gentle and just anxious. 'Wouldn't hurt a fly!'

Gary nods agreeably enough. My white lie has made him feel he is better than Liam and can look down on him, so that is helpful, at least for now. Chloe looks at me with disbelief, as though she is going to slow hand-clap. Before she can, Gary says, in a positive voice, that Liam must come to tea tomorrow. And so, we carry on eating, and that, for now, is that. I don't doubt there is more to come from Chloe soon, most likely when I least expect it.

———

THE EVENING PASSES as it normally does. We finish our tea and go our separate ways for a while. I do the dishwasher and the washing machine. Gary writes down his takings and spendings for the day. He showers. I have a bath. We sit and watch television for the rest of the evening. Chloe goes to a friend's house over on the Trimley St Mary estate. She's due back at ten o'clock.

We're watching a crime drama on BBC iPlayer. Gary likes to complete a series over two or three nights. I'm happy to relax and go with it. I sometimes ask who a character is or what is happening, if I know he is in an agreeable mood. Tonight he is, and he explains everything to me, all quite cheerfully, albeit as though I am a complete idiot. He is so patronising. He rests his hand on my arm and, later, makes us hot milky coffees and brings them through on a tray with a bar of chocolate to share. White chocolate, which I hate. He says he'll turn the series off after this second episode in case I fall asleep. I do sometimes.

He does not seem angry about Liam – my so-called second cousin – at all. Instead, now and then, he asks questions about him. Where he lives. Blah, blah. What his parents do. Blah, blah. Whether they are rich. He says it so casually, but he does not fool me. Gary always has ideas for get-rich-quick schemes every couple of months. They go wrong. People are angry. I bail him out with my savings. He promises not to do it again. But he is always seeking someone who has a lot of money, who will back his next scheme. I say I think Liam's family are rich. I can almost hear Gary purring with pleasure.

Then, suddenly, so unexpected and loud that we both jump, startled, there is knocking at the door. It is urgent and insistent. And it's that, the aggression of it, that makes me panic, fearing something terrible is happening.

It cannot be Chloe. She has a key. Even if she forgot it, she'd not hammer at the door like that. Someone to whom Gary owes money, then. We've had that twice before, debt collectors, Gary borrowing my debit card and hurrying to the nearest ATM in Felixstowe for cash whilst they waited impatiently outside by his van, ready to take his possessions. It was embarrassing and so shaming.

Gary, suddenly furious, swears loudly and goes by me, striding to the front door. I get up to follow him, ready to placate whoever is there. Gary, too. He is always aggressive, all five feet six and a half inches of him. He wrenches open the door, head jutting forward, on the front foot as ever.

It is Liam standing there, in his tee shirt, jeans and trainers. There is mud on his face, his tee shirt is torn, his jeans are muddy and so too are his white trainers; these are really filthy. He looks as though he has been in a fight. He stumbles forward onto his knees at Gary's feet. I notice he does not have his rucksack with him, and it strikes me suddenly that he has been beaten up and had his belongings stolen by a local gang of youths. Liam is a slight young man; he has a gentle, almost feminine look about him and would be an easy target.

Gary looks at him, then back at me, as if asking, *Is this him, is this Liam?* I nod, to answer 'yes, yes, it is'. And Gary is bending over, appearing concerned and sympathetic, and helping him to his feet. Liam seems confused, uncertain where he is and what he is doing. He is about to speak, and I have the sudden fear he will say Mum. He does not. Instead, he goes down onto one knee as though he has been punched in his stomach. Then, in a voice full of pain, he says he's sorry, really sorry, to come here.

"I was moving from my bed and breakfast to ..." He stops, grimacing and breathing carefully. "To another place ... a bit nicer ... but I was set upon and dragged into the bushes." He fights back tears, embarrassed, I think, and ashamed he could not fight them off. "I've had everything taken, my phone, money, all of it. I'm sorry ... I had nowhere else to turn."

Gary and I help him onto the sofa. He sits there, his face twisting in pain. Gary says we should call an ambulance. Liam says it's okay and there are no broken bones; he just needs a few minutes to recover, that's all. It's not as bad as it looks. The police, then? Liam shakes his head.

Despite what's happening, the seriousness of it, I still make polite introductions, being sure to say clearly, 'And this is Liam, my second cousin I told you about, from Chelmsford way.' I hope Liam hears and takes in what I am saying.

He seems to, trying to get to his feet, to be polite, to shake Gary's hand. But Gary puts his arms around Liam and settles him back on the sofa. "We'll run you a bath, wash your clothes, put you in the spare room, talk about the police in the morning."

And that's what we do. Gary helps Liam up the stairs, along the landing to the bedroom at the back of the house. There is a single bed, and – although the room is full of all sorts of junk, as spare rooms often are – it will do for now. I hurry to the airing cupboard for fresh bedding. We stand over Liam as he sits on the edge of the bed, insisting he will be fine and he can sort himself out.

I ask if he's eaten, and he says he has. I fetch him a glass of water and come back to put it on the bedside cabinet. Gary is out of the room, and at that moment, Liam looks at me and smiles. It's almost a smirk. I don't know why, but it looks odd, and it makes me feel uneasy. Before either of us can say anything, Gary is back with tee shirts and jogging bottoms and socks and puts them at the end of the bed. Liam says thank you.

Then, as we all stand there, Liam getting to his feet as though to undress, we hear the front door swinging open and Chloe's heavy footsteps running up the stairs. There is a moment's silence as we wait to see if she goes to the bathroom or her room. As the light is on in here, she pushes open the door and stands there looking at us. She bursts out laughing at the sight of the three of us together. It is a nasty sound. Gary says, "What's" – but she is already turning and leaving before he can say – "so funny?" He shakes his head.

I don't know what to think. I have a sense of growing unease deep down inside that all of us here in the house is a combustible mix ready to explode .

4

WEDNESDAY, 5 JULY, EARLY MORNING

Liam lies in bed late this morning. I check on him several times to make sure he is well. He breathes peacefully. I stand and watch him awhile, each time transfixed. I brush his hair away from his eyes. He has long eyelashes, so long that they curl back over.

Gary and Chloe both left later than usual, each of them finding things that just had to be done first. Stuff and nonsense. They both wanted to see Liam when he came downstairs. Eventually, they both had to go. Gary said, "Keep me posted."

Just gone ten o'clock, and I am sitting at the table at the far end of the kitchen, checking news on my phone, sipping tea, eating toast and jam, and staring out at the conifers that line the back of the garden, shielding it from the fields beyond. They need cutting, but that's a thought for another day. Liam comes in, wearing Gary's spare clothes, smiling at me. We hug, and he kisses me on the cheek and then sits opposite me at the table, taking my last piece of toast. I laugh. A happy moment.

"How are you?" I say. "Sleep well?" As he nods to confirm, I add, "Would you like a fry-up? Bacon, eggs, sausages?"

He nods again. More enthusiastically.

"I washed your clothes and dried them." I busy around the kitchen, getting a frying pan out, switching on the kettle. "Are you still in pain? Do you want me to call the police ... report it?"

"No." He pulls up the tee shirt to show his chest and stomach. "No lasting damage. I just don't have any money or my things." I tell him not to worry about that. Not to worry about anything. I want to add, "ever again," but stop myself. Too much, too soon.

He sits at the kitchen table, eating the breakfast I've made for him, whilst I fetch his tee shirt and jeans. He says Gary and Chloe both seem nice and friendly. It sounds more like a question. I reply that they are, and leave it at that. I don't really want to talk about them. He asks how I am, and I say I am fine, thank you.

Liam then looks out across the garden, and I can see he is working out what to say next. I jump in, anticipating his question and repeating, "Listen, don't worry about losing your money, your phone, your cards. Clothes. Whatever. I can let you have money ... as much as you need." I hesitate and go on, handing him my phone and reminding him of the passcode. "You'd better call ... your folks, let them know you're okay. And your bank, to get your cards blocked. Do that first, it's really important. In case someone's running around, spending on it."

He takes my phone and says he'll do it straight after his shower. He continues eating. I stand there, not sure what else to say. He says, in his matter-of-fact way, "You've told

Gary and Chloe I'm your, what was it, second cousin?" He
laughs, but it's not a nice, warm sound. I can tell it bothers
him. Like I have disowned him.

I sit down. "I ... Gary would be so ... I ... I ..." I stop, my
voice stuttering, tears in my eyes. I want to say Gary would
be so angry and upset, but don't want to admit that. I hope
Liam will reach out his hand, but he does not.

"I've never told anyone about you in my whole life ...
which ..." I take a deep breath, steadying myself. "... is crazy,
really ... because you have been my ... whole ... life." I choke
on my words.

He leans forward, pushes the chair between us to one
side and hugs me long and hard. "Stay a while?" I ask. He
nods yes, and at that my emotions get the better of me. I
break down and sob in his arms.

Later, after he has showered and made his calls and
given me back my phone, we sit in the living room and chat
some more, mostly about things to do together. I make a pot
of tea and bring it through on a tray with mugs and spoons
and milk and sugar and a half-left packet of shortbread
fingers. He demolishes the biscuits as I talk. I ask him how
long he can stay, and he says, "The summer ... if you like ...?"

I am overjoyed and say we can go into Ipswich today and
get him some new clothes and a phone. He says his cards are
being sent to his home address. I reply not to worry, and that
I'll pay for everything. I'd be happy to.

Then, he says he's going to pop to his bed and breakfast
place, as he thinks he might have left a book behind. We
agree he will return at midday, and we will head off and have
lunch in Ipswich before shopping there. I put two keys in his
hand, one for the front door and one for the back – the

kitchen – and kiss him on the cheek as he goes out that kitchen door. He then stops before he gets to the garden gate, coming back and hugging me properly. "Thank you for the keys." I think he sees it as a symbolic gesture, and I suppose, in a way, it is.

When he's gone, I text Gary. I tell him Liam wants to stay for a while … '*if that's okay?*'

Gary replies: '*Yes. If he pays for himself.*'

I say he will. I have a secret bank account that Gary knows nothing about, and will let Liam have some money from that. I don't mention I am paying for new clothes and a phone today. Gary wouldn't like that.

I lie on the sofa and daydream about how my life will now be. Somehow, my thoughts are full of Liam and me, being together and doing things and feeling happy. Sitting in the sunny garden. Days out. Holidays in lovely places. I even think of Ryan and imagine he is part of my new family. Gary and Chloe are not part of any of it. And I wonder what will happen when my daydreams and realities collide, as they are sure to do one day soon.

I look idly at my phone, at the photo I snatched of Liam as he left. I can't stop staring at it. I must ask him if I can take a selfie of the two of us. I'd like a framed photo on a cabinet or a wall. But Gary would be jealous and, anyway, that would look odd for a 'second cousin'. I'd keep it on my phone, hidden away, for me to look at now and then.

That reminds me. Curious, I click on the phone icon on my phone's home screen, interested to see if Liam phoned home. It comes up 'No recent calls', which puzzles me. I wonder if he deleted the call details. Before I can think about it, Liam is bang-bang-banging cheerfully on a window and coming back in through the kitchen, ready to go to Ipswich.

———————

THE NEXT WEEK IS, quite simply, the happiest time of my life. It is everything I could ever have wished for. And more.

Mum. Son. Spending our days together. Getting to know each other. Falling in love. My beautiful little family. We are a perfect, self-contained unit.

There are times, other than mornings and evenings, when I forget they – Gary and Chloe – exist.

Liam and I have such a happy routine. After they have gone to work and school, I do my household chores, cleaning and washing, preparing ingredients for the evening meal as necessary, vacuuming around. Liam gets up at about ten o'clock, and we have a leisurely breakfast and decide what we are going to do that day. He usually then goes for a run – he likes to keep fit – whilst I make us packed lunches. I watch him go, fiddling with his new phone, as teenagers do.

We always head off by one o'clock and visit places I think Liam would like (and he does): the castles at Colchester, Framlingham and Orford, the ruins in Abbey Gardens at Bury St Edmunds, and the beaches at Aldeburgh, Southwold and Dunwich. We wander around, seeing the sights. Then sit down and have a picnic of sandwiches, crisps, sticky buns and fizzy drinks. He whittles wood for me, making more birds, which I put on the windowsill of the box room. I have quite a collection.

And we talk – how we talk – about our respective pasts and our hopes and dreams and our future together. We walk arm-in-arm as we stroll around afterwards, ending our trip with coffees and cakes. Here, we sit close and share our dearest thoughts and wishes. He says, after university, he would like to get a job nearby so we will never be parted again. I tell him I would love that so much, adore it, and he smiles and looks delighted.

When we return home, Liam goes for what he calls 'a get to know Felixstowe' walk whilst I make tea for six o'clock. He's always looking at his phone, as teenagers do, no doubt checking where he's going to go next in and around town.

I say there's not much to see! But he says he likes to walk to the Martello Tower, the nineteenth-century fort on the seafront. And to pick up shells from the shore.

Sometimes, he brings the prettiest ones back for me. I put them in a colourful bowl on the kitchen windowsill, where the sun shines on them. Liam says he will turn the smallest ones into a necklace for me.

Early evening, we all have tea together, the four of us. Liam and I are co-conspirators in that we are as close as a mother and son can be. Yet we want that closeness, that love, to be a secret between ourselves. So we are polite and friendly – as second cousins would be – but do not, as we usually do, lean forward to talk to each other, our heads touching. And I do not, as I do when we're alone, rest my hand on his arm.

Gary, who is so often full of stress and tension at this time, is surprisingly friendly. He asks what we have done during the day, and we take turns to tell him, making it sound pleasant rather than joyful. Gary comments now and then on what he knows about the archaeology of the place, invariably wrong, and Liam and I smile and nod and then look away from each other, knowing that the slightest glance will send us both into fits of giggles. Gary is such a fool.

Chloe, the sulky little madam, veers between being aloof and attentive. She wants to play hard to get with Liam, but forgets herself when he says something amusing and she laughs a little too loudly. Gary does not seem to notice. And Liam does not, either. Truth be told, I think Chloe is wasting her time. I have the feeling Liam is not interested in girls, and I think that's part of why we have such a special bond.

In the evenings, Liam usually slips out for a 'breath of fresh air'. He has indicated to me that, as he's staying, he wants to find one or two friends. By the end of the week, he seems to be texting as he comes and goes, so I think he's found some friends at the pier. I don't ask, as he will tell me about them in his own good time.

Chloe has, a few times, intimated that she could come too, but Liam is far too smart for that and does not offer an invitation. She has, later, gone out after him on two or three occasions, but they return separately, so she could not have found him. I keep quiet about all of this.

Gary is surprisingly welcoming to Liam, saying hello and goodbye as appropriate and making an effort to talk to him. He asks about Liam's family. I think Liam realises what Gary wants, teasing him along with talk of big houses and exotic holidays and trust funds and all of that. It's hard to keep a straight face at times. Instead of wondering why Liam is here in the back bedroom when he's got so much money and could afford a nice hotel, Gary just sees pound signs.

When we go to bed, Gary is so excited most nights that he gabbles away about how much he likes Liam and would love to help him get on in the world – himself, more like, although I don't say anything.

Gary has been researching a scheme that will double his money in two years. 48 per cent a year! He's going to ask

Liam and others to invest, and he will take a cut of the profits, 20 per cent most likely. Madness, of course, but I go along with it.

Liam is far too sensible to do anything like that, but I let Gary burble away happily. Things are just perfect as they are – I long for them to continue for ever like this. But somehow, I don't think they will for long.

———

THE NEXT EVENING, when Chloe is having tea at a friend's house, Gary, Liam and I are sitting at the table, eating home-made burgers, chips and cheesy beans, Gary's culinary favourite. Gary is being cheery, asking Liam about his plans from September and making jokes as and when he can. I know what's coming.

Liam plays along well enough, making responsive comments and smiling as and when needed. Liam and I don't look at each other, in case we set each other off. We're always giggling about something or other we see when we are out and about. We hurry our food, as if we both know what Gary is about to ask, and we want to eat up quickly and go before that. It's not going to happen, of course.

As we finish our main course, Gary picks up his empty plate and puts it on top of Liam's and then mine, adds the dirty cutlery, and smiles as he hands the pile of plates to me. Like I'm the waitress. I go along with it. Liam can handle what's coming. I head for the kitchen, loading the dishwasher and putting bowls, spoons and a tub of chocolate ice cream on a tray to carry through. I stand in the kitchen, the door slightly ajar, seeing and hearing everything.

"I, um ..." Gary takes a sip of lemonade from his glass

and then hesitates before going on. "I wanted to talk to you about money, Liam. Before you go off into the world."

Liam glances at Gary, and I can see he does not really want to have this conversation but knows he has little choice. Gary has to be kept onside if we're all going to live happily under this roof. So Liam just offers a neutral smile.

Gary continues, "I've, ah, been investing in this scheme ... very successfully." He pauses, and I now know why he waited until I had left the room – this is a bare-faced lie. "It pays out 48 per cent a year." More nonsense. Gary nods enthusiastically. Liam just looks at him.

"Shall I tell you how it works, Liam? It's very clever ... but also very simple ... by the time you've left university, you'll have tripled your money." I cringe at the stupidity of the man. He embarrasses me.

"No, I'm fine, but thank you, Gary. Thank you very much for thinking of me." Liam is polite rather than out-and-out dismissive. I take a deep breath, waiting for Gary's reaction.

"I thought you said you had money ... a trust fund. That needs to be invested properly, doesn't it?" Gary's voice sounds strained. I can sense the disappointment and anger, and I try to head off what comes next by bustling back in with the tub of chocolate, bowls and spoons.

"The issue is, Gary ..." Liam says, turning to me as I scoop chocolate ice cream into bowls. "Gary was just asking me how I'll get on money-wise at university ... and I was saying my parents, Tracey and Peter ... your cousin ... have put everything into a trust fund for me after Grandpa Roger died. I can't touch it."

I look at him, a sudden smirk at me, and think how smooth and effortless these little white lies seem to be for him. And how clever he is to stop Gary in his tracks without triggering his anger. Gary looks disappointed, of course, but I don't believe he's going to lose his temper. Gary is about to reply, but Liam carries on.

"Dear old Grandpa Roger and his fortune from the Springham property estate ..." Liam looks at me again, another silly smirk, and it occurs to me, for the first time, that he's gone too far. That he may now go even further, adding other pointless embellishments that are simply unbelievable. He then adds, "But all I get is a monthly allowance that's little more than I'd get from a student loan." He looks at me again, and we both smile at each other. I am relieved.

Gary has his head dipped, scooping mouthful after mouthful of ice cream into his mouth, like he can't wait to be finished and go to the pub as per usual. I can tell from his expression and body language that he's bitterly disappointed. All he says, mutters really, is, "Shame none of it came this way." Like he's been somehow disinherited. Not me. This fictional nonsense.

"I ... ah ..." I hesitate, knowing I need to respond to head off a possible angrier outburst but, at the same time, not wishing to make things worse. "Liam's grandpa was my father's brother ... they did not get on ... as you know, my father was religious. Liam's grandpa was not." I leave it at that; as little as possible is best. Even so, Gary looks really sour-faced, and I wonder, not for the first time, if he is in more significant financial trouble than I have thought.

But then Gary is up with a muttered, "Got to be going." And he pushes his empty bowl across the table so hard that the spoon clatters out, and then he is gone, upstairs to change, back down to get his wallet, and then he is out, with a hurried, "Bye."

We sit there a while, Liam and I, pulling rueful faces at each other. I am about to suggest we wash up and watch TV for a while. But his phone beeps, he reads a message, and with a quick hug and a peck on the cheek, he is up and gone as well.

5

WEDNESDAY, 12 JULY, LUNCHTIME

A week on from Liam moving in, we are back in Ipswich town centre, where we went that first day together to buy him clothes, a phone and to arrange for him to have a card he could use on my secret bank account.

Today, we are here for lunch in a new restaurant that's opened by the quayside, a pretty place full of bistros, boats and, whenever I have been here, endless sunshine. It's a bright and sunny day.

We sit outside the restaurant, sharing a large pizza, and I am about to raise the subject of him maybe staying here beyond the autumn, maybe even forever, when everything changes in a split second.

Ryan, my first love, my true love, is walking towards us around the quayside. He has a man either side of him, both suited and booted as Ryan is. He looks rich and successful – there are so many new buildings going up here that I wonder if he's involved with property: a surveyor, an estate agent, maybe even an investor buying up apartments for rentals.

I am staring at him, open-mouthed. I have seen him out and about over the years in Ipswich. But not here. And never looking so well. I put my glass back on the table, clattering it clumsily. Liam does not seem to notice, and continues eating.

As Ryan approaches, I am torn what to do. Whether to wave my hand at him, saying, "Ryan, remember me?" Then adding, "This is Liam, our son." But how can I? He is with work colleagues. What an unspeakable thing to do.

I wonder if I should turn away, clearing my throat and starting a new conversation with Liam. But I am frozen, unable to move. Ryan sees me – our eyes meet, and I watch as he looks at me first, then at Liam, for a moment or two, taking it in, working it out. Then he looks back at me. Half a dozen words pass silently between us with that single look.

I can see him thinking, *Is that our son, Nina?* And the reply in my head, as I am too stunned to speak, is a simple one, *Yes.* I nod slightly. Then he is gone, striding by with his colleagues, talking of indemnity insurances and rates and other business matters.

I think, for a fleeting second, of telling Liam that the man who just passed by, the one in the middle with the prematurely greying hair, the sad eyes, and the dark grey suit, is his father. But I imagine Liam going after Ryan, and I could not bear it. The embarrassment of watching Liam's approach. The horror of seeing Ryan pushing him away and hurrying off.

As Liam smiles, sips his drink, and eats another slice of pizza, I sit and watch Ryan and his colleagues walking around the curve of the quayside towards the car park up by the main road. My car is parked there, too. When they get to the car park, they stop and shake hands and say their farewells, and part company. One goes to the left. The other to the right. Ryan stands by his car, a smart black Audi, looking one way and then the other and, finally, towards me.

I hope, for a moment, that he will come striding back. But it is a split-second daydream, wishful thinking, something that will never happen. He will turn and get in his car and be gone. I will bump into him again in the town centre in a year or so, as we so often do, and we will pretend not to see each other. As we've done before. And now.

I turn back to Liam to start a fresh conversation, but something catches my eye. It is Ryan. He has his arm up. Then he waves, beckoning me over.

———

I AM up on my feet instinctively, without thinking whether it is the right thing to do. Wrong, most probably. God knows where this will lead.

I say to Liam that time's running out on the parking ticket, and I need to put some more coins in the machine. Then I tell him to order desserts; I'll have a tiramisu. I almost laugh at the incongruity of my mundane request in this life-changing moment.

Liam reaches for the last piece of pizza, gesturing at me, asking if I want it. I shake my head and walk away, trying to act as calm – as nonchalant – as I can.

I smile at Ryan as I approach. He smiles back. He looks as nervous and ill at ease as I feel. Maybe this is a dreadful mistake. I should have just ignored him waving at me.

We stand, a metre or so apart, looking at each other,

neither of us able to speak. He looks much the same, with his gorgeous brown eyes, but he seems somehow older than his years. The weight of life on his shoulders. I expect he's thinking the same of me. And that I have put on weight. Not that I was ever slim.

Then, suddenly, the tension breaks. He smiles that lopsided smile. The one that made me fall in love with him. I think for a moment he is going to step forward and hug me, but he does not. He speaks warmly enough, though.

"Nina," he says simply. "How are you? You look well ... happy."

"I am. Happy. And you?"

He nods thoughtfully. "I guess. Life has its ups and downs. I'm up at the moment."

I'm not sure what to add, to say, to ask. This moment feels surreal. And the conversation is inane given that we were each other's first lovers – we once swore to spend our lives together – and now have a nineteen-year-old son sitting not so far away in sight of us. But how do you go from the superficial to the profound in a sentence or two? So I smile and ask him what he's been up to ... since ... 'you know'.

"Ah." He purses his lips, blows air through them as if saying, *Where to start?* He thinks for a moment or two. "Um, I did A-levels in Ipswich ... trained as a dentist up in the North-East ... I now have a practice in town, but we're looking to open an implant centre here on the quay ... married ... divorced ... two daughters. And you?"

I note how he hurries through the married-divorced bit. I guess he's now single. Not so 'up', then. And it occurs to me, all of a sudden, why I've not been able to find him on Face-book or Instagram. Being a private dentist. He needs to be above all that, this professional man.

"Um." I wonder if I should talk about Liam, saying, *Our son – he's sitting there right now at the restaurant.* Instead, I keep it light. "I did my A-levels in Felixstowe ... worked in an office ... insurance ... shipping ... sales ... hated that ... I'm now taking some time out ... bit of a breather." I don't mention the baby, or that I'm off work because of my loss and my anxiety and other mental health issues. He nods agreeably, as though what I am saying is good to hear. He seems to be looking beyond me.

I wait to see if he asks if I am married ... or divorced ... or single ... but he does not. He just smiles at me, looking rather a simple soul.

So I wonder if I should ask about his daughters – names and ages and what they're like – or if he is alone now, estranged from his family. But I cannot bring myself to do it. To open myself up to him.

That's it. All this time, all these years, I have dreamed of this moment and what would come of it. But it has come to nothing; like you've just bumped into a neighbour you lived next door to years ago and have little to say. I turn to go.

"Is that ..." he says suddenly,. "The boy ... that young man ... with you at the restaurant ... is he ..." He cannot bring himself to say *our son,* and he never knew what I called him. Alex. I want to shout back, *Yes, that's our boy, Alex. He calls himself Liam these days.*

But I don't. For me, this meeting should be a wonderful, pivotal moment in my life. We'd be thrilled to see each other. I'd tell him everything. And fall into his arms. But his look, his whole manner towards me, is of politeness and professional detachment. No more than that. He's not rude, just ... bland. It's the lack of personal interest that upsets me most.

I turn so that he cannot see I am hurt, and start walking

away. Liam looks up and waves at me, gesturing towards the table, as though saying, *Two puddings ... our puddings are here! Hurry up!* I should laugh, but I am so hurt and angry with Ryan that I do not.

"Wait!" Ryan calls after me. I half turn, but he is not following, just standing there, waiting for me to go back to him.

I stop and look at him, unmoving, and then I reply, "What?" I raise my hands, indicating I'm saying, *What is it you want?*

"Is he ...? Who I think it is? Is it him?"

I nod.

He seems flustered momentarily and then says, "I'd like to, you know, see you maybe?" A long pause, and then I nod, *okay.* I try not to think of Gary or Chloe, especially Gary.

He comes towards me and stands for a moment or two, thinking. I can smell his aftershave, all lemony, which I like. "May I have your number?" he asks. "If that's okay?"

I hesitate, really wanting to have time to think about things, to mull it all over, see which way things may go, before committing to anything.

He adds, "Please." And so I relent, handing him my phone and giving him the passcode. He taps away before handing the phone back, smiling. Then he hands me his phone. I hesitate, then put my name and number into his contacts.

I nod and look at his face, trying to make sense of this, what seems to be a sudden turnaround. Feigning interest to actual interest. I wonder, with a flash of anger, if it is Liam who interests Ryan and not me. Maybe. After all, he's walked by me over the years and not shown a jot of interest. So why now? Liam. That's why. I smile and say goodbye and make my way to the restaurant.

"Who was that?" Liam says as I sit opposite him. He is waiting to eat the tiramisu. I take a spoonful of my tiramisu, and he starts eating his. I think quickly, not wanting to share the truth right now. I need to give it some thought. "Just someone from work, asking how I was and when I was going back."

Liam nods, seeming more interested in dessert than conversation, so we eat on and finish our meal. I worry my little fib may come back to haunt me one day soon.

———

As WE DRIVE HOME LATER, listening to Radio 1 and chatting more about our music likes and dislikes, my mind is restless. My spirits, too. I feel love for Liam. I don't know what to think about Ryan. I am tiring of Gary and his nuisance of a daughter. I need to do something about all of this, and soon. I need to make some life-changing decisions.

I stop the car at the top of the close, as Liam says he wants to go for a walk to the pier. I glance at him, thinking perhaps he has met someone, which would be good, as it may encourage him to stay here permanently from now on. But he does not glance back at me, just sits there looking out the side window, a neutral expression on his face as he gets out and, finally, as he waves goodbye, a sweet-enough smile.

As I drive on and into the close, approaching the driveway, I see a black Mercedes where I'd normally park my Fiesta. It's next to Gary's white van. He's home early, and the Mercedes belongs to his ex, Gemma. My spirits sink. He's obviously come back to meet her. I've only met her once or twice, and she is what she'd call assertive. I'd say gobby. She is certainly hard and demanding. What Gemma wants, Gemma gets. End of. I walk up the path to the front door, my keys in one hand, my bag over the other shoulder. My heart is in my mouth. I'm dreading this.

I can hear shouting. Gemma's voice is shrill and angry. Gary's is its usual monotone, but raised and defensive. Chloe's here too, echoing her mother's voice. I cannot tell who she is shouting at. Herself, possibly.

I put the key in the lock and pause, wanting to turn round, go back to my car, and drive somewhere else for a while, maybe sitting on the beach by the pier, until Gemma has gone. But that would be cowardly. It is, after all, my house, though nobody ever seems to acknowledge that. I turn the key in the lock and step through the small hallway into the living room.

Gary, Chloe and Gemma all stop shouting and turn towards me. They look at me, a stranger in my own home, with the same expression on their faces, as if I have no right to be here, interrupting a private conversation.

Gemma raises her hand, holding envelopes and pieces of paper. Chloe says, "Mum, no, don't." And I see, for a split second, such fury on Gary's face that I think he's going to step forward and strike Gemma.

She sees it, too, and reacts with venom. "You dare. You just fucking dare. Glenn will cut your face off." He stands there, a glowering, shame-faced child, as she turns and thrusts the envelopes and papers at me. I take them without thinking.

"Here." She says, "Rich bitch ... you pay his fucking debts." Then, without taking a breath, she adds viciously, "That's why he's with you. It's not for your looks, is it?"

She turns to Chloe, and I see, for the first time, that there is a holdall, packed so full that the top is unzipped, by Chloe's feet. "You coming or not?" Gemma says and then adds, "She's coming to live with me."

Chloe hesitates, glancing at her dad, who is so angry that he can't seem to meet her eye let alone speak. She doesn't look at me. That would indicate I was of some significance. I'm not, to her anyway. She picks up her holdall and follows Gemma to the hallway.

That, if that was it, would be enough of a nasty conversation. But Gemma, being Gemma, cannot leave it there. She has to not only win, and be seen to win, but to deliver a final, knockout blow.

"He's here," she says to me but looking at Gary, "because no one else will have him. He wants a roof over his head ... his home comforts ... your money ... to pay his bills ... and your bed, although God knows how he could do it with you." She puts her fingers to her mouth and makes a gagging noise.

Then one last look at Gary, a gesture to Chloe, and she is in the hallway by the front door. Gary stands there ready to explode. Chloe looks across at him, but he still won't meet her eye. He is ashamed, I think. And then they have gone, the door slammed hard behind them.

There is a long, shattered silence. I am shocked by the anger and hatred Gemma has shown towards me. Gary looks like a naughty schoolboy. More than that, really, as if he is the prisoner in the dock, just found guilty of an horrific crime. I wait, expecting him to say something, explaining what all of this is about, and to offer words of comfort for what Gemma has said to me. The way she spoke. But he says nothing.

I look down at the envelopes and letters in my hands, checking the first few of a dozen or more. His old address. Variations of his name. £3,827 unpaid here. £5,240 there. I don't recognise the business names. I don't understand these debts. I don't know what they are. Payday loans, gambling, maybe. Before I can ask, Gary shouts, "No!" and moves towards me. I think he is going to strike me, knocking me to the floor, somehow blaming me for whatever he has done.

I step back instinctively as he lunges forward, and I stumble over, falling awkwardly onto my elbow, the other arm flailing. Envelopes and letters scatter across the carpet. Gary does not help me up, nor offer kind or consoling words, let alone show concern for me. Instead, he turns and snatches at the envelopes and letters, absorbed in himself, cursing angrily as he fumbles over them. Then, without a glance or a word to me, he is up the stairs, two at a time, to the computer in the box room at the front of the house, slamming the door shut. He seems more worried about his unpaid bills than Chloe leaving home. Or me here, flat on my back.

———

AN HOUR OR SO LATER, Gary, Liam and I are sat around the little table in the conservatory. I thought it would be nicer here than in the busy kitchen with the washing machine rumbling away. The sun is low in the sky, and the evening is pleasantly warm.

I've made a chicken Caesar salad, with plenty of shredded chicken pieces and heavy on the dressing, just as Gary likes it. But as he sat down, he muttered, "Bloody rabbit food." So no apology for earlier, then, just more aggression.

Then, when Liam came in and wandered through to find us, kissing me on the cheek and saying hi quite cheerily to Gary, his reaction to Liam was to snarl, "Wash your bloody hands." Liam did.

I should have known better than to have this meal for the three of us this evening, but what else could I do? I wish we weren't sat here like this, the room so full of tension.

I listened at the foot of stairs when Gary shut himself in the box room and made various phone calls. Heard his cajoling, whining and, finally, his pleading. I saw his bubbling-over anger, his impotent rage, as he came back downstairs. He has no savings and can barely pay his share of things. He is dependent upon me and hates that.

If I had somehow avoided preparing this meal, said I was feeling sick and texted Liam to eat at the pier, Gary would have been even angrier, rummaging through the fridge, complaining about a packet meal, struggling to turn on the oven. Getting ever closer to exploding.

So we sit here now, a massive fallout waiting to happen. Gary is focused on his plate, pulling the chicken pieces out with his fingers and flicking the salad to the side with a sigh each time.

Liam notices this and tries to jolly things along with comments such as "Loving the chicken, Nina." I can tell, from Gary's laboured breathing, that these cheery words, the jolliness of them, are winding him up.

Then Liam says he loves the dressing, too, and, although I am sure he knows, he asks, "What is it?" He's trying to start a conversation. Gary snorts derisively. I answer Liam, and we carry on eating in an increasingly brittle atmosphere.

Liam is an innocent, with his fresh-air walks on the seafront and spending his copper and silver coins on the amusements at the pier. He doesn't understand what Gary is like, an earthy, physical man.

I should have texted him before he came back: *Stay away this evening. Gary's in a mood.* But how could I? Even making it jovial, with an exclamation mark, would have revealed the fracture at the heart of my relationship with Gary.

So we must muddle through, and I hope that Liam does not say anything more that will trigger a proper argument with Gary. If he does, I fear it will escalate quickly into something far worse. Gary is a strong man. Liam is not.

"Where's Chloe?" Liam asks innocently, smiling first at Gary and then at me. It's just meant to be another conversation starter, that's all. He's not to know.

He looks alarmed as I pull the slightest of faces and make an almost imperceptible shake of my head. A secret message between us. Too late, though.

Gary looks up and sees this, and I know he's going to react badly, taking my expression and reaction as some sort of betrayal of him.

"Why? What's it got to do with you?" is Gary's instinctive, belligerent response.

It's ridiculous and unnecessary, but as long as Liam now says something placatory, maybe slightly apologetic, I should then be able to change the conversation to something more cheerful.

Liam laughs, clearly mistaking Gary's abrupt and gruff response as a joke, banter even. It's the worst thing he could do.

I should speak, but find myself holding my breath, waiting to see which way this conversation is going to turn.

There is a pause. I do not know if Gary is going to swear at Liam, maybe insult him, perhaps even reach across and grab him by his tee shirt, yanking him forwards so their faces are centimetres apart.

I feel I am about to have to make a choice between my beautiful boy or my partner. Such a choice will be forced upon me. I cannot lose my boy.

Gary pushes his plate away and stands up. He looks at me and then at Liam. He's so full of venom. We wait on what he has to say, although I have the sudden sense the moment of danger – the risk of violence – has passed.

"You." He points at Liam. "You need to shape up or ship out." More inarticulate nonsense.

Liam swallows, uncertain, and nods his head and then lowers it, looking at his plate. It is enough to satisfy Gary, at least for now.

Then Gary turns to me. I look at him with a neutral expression. He stares at me, and I can see he is struggling to know what to say and how to put it. Something sharp and clever. "You fucking watch it," he says finally, like we are two schoolchildren. Him the bully. Me the victim. Then he stalks off, heading upstairs.

We sit there quietly, Liam and I, eating and listening to Gary stomping about, opening and shutting drawers, slamming doors.

I am choking on my food, struggling not to cry, so upset that Gary spoke to me like that, and in front of Liam, too. I am ashamed of him. The way he treats people. I wonder what he would be like if we had a baby. Not good, I fear. He would beat the child, with his looks and aggressive words, into submission. Maybe more than that.

Liam eats with a fork in his left hand and reaches out his right hand to hold mine. Then he inclines his head towards me, and I do the same until our heads are touching.

We say nothing for a minute or more, just sitting there like this listening to Gary still storming about upstairs. It is a comforting gesture.

"Chloe's left," I say. "Gone to live with her mum. Don't say anything."

Liam nods. "I'm here for you ..." Liam says, pulling ever so slightly away. A pause, and then he says, "Mum."

I am thrilled, utterly thrilled.

He continues, "Why the hell are you with him? He's such a ..."

I put my finger to my lips, indicating, *Ssshhh, not now.*

We sit up. Gary is hurtling down the stairs, dressed up smart and smelling of that pungent body spray of his that I hate. It's cheap and nasty. "Off to the pub," he says as he moves to the door. "Don't wait up."

I wonder where he's really going, what he's up to smelling like that, but say nothing.

We've been here before, of course. Him dressed up and soaked in body spray, coming back in the early hours, stinking of perfume. I asked where he'd been. "A club," he blustered, "In town ... a casino, actually ... with a couple of the lads. I won."

I let it go, but he never showed me his so-called winnings. And his jacket smelled of perfume and had blonde hairs on one shoulder. More fool me.

Liam shakes his head, an almost disbelieving gesture. But I do not want to open up further about Gary, at least not yet. I want to be loyal. I demean myself if I am not. So we carry on eating with barely a word spoken. We are kind of at ease with each other, though. I never feel I have to fill a silence with Liam.

After our salad, I bring through bowls and spoons, and

we share a large pot of cherry yoghurt smothered over meringue nests, one each. Liam asks if he'd like me to stay in this evening. But I say "No, go and find your friends."

So, after a kiss on the cheek and a hug goodbye, he does, and I am left alone with my increasingly troubled mind.

I LIE HERE IN BED, still thinking my awful thoughts. I must try to fall asleep before Gary returns from wherever. I wonder, if I'd had the baby, whether things might have worked out between Gary and me and Chloe. The baby could have been the glue that somehow kept us together against the odds.

Without the baby, I realise Gary is not the man for me. He is so full of rage. That's the worst of it. And Chloe is a hard-faced teenager, damaged by her parents' nasty divorce. There is no love lost between us. How could there be?

During the day, keeping myself busy, I have allowed my life to meander on. Gary is happy only when everything is how he wants it. He has never hit me – not yet anyway – but he will do soon. The day is coming. As I start to fall asleep, I decide I must do something before that happens.

I am hiding, squatting and crouched over, my forehead resting on my raised knees, in the cupboard under the stairs. I am shaking. I hug my knees tighter. Still I keep shaking.

I hear his heavy footsteps above my head. He is stomping up the stairs, going from one room to the next, searching for me. Furniture is tipped over and pushed aside. Belongings are hurled across the room. There are guttural grunts of rage.

"Where are you? Where are you?" I hear fury and frustration in his voice. "Come out! Come out!" I know, when I am found, I

will be beaten heavily, or worse. I fear for my life. I stay as quiet as I can.

My mind reels back over the evening. I cannot remember all that I did. Only that everything was wrong for him.

He kept shouting, telling me I was stupid and to do it again. Whatever I did, it was never enough.

However much I tried to please him, he just shouted more and more. When his back was turned, I ran to hide.

I hear doors slamming upstairs, and his heavy footsteps storming back and forth, opening cupboards, searching inside, then wrenching them over onto the floor.

He moves now from fury to frenzy, and I know he will kill me. There is a light bulb under the stairs, and I feel for it in the dark, finding it, unscrewing it, breaking it gently by my side, holding onto the base below the jagged pieces. I feel blood running down my fingers.

I hear him running down the stairs, still bellowing for me to show myself. It's some kind of sick game now: "Come out, come out, wherever you are!" I cower.

I hid in the cupboard under the stairs. It was the first place I found, opening the door, pulling it to, sitting in the dark.

There was nowhere else. Behind curtains. Inside a wardrobe. In the shower with the curtain pulled across. Like I was a child playing a game of hide-and-seek.

He rushed by the cupboard under the stairs. Upstairs first, his anger rising. Downstairs now, ready to attack. He pulls the cupboard door open.

I am up and at him, the broken light bulb in my hand, slashing at his throat. He steps back, raises his arm and knocks the light bulb away.

He slams me back against the staircase, his full weight

pinning me tight. He has his hands over my face, pinching my
nose and clamping my mouth shut.

I cannot breathe, and I know that this is the end of me. He is
too strong, and all I can do is to twist and turn my head to try to
shake his hands loose. I feel myself passing out.

As I do, I snap out of the nightmare. I lie here in bed,
reliving the horror in my mind, with Gary snoring by my
side. The rain is hammering at the window. It has been
sunny for so long that I thought it would never rain again. It
will at least water the grass and plants.

I turn and look at Gary, on his back, mouth open,
snoring loudly. I could never wake him up and say he was
snoring, as he would not believe such a thing were possible.
I have 'accidentally' kicked him awake once or twice and
pretended to be asleep.

Now, he moves, slowly and heavily, onto his side. He
stops snoring, but is making a wet slobbering noise as
though he is blowing air out through his lips. I wish I could
leave him. I don't know how. To be frank, I don't think I'd
have the courage. My fear is that, if I do not, my nightmare
will soon turn into reality.

6

THURSDAY, 13 JULY, DAYTIME

I put the breakfast things on the table the next morning, keeping away from Gary whilst he eats and drinks by pretending to scrub the oven. He likes everything to be sparkling clean, although he never lifts a finger to do anything himself.

"Where's numbnuts?" he asks as he comes through to say goodbye before he leaves. He expects to kiss me on the cheek, and although I'd rather push my oven-cleaning cloth into his face, I let him. To keep the peace.

"He came in late." To this white lie, I add, "I expect he's got a hangover."

I regret the words as I say them, as Gary mutters an obscenity under his breath. I think for one awful moment that he's going to go upstairs and drag Liam out of bed. But he does not. He just turns and goes, slamming the front door behind him. I doubt that's the end of his issues with Liam.

I hear Gary revving and reversing his white van down the driveway and then roaring up the close and off to Ipswich.

Another day of rising resentment coming to the boil when he returns home, no doubt.

Liam is up and out of bed, walking across the landing into the bathroom. He's always in and out quickly. I'm not sure he washes properly. I hope he does his teeth.

I clear Gary's breakfast things away and re-set the table for Liam and me with toast and jam and marmalade, cereals and orange juice and a pot of tea. There's plenty there to eat and drink.

As we have our breakfast, I can sense that Liam wants to say something to me – there are little glances and jigglings in his chair as he prepares what he is going to say.

I wait, neither encouraging nor discouraging, just chattering away on the usual weather, what are you doing today, I'm going shopping nonsense so that he can formulate his words and sentences.

For one desperate moment, I think he might say that he's in the way here, is upsetting Gary and that he should leave. He's texted his adoptive parents, and they're going to pick him up later today. I panic and am about to speak, to say something about staying. *Please.* But Liam talks first.

"He doesn't like me ... Gary ... does he? He'd rather I left, wouldn't he?" He stirs his cereal around the bowl, splashing the milk. He seems agitated.

"He's ... ah ..." I'm not sure how to reply. I think and then say, "He's under a lot of pressure at work ... and he's upset about Chloe ... and he's ... well, he's just on edge."

"I think he only wanted me here to invest in his scheme. Honestly, if I said I were a piss-poor orphan, he'd never have let me in. And now he wants me gone."

I feel ever closer to making that choice between Liam

and Gary. There's no contest at all, but I'm not ready to make life-changing decisions at the moment. Not just yet.

"It's alright," I reply. "About your money. Gary's just ... he's ... keep your head low, and it will all blow over. He'll be okay later, you'll see." I have my doubts – he could be ten times worse – but I don't want to upset Liam and scare him away.

There is a pause, and it turns into a long silence. He sits there, not moving, framing his next comment. I sit patiently.

"You can do better than him," he says finally, glancing upwards as he speaks. "He's ... a horrible man." Another pause. "He treats you like shit." One more thing, a question. "Does he hit you?"

I look up. Our eyes meet, and I glance away. I feel ashamed; I'm not sure why. I am torn between defending Gary and confessing, sharing my innermost thoughts with Liam.

I shake my head, dipping my head, not wanting to look into his eyes at the moment. "No," I say, in as steady a voice as I can. In truth, it is not steady at all.

I reach across to his spoon and now empty bowl, picking them up and placing them with my spoon and bowl. I finish my mug of tea and put it into the bowls, feeling awkward, ready to get up, clearing away.

Liam reaches out his hand as I stand, putting it on top of my hand, holding the cup and bowls. "Do you want me to speak to him, tell him to go?"

I laugh. I can't help myself. It's not a nice laugh, though. It sounds rather tart, I know. If Liam were to say anything like that to Gary, the response would be immediate and savage. Gary, quite simply, would knock Liam out. Then drag and dump him on the pavement. Then come in and go for me. It would be the worst possible thing. The last straw.

"No, no." I pull away and take the breakfast things to the kitchen. "Leave it for now ... I'll sort it out later." I sound like I'm talking about forgetting to pay someone back a fiver I borrowed. As though it's nothing. It is, of course, everything, really.

He follows me into the kitchen, carrying more breakfast things, then hesitates after he's put them on the side and is about to go out for the day. "If you're sure ... I'm happy to speak to him."

He moves towards me as if he is going to put his arms around my shoulders and pull me in for a big hug.

I could not bear that, not at the moment. I would collapse into his arms and let him talk me into agreeing to anything, however foolhardy. So I am moving here and there, loading the dishwasher, fiddling about, loading cups and bowls and plates. Busy, busy, busy.

"Well" – he says at last – "if you're certain?"

I nod my head emphatically as I turn away and fill the kettle with fresh water from the tap.

He does not see me crying softly as he turns to go with a cheerful, "See you at six!"

I love him. I don't love Gary. I don't know what to do about all of this.

I HAVE a lazy day at home, spending the morning tidying and cleaning around, from top to bottom. I have found, when I am feeling low, that it helps to take my mind off things, keeping busy with gentle physical work.

I have a phone conversation with someone from the office – not my line manager, but a new person in HR who speaks in practised, soothing tones about going back to work. They have been understanding since I lost my baby and are not pressuring me at all. Not yet, anyway. I don't feel right at the moment, though.

Later in the morning, I clean the bath and the shower and the toilet and the sinks in the bathroom and the kitchen. Silly, I know, but I find this so soothing – the mindlessness of it, I think – yet, even so, thoughts of Gary, Liam and Ryan fill my mind.

Now, after a light lunch of cheese and biscuits watching the one o'clock news – the usual anger and misery – I am sitting quietly in the living room, looking out the front window, with my mobile phone on my lap.

I like it here, in the close, in this quiet and sunny spot. I don't really know the neighbours, just waving and smiling when I see them, that's all. The man next door, Tony, is a sweet, older man in his sixties. We pass the time of day when we bump into each other, sometimes up the town, as he works in a shop there.

There is a creepy man, late fifties, over the way who lives with his yappy Jack Russell terrier and his elderly white-haired mother. Terry and Yona, or it might be Mona, I'm not sure. I don't know what the dog is called. I see him walking it sometimes in the fields behind my house, mornings and evenings. I don't think Terry has ever worked, or at least he always seems to be here. I ignore him even when he shouts over at me. I never see her anymore; I think she is in a wheel-chair or may be bedridden by now.

Other than that, everyone else in the close is mostly anonymous. I see them coming and going – mostly older folk, white-haired couples – and try to be doing something when they look across. I smile and wave if I have to. It's not that I am rude. I just want to keep to myself and not get involved in watering their plants and feeding their cats and putting their bins out when they are on holiday.

I stare at my phone, the contacts list, Ryan and his number. I have a horrible feeling that I gave Ryan the wrong phone number yesterday. I was so flustered that I'm sure I put 4343 in the middle instead of 4334.

If so, he cannot contact me, and I do so want to hear from him. I don't want to chase, to seem desperate. But a text: *Ryan, it's Nina. I'm not sure I gave you the right number yesterday. It's ...* could do no harm, could it?

I know in my heart what it is I want. Ryan and I to be together. Here. With our son, Liam. The perfect little family.

I also know what I don't want. Gary. And a baby with him. Tied to him for the rest of my life. Forever. And Chloe coming back when she next has a falling-out with Gemma. More hate coming from her.

I don't know how to go from where I am now to where I want to be. I don't even know if Ryan would want me. Us. This home. He may still have feelings for his ex-wife. And certainly his daughters.

I hesitate and then put my phone away. I need to deal with Gary first, however and whenever I do that. I need to work it out.

I do not want to encourage Ryan now, not when I am unable to really progress anything with Gary still here. And although I don't think Gary has ever looked at my phone, he could do; I do not want him to see messages between Ryan and me. I set up fingerprint security on my phone so only I can access it.

I suddenly have a terrible image in my head of me lying unconscious on the bedroom carpet, with Gary kneeling nearby, holding my mobile phone. He turns my hand sharply, then my fingers, pressing one after another against the screen of my mobile phone. "Aha," he'll shout as he drops me back down and accesses my messages.

I shake my head, trying to blot out the image.

Anyway, if Ryan is truly interested in me and I gave him the wrong number, he can come and find me. I'm not hard to find. My name is distinctive, and I am sure there are various online search engines to uncover me. Not that that would be any better, with Gary here.

Later, I drive over to the Tesco superstore at Martlesham Heath to do a big shop. I find myself stocking up on all the things that Liam likes to eat and drink; I think, subconsciously, that I want to do everything to encourage him to stay.

Then, and I know it's mad of me, I drive to Ipswich, a detour on the way home, to go by Ryan's dental practice. There is a road that seems to have lots of private dental practices in it, and Ryan's is one of them. I notice his black Audi on the drive as I slow and take it all in: the name and the grandness of it. So upmarket.

I pull into a McDonald's car park on the way out of town, and Google Ryan's business. He looks successful and wealthy, and I am pleased that he has done well for himself. More so, that he would not want to be with me for my money as I suspect Gary is. It's certainly been a motivating factor, and I hate him for it. Despise him, really.

Then I drive home. As I come towards Trimley St Martin, I decide I will tell Liam how I feel, what I want from life, and what I don't want. And we will see if we can come up with a plan between us. The thought thrills me, filling me with joy. It doesn't all have to be done today, or even soon. But having a plan will be enough to keep me happy.

I pull over into a layby and decide to text Liam, to see if maybe we could meet at the café on the pier in an hour or so. We can then talk, and I can say how I feel about him and Gary, and we can come up with that plan. He can come home with me in the car and help me get tea ready for six o'clock, when, together, we can set the plan in action.

'HI LIAM. ARE YOU ABOUT?'

I then press 'send'. As I do, I realise, and it's funny, really, that, even though we have each other's numbers, we don't text.

I don't know why. I think it's because I don't want to bother him – to be a nagging mum! And he's a teenager and is, like all of them I think, wrapped up in the here and now. He doesn't want to have to text his mum when he's larking about with his mates.

But this is different, a chance for us to share our innermost thoughts and feelings and to work together to achieve our dreams. When all is said and done, I'm sure they are shared dreams.

I stare out the window, watching the cars passing by, this way and that. There is a thirty-mile-per-hour limit on this stretch of road, but some of the cars are going much faster.

The road, making its way from Felixstowe through the villages of Walton, Trimley St Mary and Trimley St Martin to the A14, is a funny old thing. It used to be a quiet, rural road almost, just pottering along, minding its own business.

Now it's packed and edgy. There's been so many changes lately, new houses, roundabouts, and it's hard to get up speed until you get to this end close to the A14. And then the cars accelerate. My car shakes as one passes by, too fast, too close.

I look at my phone, hoping for a quick reply from Liam, an enthusiastic *Yes!* and an invitation to meet me at the pier or the Wimpy bar in town; I'd be happy anywhere.

But there is no reply. I sit staring at it for minutes, clicking in and out of Messages over and again as if that will somehow pull in his response.

I am tempted to drive to the seafront, park, and go and find him on the pier or the amusements. But I hesitate, thinking he might be embarrassed, angry even, if I see him with his mates, like I'm checking he's changed his pants and socks today.

Instead, I write what it is I want to tell him. *Liam, my darling boy, I want you to live here with me forever. We will be happy together. Just you and I. Let's meet and talk about it.*

I hesitate, thinking, perhaps, it is far too strong, too emotional, and that he may cringe. I imagine one of his mates looking over his shoulder as he reads it and shouting, "Darling boy!" and all of them laughing at him. I can't have that.

I wonder if I should make it more kind of take it or leave it. But I want him to know my feelings. I also need to say something about Gary, that I want him gone. But I am not sure how to put that, either.

I look up suddenly, hearing a car braking, another hooting, and see two cars, one behind the other, with the man in the following car gesturing and waving his fist. It's always like that on the roads round here, with these red-faced, angry men spoiling for a fight.

The car at the front accelerates away with the one behind hoot-hoot-hooting in pursuit. I wonder how this will end. I once saw two men fighting outside the village stores in Trimley St Mary over a parking space. Most likely, the car behind will overtake the one in front, there will be more gestures, and then they'll go about their business, honours even. Some men are so pathetic.

I look down at my text, ready to change what I've written. But then I see, coming along the road, a white van and the unmistakeable face of Gary, leaning forward, intense and concentrating, and driving way too fast. He's heading home in a hurry.

I have an appalling sense of fear, all of a sudden. I note from my phone that it's later than I thought, but still not yet teatime. Gary is early, which he is now and then. But not often. And it's the expression on his face that's alarming me.

It's possible that Liam may already be home. He does not usually turn up more than ten or fifteen minutes before his meal. But who knows? He could be there now, with Gary racing towards him. After last night and this morning, I need to be there too, getting between them, calming things down.

I look at my message to Liam, deciding it's not quite right, and it can wait anyway. I delete it and then drop the phone on the passenger seat. Mirror, signal, manoeuvre, and I pull out into the fast-flowing traffic and away, pursuing Gary's white van.

7

THURSDAY, 13 JULY, EARLY EVENING

As I open the front door and go into the hallway, I can see Gary is in the living room, all jerks and twitches. I hope I've got the wrong end of the stick, that he has simply lost more work or has had an argument with a customer who wants a cheaper job. I wonder if he's now not earning enough to even pay his share of our outgoings.

I know better than to ask or even to say anything other than, "Dinner will be on the table in thirty minutes," giving him a chance to change his clothes or wash his hands. Not that he ever does. At most, he rubs the palms of his hands on the back of his jeans, like that will clean them.

He glances towards the staircase, as if checking Liam is upstairs – he isn't, but I don't say – and then rushes towards me, grabbing my arm. Too tight. It hurts. I say nothing, though, as he tugs me round to face him.

"Who is he?" Gary says, cocking his head at an upwards angle. I feel myself flushing.

I have a sudden surge of fear that he has uncovered the truth. I don't know how. I struggle to reply.

"He's not who he says he is." Gary answers his own question. He is angry, but not with me. Not yet, anyway.

I shake my head, bewildered, and swallow and choke out the words, "What do you mean?"

He hushes me, listening for sounds from upstairs, and then pulls me through into the kitchen. I do not resist.

Gary pushes the door to, stands by it, listening, and then gestures me to come towards him. I move a little closer as Gary starts talking.

"I don't know who he is. But he's not Liam Riley; he's not your cousin." He says this in a strained voice.

I say I don't understand. He sighs, like I'm stupid, and goes on.

"There's just something about him." He looks at me. "Something not quite right. Never has been. You must have felt it, too."

I pull a non-committal face. I think Gary takes it as a confirmation because he nods, not once but twice, and it then all comes pouring out.

"I've been texting with Chloe; she noticed it first. He's just ... odd with her. Bloody creepy. So we've been checking him out ... we met at lunchtime at McDonald's to compare ..." He tails off, listening at the door before continuing.

"He's not on Facebook ... Instagram ... or TikTok or ... whatever bloody Twitter is called these days. He's not on any social media at all. Chloe can't find him anywhere. That's kind of weird, isn't it?"

I go to nod, but he hasn't finished yet. He's just getting started.

"And there's this site, see, 192.com, where you can search

the electoral roll and stuff ... for people ... and he mentioned his parents' names once ... and where they lived ... and they're not there. They don't exist, either."

"Chloe says he's some sort of con artist, and he's here to take you for your money ... your savings. Has he ... what's he said to you? Has he asked to borrow money?"

I want to reply that Liam is my cousin, I know he is, but I am rattled by what Gary says. I don't know how to respond. I stand there open-mouthed. That obviously angers Gary, and I know he's now going to turn on me.

"He just came to the door, didn't he, selling tea towels? He must have sweet-talked you into telling him all about yourself. Jesus Christ! You're so fucking stupid. Wait here." He swings round, and I watch as he pushes open the kitchen door. He pauses, and I think he's going to shout upstairs, "Liam? Liam? Get your arse down here now." He moves to the staircase.

I am outraged that he is doing this, taking charge, being so aggressive, expecting me to stay in the kitchen like the little woman he treats me as. Whilst he, the big man, will talk to Liam – 'man-to-man', as he'd put it. He storms up the stairs.

I have a moment or two before he realises Liam is not here. Then he will come down and start interrogating me as though I, this house and all my money are his belongings to be protected at all costs. For him. I reach for my purse and handbag, and keys in hand, I head out to my car. I imagine Gary watching from the front bedroom window, furious, as I drive away to find Liam.

I PULL the car over at the top of the close, out of sight of my house, but before I get to the main road to Felixstowe. I'm not thinking straight.

It's madness for me to go searching for Liam at the pier, along the amusements, even up the town. He could be anywhere, and I'd never find him.

I just want to get to him before he returns to the house and there is a confrontation. Maybe I should have stayed at home and tried to act as a peacemaker when Liam arrives, but I am frightened of what Gary might do.

I have to tell Liam what Gary has said to me. Then insist he go and stay in a bed and breakfast for the night, whilst I go back after a while and listen to what else Gary has to say, trying to calm him down. If I can't, Liam can never come here again.

I'm certain that, if Liam and Gary meet tonight, there will be bloodshed. And Liam may be forced to reveal he is my son. And the thought of what happens after that frightens me.

I also want to know more about Gary's online searches for Liam and his adoptive family, though. Neither Gary nor Chloe is a clever or diligent person. I think they've somehow got it all wrong. Even so, something nags at the back of my mind. A troubling thought I can't quite get to.

I pull my mobile phone out of my handbag, my hands shaking, and press my way through to 'Liam' in my contacts list.

I call him, muttering, "Answer ... answer ... answer!" under my breath. It just rings out.

I try again, once, twice, three times. It does the same. Just rings on and on. It does not go to voicemail, so I cannot leave a message.

I decide to text him, thinking quickly what to put and then stabbing at the buttons.

'*Gary suspects all. Don't come home tonight. Meet me by the pier 10am.*'

I press 'send' and hope that he will read it before he gets to the house.

I sit here a while, ages really, expecting a call or a text from Liam at any moment, or to see him appear suddenly from along the main road.

If they were to meet now, Gary would ask Liam who he is, demanding an answer. As Liam hesitates, trying to find the words, Gary will have his hands on Liam's neck, slamming his body against the wall.

He will then bang Liam's head repeatedly against the wall, shouting, again and again, "Who are you? What do you want with Nina?" And Liam will struggle to speak, his eyes bulging as he gasps for breath.

Gary has such a temper. If he thinks he is right, and someone is lying, he will go on and on and on. Until Liam falls to the floor. And Gary will step forward, standing over him. "Last time, who the fuck are you?" he'll say. Liam will look up at Gary's furious face and have no choice.

"I'm Liam, Nina's son; she had me adopted nineteen years ago, just after I was born." And Gary would explode in complete and utter rage, yelling his pain and fury out loud. And then he would bring his boot down on Liam's head one last time.

I would find Liam lying there, at the foot of the stairs, his face a beaten and bloodied pulp. Gary will turn as I come through the front door. "So," he'll say, "he's your son. All this ... cousin bollocks ... just a bare-faced lie. How dare you do this to me ... laughing at me behind my back." All these weeks and months, when he has struggled to control his temper, never to lay a finger on me, will count for nothing.

He will stride towards me, his arm raised above his head, his hand clenched in a fist, and he will club me to the floor and then move in to kick my back, my legs, and my tummy, where our baby used to be.

I check my phone, hoping to see a reply to my text message. There has been no response. I shake my head in frustration.

I text again, in capitals, with as much emphasis as I can. *'DON'T COME HOME TONIGHT! GARY ON WARPATH!'*

I press 'send' with a sense of hopelessness, that Liam's just going to come back all bright and breezy, without checking his phone, walking straight into Gary.

I check for recent phone calls. There have been none. I call Liam's number. It rings out as it did before.

I stop and try again and then once more, almost close to obsession now. He's not answering. I cannot leave a message, my voice shaking so much.

All I can do is sit here, my car parked at the top of the close, waiting for him to come by. And that's what I do.

Then it hits me. He'll be back by now, Liam, at this time of the evening. He'll have cut across the fields and come in through the back gate, all whilst I'm sitting here fretting and worrying.

He will have walked in on Gary standing there, ready to attack him. Smiled cheerfully, not realising what was about to happen.

I start my car, revving and roaring into a three-point turn. I have to get back and save Liam from Gary's attack.

I PULL my car onto the driveway next to Gary's van and get out, standing there, looking and listening.

The front door is shut; the curtains are still pulled back, the windows slightly open for fresh air. I cannot hear any noise, neither shouts nor yells, nor music or any household sounds. It is quiet. In fact, the whole close is unnaturally silent.

I walk up the path and put the key in the lock. I open the door and step inside, not knowing what to expect.

The living room as I left it, a folded-over *Daily Mail* on an armrest, a half-empty mug of tea on the coffee table. It's as though I had just got up and gone – which, of course, I did. And it is as if Gary, when Liam returned, had called out, "Liam, let's go and have a beer at the pub ... leave everything to the little woman!"

But this is where the fight would have taken place, as Liam came in the front door, through the hallway to here, when Gary would have pounced on him. Armchairs should have been turned over, knick-knacks sent scattering, the walls spattered with blood. Perhaps even Liam lying behind the sofa, groaning in agony. But there is nothing amiss. There is nobody here.

I move to the kitchen, which is just as I left it when I hurried out the back. The plates and dishes are in the dishwasher, the door upright at an angle, not quite shut. I went out in a hurry. No one has been in here since. At least, if they have, nothing has been moved.

I stand, looking out towards the conservatory, my peaceful place, where I like to sit and watch the birds in the garden. And it seems quiet now, and I wonder how that can be. I had expected mayhem, perhaps even horror, Gary beating up Liam, leaving him a sobbing mess, blood all across the carpet. But there is nothing like that at all.

Liam has not come back yet, then. Maybe he has hooked up with someone down on the seafront, back to their place for the evening, perhaps for the night. The prettiest girl or boy from amongst his new-found friends. Gary waited and waited, got bored, and then went to the pub to play darts.

I tidy around, on autopilot, just going back and forward, straightening this, moving that. Chores I have done thousands of times before and will do so again. I want to have a bath, but will wait for Liam to return, so I can talk to him before Gary comes back after the pub closes.

I get the vacuum cleaner from under the stairs and run it around. It is a soothing feeling, cleaning the carpet, and I relax slowly as I manoeuvre the vacuum into the corners and along the edges. I think, possibly, I have been worried over nothing. Maybe Gary and Liam have already had words, but Liam has been quick-witted and placated Gary in some way; perhaps they have even gone out together. I will vacuum upstairs and then have a relaxing bath.

I struggle to lift the vacuum cleaner up the stairs, the weight of it in my left hand, the hose wrapping itself around my left leg as I try to untangle it with my right hand.

I put it back on the carpet at the bottom of the stairs and glance up as I hear footsteps on the landing. Liam stands there, wild-eyed and speechless. I stare at him. Neither of us speak.

Eventually, Liam raises his blood-soaked hands and speaks. Six words. "I'm sorry, Mum. I've killed him."

PART II

TRUTHS OR LIES

8

THURSDAY, 13 JULY, NIGHT-TIME

Gary – his body, his corpse – is flat on his back on Liam's bedroom carpet. His white tee shirt is dark with blood that still seems to be running down onto the cream-coloured carpet.

My mind, frozen in the horror of the moment, thinks only that it was a really stupid colour to choose. For the carpet. And that I will never get the stain out. Madness.

Then I imagine the blood dripping through the carpet and the ceiling below into the living room. A never-ending cascade. And I suddenly come to, shaking off these nonsensical thoughts in my head.

I look towards Liam, half-hoping, expecting, that he will take charge, deciding what to do. I will follow his lead. But Liam appears to be stunned by what has happened, this awful turn of events. He is motionless, his arms by his sides, his thumbs in his pockets. He looks transfixed by what is in front of him.

I take in as much as I can. Gary is clearly dead and has, looking at the cut and shredded tee shirt, been stabbed many times. The knife, Liam's whittling knife, lies beside the body. It has been wiped clean. I wonder for a second how Liam could be so matter-of-fact after such a shocking act.

I find myself swallowing, trying to anyway, my mouth dry, my tongue feeling twice its normal size. I shake my head, my mind seeking the words to say. My clothes are drenched in sweat, my body reacting to the slaughter by our feet. Strangely, I do not seem to feel sorrow or anger because of what has happened – Gary's death, the loss of the man who might one day have been my husband and the father of my baby. Truth is, I know now, I never loved him.

My mind starts taking a more practical turn. But before I can say anything, Liam starts to speak in a flat monotone of a voice. He sounds like a different person as he provides an explanation of what happened.

"I came in ... upstairs ..." He breathes unevenly. "I was ... he came storming in, pushing me against the wall, banging my head. He kept shouting, 'Who are you?' I thought he was going to kill me."

He gulps. "I said I was your son. I had to ... I thought ..." He slows, steadying his voice. "I thought that was the only way to stop him. But he just went mad ... he saw my knife on the side ... went to grab it ... I got it first ..."

We stand there, side by side, Liam waiting for me to take over, to tell him what to do. My mind flicks through the options. We should, I know, dial 999, call the police, explain what happened. That Gary attacked Liam, was going to kill him, that Liam acted in self-defence. But something about this bloody scene nags at me, at the back of my mind, telling my subconscious that this would be the wrong thing to do.

It hits me that Liam, my precious boy, may be charged with manslaughter, that he may be sent to prison. I could not bear it, being apart from him, seeing him at most at once-a-month visits. His future, all his hopes and dreams, snatched away from him by this one awful act, a tragic mistake. I glance once more at the body, and my mind reeling, I try to guess how many times Liam stabbed Gary. So many, I believe, that manslaughter may actually be murder.

So I think, with such a sense of fear, that there is only one thing to do. For me to claim this killing as my own. To put my fingerprints on the knife handle. My hands on Gary's face and body and hands and arms and legs. His blood on my hands, my clothes, and my face. To send Liam away into the night, urging him to go back to his adoptive parents, where he will be safe. I stifle a sob at the thought of never seeing him again. Not for ages, anyway. But he will be safe. I will plead self-defence, saying Gary attacked me. What else can I do?

Then, suddenly, unexpectedly, Liam steps forward, taking charge. "We have to dispose of the body so it's never found." He looks at me, presenting this new and shocking option, waiting for my agreement. There is the longest pause. My mind goes this way and that. The option is such a nasty one. Horrific. Beyond any sense of basic decency.

And yet it is the only one that gives Liam and me the chance of a future. My mind races through what we will do with the body, and how we will explain his disappearance. I have some ideas. I work through them quickly. "Yes," I say finally. God help us.

Liam nods. The decision made, he seems to become a stronger, more decisive person. "We can bury him here or elsewhere ... cut him up ... take him in his van miles away and set fire to it ... use his phone to text you a suicide note ..."

I sink to my knees at this, sobbing at the thought of what has happened and what is about to unfold. I cannot bear it. But then, breaking the silence, we hear the ringing of the front doorbell.

LIAM and I stand here looking at each other, neither knowing what to do. I'm worried it's Chloe coming home. She will run up the stairs, see this bedroom door is open, and look inside, her slaughtered father before her. I wonder how Liam and I will react, one or both of us instinctively reaching for the knife in an act of self-preservation.

I shake my head, realising she does not need to ring the doorbell. She has her own key. She'd have come straight in. Someone else, then. I don't know who it could be, coming here after nine o'clock. Closer to ten, really.

Neither Gary nor Chloe have ever had any friends or family visiting the house. Other than Gemma, but I don't think she'd be here on her own, ringing. A neighbour, then, but I only ever smile and wave at most of them; I don't pass the time of day. Perhaps it's someone Gary owes money to.

"Don't answer it," Liam whispers urgently. He looks hot and clammy, and I notice, for the first time, that he is splattered with blood. I can't believe I did not see it before. My mind playing tricks, protecting me, I suppose.

I shake my head and answer, "They'll ... go ... soon." I struggle for breath and to speak properly. I breathe in long and hard through my nose, pushing the breath out of my mouth. It makes no difference. I am still terrified.

"Who is it?" Liam asks. "At this time?" He pulls a disbelieving face. I look at him, one scared person to another, and shrug my shoulders. He shakes his head. We both look at the body, feeling helpless.

I imagine whoever it is, a policeman, a firefighter, a concerned neighbour, then banging on the door, again and again and again.

With no answer, they'll break the door in and shout, "Anyone in? There's a fire! Fire! Hurry. Hurry!" Up the stairs they'll come. In here. Seeing the corpse. We can't pull the knife on them. These fit young men and women. I am in torment, my mind playing out this vivid nightmare.

But there is no hammering or cracking and splintering, just another incongruous ring-a-ding of the doorbell. Whoever it is isn't going to just leave. I will go downstairs and send them on their way. I step towards the bedroom door.

"Don't," Liam says. "Don't answer it." He gestures towards the body, as if to say, *Look, look, what if they come up here? We're done for.* Instead, he says, in a cracking voice, "You look ... your face ... like you've just murdered someone."

I stop and gaze at him, my mind searching for an elusive, troubling thought. So I reply, "I'm not going to. I'll look out the window and see who it is. Wait here."

And so I am at the window of the box room at the front of the house, looking down. The close is full of cars. I think someone, here somewhere, is having a dinner party. In my troubled mind, they are police cars, as if they have already discovered what has happened. Insanity, really. My thoughts seeking out the worst scenarios.

It is a man standing below, the outside light shining on trousers and shoes. I think it must be a neighbour, asking for a bottle of milk, or to say he's noticed my car has a flat tyre, whatever. He steps back suddenly, and I see it is Ryan. I gasp in surprise, not only that he has found me, those online searches, I guess, but that he has come to me.

As he turns to leave, he looks up. He sees me before I can step away. We look at each other for an age, and then he inclines his head towards Gary's white van, as though he's saying, *You're with someone, then.* I wonder why he rang the doorbell if he thinks that. I guess discovering you have a son triggers something close to madness in you. With Gary lying dead, I have to let him leave. Then he is gone, to his car and away, and I stand and watch with a sense of utter desolation. I wonder if I will ever see him again.

———

I SHRUG as I go back into Liam's room, and he looks at me quizzically. "No idea," I say. "Neighbour wanting a cup of sugar, most likely. I don't know." I don't want to say it was Ryan. Not now. Perhaps not ever.

"They've gone?" he asks, letting out a sigh. "Now what do you want to do?" He waits for my decision.

We look at the body. The stiff-set face. Eyes still open. The chest. Bloody and mushed. The smell makes me feel sick. Is there one? Perhaps I just have an overactive imagination. But there is no mistaking we need to dispose of the body fast. We talk quickly.

I ask what we should do. I add I could not bear to cut – I stumble, choking over the words – him up. I don't think I could even touch Gary.

He replies we should take 'the body', as he calls it, to woods or forests far away and set fire to everything. "Fire destroys all evidence. It's the safest."

I cannot bear that idea, either, and say so: "I can't. I just can't." Whatever is done will have to be done by Liam.

I go on, "Surely, even if it could be done ... they'll know petrol was used ... so that's clearly murder ... if the engine doesn't burn, the number on it may be traceable ... anyway ... if ... when he's reported missing, the police will put two and two together and come here." My thoughts come tumbling out. All of them alarming me.

He mulls it over and then laughs and says he can't drive anyway, so I'd have to drive the van and then walk home. His laughter unsettles me; there is nothing funny about this horror. He is off-balance. It is like people sometimes laughing when a hearse goes by. Why would they do such a thing? Nervousness, I suppose.

"We'll bury him, then. Here," he replies, leaning forward and picking up the knife before handing it to me. I take it by the handle without thinking, folding it closed, tucking it into a pocket. He then starts stripping the cover from his duvet, asking me to get bin bags, tape, whatever else I have, to wrap the body. I feel sick at the thought, but go to see what I can find.

We wrap the body – Gary, I must say his name – in the duvet cover. We leave the duvet on the bed. We could have used it to wrap the body and soak up the blood. But it is too bulky, I suppose. We then put bin bags over and around the body – head, torso, legs and feet – and tape them together. It's a blur.

This is stop-start, stop-start. Liam is calm and methodical. It is as if he has a checklist of what to do in his head and is following it step by step. His face is grim, but shows no other emotion. I am sobbing and wiping my eyes constantly. I go to the bathroom to be sick twice, a third time just bringing up bile. Eventually, the task is done, this black-binned mummy by our feet. I'm sure I can see the contours of Gary's face.

And then Liam and I are out in the garden, digging a hole out of sight behind my garage. It takes what seems like hours. The hardest thing I have ever done physically. And mentally, too. Working in desperate silence. Noises from the close. People leaving the dinner party. Going home. There is an ever-present fear of discovery. A street light shines into some of the garden, but not this hellish corner, thank goodness.

Half-carrying, half-dragging Gary downstairs, out the back to the shallow grave, is the worst thing ever. This is a mistake. I understand that, but don't know what else to do. I help Liam lift him in, then say – a stubborn memory from my disbelieving childhood – the Lord's Prayer. That's it. I cannot bring myself to shovel soil back over Gary, treading it down flat and even into place. I gag one final time, my heart breaking, as I go back indoors, heading to the shower to rub my hair and face and skin until they are red-raw clean.

As I shower, rubbing madly everywhere with the most powerful spray and a soapy nail brush, I feel sick with dread. I know this is not the end of everything. I have to dispose of the clothes I've been wearing, Liam's too, and clean or burn everything between here and the garden, the blood on the carpet and more, a trail of potential evidence all down the stairs and beyond.

Then there are Gary's clothes and belongings all over the house, and his work equipment, ladder and brushes in his van. And the van itself. That great big white van sitting on the driveway. A constant reminder of Gary and that he's going nowhere. Somehow, that van will have to go.

And there will be customers, wanting to know where he is. Debt collectors. And Chloe, wanting to see her dad. Gemma too, asking him for something or other. I do not know what I will say to them. Nothing will sound believable. And, of course, there is Gary out there in the garden, waiting to be discovered. This is not an ending but a beginning, the beginning of the end of my life. I don't where this will all go. At best, I will live in fear until the day I die. Somehow, I don't think it will get that far.

9

FRIDAY, 14 JULY, EARLY HOURS

The illuminated clock on my bedside cabinet clicks to 3.41am. I have not slept yet. Not properly. Just nodded on and off through exhaustion. My mind is in turmoil. I doubt it will ever be still again.

Shame. Fear. Dread. So many hideous emotions come and go through my mind over and over. Yet one persists. And it is shocking.

Relief. That I will not have to spend my life with Gary. The feeling is matched only by the certainty I will be caught. I can never relax.

After Gary's makeshift burial, we came back into the house, the kitchen and then Liam's bedroom. Liam stood over me in the same stained tee shirt and jogging bottoms as I scrubbed the carpet, wiped the skirting boards and walls and cleaned anything that might have Gary's blood, skin or DNA on it. I gathered up the bedsheet and various tee shirts and shorts he'd left on the carpet, and gave them to him. "These need to be put in the washing machine." I said, sending him on his way. "I'll turn it on later."

I showered, and Liam then had one too – he was so fast I felt he could not have scrubbed himself clean. I did not say anything. Instead, we went off to dress in fresh clothes. I then gathered up the clothes I had been wearing, Liam's, and even the towels we used, and put everything, with the summer duvet and more, in the hottest cycle in the washing machine. My fluttery mind then decided, to be safe, to get rid of them later after tumble-drying, putting them in a black bin bag in the garage, ready to take to the dump.

Liam got clean bedding from the airing cupboard and put it in the box room. It's a bleak place, half-full of bags of winter clothes that should have gone in the loft at the end of spring. And baby clothes and toys I cannot bear to throw away. It's where Liam will sleep from now on.

I moved some of the clothes and toys into my bedroom to give Liam more space. I noticed, suddenly, that the carved wooden birds on the windowsill had disappeared. My little flock. I wondered when and why. Perhaps Gary saw and then threw them away, consumed by his childish jealousy. I felt sad somehow – I don't imagine Liam will carve any more now.

I then took a bucket of hot water and cloths and sprays and cleaned, time and again, everything between the bedroom and the garden, wiping, scrubbing and scratching at blood spots, hairs and skin and DNA, real and imagined. Liam just stood, watching silently.

I lie here now in my bed, approaching 3.50am, and know that the carpet in Liam's bedroom and the underlay beneath, both soaked in blood, will have to go.

I don't know how. I cannot take them down to the dump with the bin bags. Even those may prove dangerous, with the disposal of clothes under the watching eye of a CCTV camera. Evidence waiting to be looked at. So much to do. I cannot take everything in.

It all has to be obliterated, not just put somewhere or hidden away. 'Fire destroys everything,' Liam said. We must have a bonfire, although even that will draw attention to ourselves. People don't have bonfires these days. Not round here anyway.

After I'd cleaned, wiped, scrubbed and scratched at everything between the bedroom and the garden, I tipped the contents of the bucket, along with the cloths I'd used, into the toilet and flushed them away. Liam stood behind me, so close that I felt uncomfortable. I was not sure if he were monitoring me, to check to see if I missed something, or just felt scared and wanted to stay close. I turned and looked at him. He glanced down at the toilet, unable to meet my eyes.

Something, the turning away, saw part of me, my heart, my love, wither a little inside. Liam was always the most important thing in my world. I kept going all these years because I thought I might one day find him. Meeting Liam, being with him, transformed my life. Now, this, this monstrous killing, has ruined everything. We are locked together forever because of it, but I don't know how we will survive it, let along get back to any sort of happiness. We are bonded now: not by love, but by murder.

"That will do for tonight," I said, feeling utterly exhausted and close to despair. I was at breaking point. "Let's go to bed."

He nodded, hesitating, and I wondered for a second if he were going to say something nice to me, maybe a few reassuring words, or even step forward and hug me. But he did not. He turned, as if relieved, and almost hurried away. I had the most horrible feeling that, in some way, this killing – this murder – was down to me, and nothing to do with him at all. It was an extraordinary, repugnant feeling.

As the bedroom clock turns 4.00am, my mind is ever restless. I think it will always be like this from now on. My thoughts swirl repeatedly through so many more things.

I keep thinking about Gary's clothes and belongings. I cannot just leave them untouched. I have to decide what to keep and what to throw away or destroy.

His van and his equipment worry me more than I can say. I cannot have the van and its contents out there for the world to see. I don't know what to do with them or where to go.

When Liam had gone into the box room, I went after him. I stopped as I got to the door, rehearsing what I was going to say, to agree on a story for anyone who asked. 'This is our story ... You went out for the evening. Remember what you did. I went out, too. We came back, and Gary was gone. We both said goodnight and went to bed. We assumed he was at the pub.'

'We got up the next morning, and he was not back. We agreed that he must have gone away. I will say he was unhappy and had money troubles. He did not leave a note, so we did not think there was anything to worry about.'

'We assumed he would come back in a week or two after he had sorted himself out. Later, we can't remember when, one weekend, we came back from having a coffee up the town, and some of his clothes and belongings had gone, along with his van and equipment.'

My head resting on the door, I did not enter his room. I

heard Liam crying softly, sobbing out words, although I could not make them out. I was not sure if he was on his phone or just talking to himself in his grief, his own madness, so I just walked away and came to bed. Hours ago now.

As the sun comes up, a shaft of light streaming through my half-open curtains, and I am nodding off, my last thoughts are that I am under siege in this house.

There will be so many of them coming to the door, from customers to creditors, through friends from the darts team to his family, Chloe and Gemma. Some may be sent away easily; others will be more persistent, demanding answers from me, maybe even going to the police.

I imagine, as I am falling asleep, that someone is at the house, outside, ready to demand where Gary is. And I awake with a start – because someone really is outside, and it sounds like they are breaking in. I reach for the whittling knife that is now under my pillow and will forever be close to hand.

I AM UP and out of my bed, pulling on my dressing gown and slipping the unfolded knife into a pocket for my own safety.

I would never use it, but I need to stand tall if a man is breaking in. I have to protect myself if necessary from an unprovoked attack.

I am on to the landing, my hand on the knife, calling furiously to Liam, "Liam, Liam, help me."

There is no reply, no sound of movement, from the box room. I turn and stand at the top of the stairs, looking down, listening to the silence.

Nobody is in the house, nor breaking in. I was, in my exhausted state, imagining the noise. My mind playing tricks.

I wonder what with all that has happened – losing my baby, Liam's arrival, Gary's death – if I am now unhinged.

I look down the stairs, and for one awful moment I have a sudden urge to throw myself from the top step. I move back, resisting the horrible sensation.

I stand there, looking into space, swaying slightly, breathing in and out, calming myself. Gary's death and the long, sleepless night have unbalanced me.

But then I hear that breaking-in noise again. I can now tell, from here, that whatever is happening is outside.

It's Gary's van. Someone is trying to break into it, to steal his equipment. He leaves it in the van overnight, always has.

He had everything stolen once before, years ago. But he says – he said – it wouldn't happen round here. It's posh compared to where he used to live. And besides, his stuff's not worth much.

He has – had – an alarm on the van, but it went off by itself two or three times after he moved in, annoying the neighbours. So he turned that off.

It will be teenagers – they are a plague on this estate, with their petty acts of vandalism, scratching cars, spray-painting walls, and more.

I hurry down the stairs, pulling my dressing gown around me, checking my pocket, opening the front door to shout at them to 'Go away, or I'll call the police.'

As I look across at the van, I see two shaven-headed men, in tee shirts, jeans and boots, at the back door. I think they are trying to force it open. They see me.

I fear they will come storming across, knocking me aside,

coming into the house, going up the stairs, searching for Gary, and seeing the unmistakeable pool of blood on the carpet – and then pressing 999 on their phones.

I put my hands up in a gesture of surrender, indicating I'll leave them to it. If they take the equipment, I can say that was the final straw that led to Gary leaving.

But then I notice a glint in an upstairs window of a house opposite. The creepy man who lives there with his elderly mother is filming them on his mobile phone. I point upwards, and the shaven-headed men see him too.

They stop what they are doing. One gestures with his middle finger towards the man in the window; the other turns towards me. "Tell your fucking husband to keep off our patch ... or else."

And then they are going, striding away to a dark, nondescript car parked at the top of the close. The man at the window follows them with his phone camera. Then turns and salutes me. I pretend not to see.

I step back inside the house and find myself breathing heavily. The two shaven-headed men came here to steal Gary's equipment so he could not work on their territory. I don't know how they found his van, but it chills me that they did.

Most likely, they saw the van's number plate from when he was on their patch, maybe spoke to a customer to find out where he lived, and then drove round this estate until they saw it parked outside. I wonder if they will come back again, in the night, and maybe break in next time. The thought scares me.

AN HOUR OR SO LATER, after I have checked the makeshift grave has not sunk, Liam and I are eating our breakfast of toast, cereals, coffee and orange juice. It's as though everything is normal and just so, as it was before. But, of course, it is not. How can it ever be again?

We are tense and nervous and barely speaking. All I can think of is all the things that still need to be done to cover up Gary's death. Liam has his head down, eating and drinking well enough. I drink a mug of black coffee and struggle with that.

Liam checks his phone and then says he's off to the amusements at the pier. It's as though nothing much has happened. A hamster or a guinea pig has died of old age, that's all. He's leaving all of this horror to me. I say nothing. I cannot think of any comment to make other than a critical one that might drive him away.

Eventually, I have to say something, though. "What do we do? With his clothes, his belongings ... the van, his equipment, his customers, Chloe ..." I do not mention the shaven-headed men from earlier or the debt collectors I expect to arrive any time soon. I have no experience of dealing with these sorts of people. The thought frightens me.

He thinks for a moment, his elbow on the table, a slice of toast and marmalade dangling nonchalantly from his hand. "Um." He shrugs. "You just say he walked out and left you." No big deal!

The insouciance angers me, but I do not react with a sharp comment. We have to get through this together, mother and son. I reply, thinking over what I was going to say to him last night, about the story we need to stick to. I'm not sure now if that was the right story to suggest. So I say,

"He'd only walk out and leave everything behind if he were going to commit suicide."

He stares into the distance, thinking again, and then says, "Yes, say that ... that's what you need to say." I note it's now 'you', not we. And I could scream at the thoughtlessness.

I try to retain my anger, but it comes crackling through in my edgy response. "If anyone thinks it's suicide, they'll all be here – police, everyone – crawling over everything."

He looks awkward suddenly, as if he is embarrassed by his stupid comment. He nods, finishes his toast in two big bites, swallows the last of his orange juice and looks at his watch. "Okay ... yeah ... that's true. Anyway, got to go." Conversation over.

I think for one appalling moment that he is about to disappear, to go away forever. I want to hold him tight, tell him I love him and to plead with him not to go and leave me to deal with this.

But I hold back. I don't want to spook him, nor drive him off by being clingy and needy, even though it's only because I am so scared at this moment. He picks up his rucksack, swinging it over his shoulder. I don't know what to do.

He looks at me, sees my face, my fear across it, and then hesitates. He comes over and hugs me briefly, even though I want to sink into his embrace. "Let's talk tonight." He lets go.

And then he is gone, leaving me with my mind spinning, that he is going off and having fun with his new friends at the pier so soon after what has happened. I do not know what to do, how to cope with any of this. This house now feels like a prison. It strikes me that Chloe might turn up at some point to collect something she forgot to take with her to Gemma's. I could not handle that. What would I do? I feel the folded-over knife in my pocket, but feel sick at the thought of having to use it. How could I do such a thing? I don't think I could. But what would happen if not? My mind whizzes through these conflicting thoughts.

I take the breakfast things and put the cereal packets and jam jars back where they belong, and stack the mugs and plates in the dishwasher. Then I stand and look out the window across the back garden. I see the uneven bumpiness of the soil by the garage. A black cat I've never seen before walks daintily – almost tiptoeing – along the back of the garden, as though heading for the grave. I open the kitchen door, running towards it, flapping a tea towel, shooing it away.

I stand in the garden, my mind here and there, before going back onto the patio, lifting and carrying two of the plants in pots over to the soil. I place them side by side in the middle, gagging at the thought of Gary exposed down there. Close enough to the surface to attract cats and foxes and rats. I imagine the soil sinking as his body decomposes, and having to add more soil constantly every few weeks, maybe even weekly; the thought revolts me.

I try to think again of all the things I need to do, a checklist to cover what's happened, but I jump, startled, by a sudden knocking at the front door. It's not a gentle ringing of the doorbell nor a tap-tap-tap with the knuckle of a forefinger on the glass. It's a thump, thump, thump. *Open up!*

My mind thinks immediately that this is the police, that, somehow, they have uncovered the murder – for that is what it is – and they are here to arrest me. I sink to my knees in despair, giving up before it's even started.

But no one could have seen – the garden is so sheltered,

and nobody would have heard Liam's grunts of exertion or my sobs and gagging noises, as they could not have got that close. Liam, then. He has reported me and gone running back to his adoptive parents. I cannot believe that, though – he has as much to lose as me. More, really; he committed the crime. I had to help him under duress.

I move back into the house, as quickly and as quietly as I can, pulling the kitchen door closed and moving forwards into the living room, where I can see out to the driveway. I see a lorry, a pickup truck, with a trailer.

Emboldened that it is not the police, I move into the living room and up to the windows. There are blinds here, at an angle, so I can see out between them. It would be hard to see in, although anyone outside may spot the shape of my moving body. I don't know. I stand still.

There are two men, in some sort of matching uniforms with hi-vis jackets, and they are walking around Gary's van. An echo of the shaven-headed men's visit, but more official. The back has been opened, and Gary's window-cleaning equipment is being laid out on my postage-stamp-sized front lawn. They must be repossessing his van.

One of the men comes back to my front door. He knocks again. This time, I answer it. I try to compose my face to look calm, to disguise the fear I feel inside. This is all new to me, and I don't know what to say or do.

"Hello," the man says politely, although I think it's a struggle for him. He's big and thickset and looks like he'd rather have an argument, if not a fight. If Gary were here, they'd be brawling soon enough. "Is Gary Morris in?"

I shake my head and swallow. "My name's Nina Bolitho ... Gary ... Mr Morris doesn't live here anymore." I don't know what else to say or do. But then I think of something. "He left for another woman ... a while ago."

The man just checks his clipboard, as though confirming facts. "His ex-wife gave us this address. That's the van, alright. He's seven months in arrears; he'll have had all the default notices and then the notice to repossess. He's had plenty of time, and he's never been in touch. We're repossessing."

He hands me sheets of paper. I look at them, all the statements and legalese, and my mind struggles to take it all in. I go to say, *Don't take anything that's not yours.* But I stop – the comment suddenly seems nonsensical, as they have left Gary's window-cleaning equipment from the van across the front lawn.

I watch as the van is driven onto the trailer. The men both get into the lorry, and it loops slowly, grinding through gears, around the close and away, neither of the men looking back at me. I go to the lawn and start picking up Gary's equipment, taking it to the garage. When I stand there, looking at it all over the floor, my mood lifts suddenly and unexpectedly.

The van, sitting there, was always going to be a telltale sign of wrongdoing. 'Why?' Everyone from Chloe to, finally, the police would ask, 'Why is his van still here if he's run away?' I would have had to have driven it somewhere, to a forest perhaps, maybe even to set it alight, and that would have sat there, waiting to be discovered. A police officer, one day sooner or later, knocking on my door to ask about it and Gary and what has happened to him.

Now it has gone. And I have a ready-made story to tell everyone who asks. Gary was down on his luck, short of money, angry and violent towards me. His van was repossessed. He then stormed out, saying he was going to start a new life away from all of this. And so he went, I would say, to somewhere far, far away. And I hope, I truly hope, that it will be enough for me to live my life without being in permanent fear.

10

FRIDAY, 14 JULY, LATE MORNING

I spend the morning in a daze, going over everything I cleaned last night, scraping and rubbing and brushing, with my mood plummeting lower and lower as I discover more spots of blood: telltale evidence I missed before. How could I be so blind? It is never-ending. I shower several times, I feel so dirty.

I open all the windows to freshen the air. But I jump each time I hear a noise outside the house: a car pulling up, footsteps on the pavement, a conversation. I keep thinking the police are coming for me any moment. Crazy, I know. I check regularly, but there is nobody lurking outside. I am going insane.

I leave the blood-soaked carpet and underlay as they are in Liam's old room, moving the bed, covered with a clean duvet, over it and then rearranging the furniture as though having a move around just for a change. The carpet does not seem to smell. Not yet, anyway. It will have to do for now. At the back of my mind, I keep thinking Chloe may turn up suddenly. I can't imagine she will stay with her mother and her new partner for long. Gary always described Gemma and Chloe as 'explosive'. She'll come and go for sure.

I have to match everything up with the story that Gary walked out in an emotional state to start afresh elsewhere. So he would, at most, have just grabbed a rucksack and filled it with whatever clothes came to hand.

I find an old rucksack in a cupboard and fill it with as many of his clothes as I can from his wardrobe and chest of drawers. As he might have done in a hurry. I put it out of sight behind the lawnmower and the window-cleaning equipment in the garage. The rucksack and contents will have to be disposed of later; permanently, I think. I don't know how yet. There is so much to think about. I'm sure I'll miss something crucial. That will give the game away. And lead to my downfall.

The rest of his clothes and belongings, I gather up and put in our two big holiday suitcases on top of the wardrobe in the box room where Liam is sleeping. As though I packed them up in anger. They can stay there a while. Like the equipment in the garage, it all looks right and proper, as it should be if he'd left.

By the early afternoon, I am sitting at the top of the stairs, hot and sweaty and feeling grubby. I am not sure if I should have another shower and then try to eat and drink something, or vice versa. Later this afternoon, until Liam appears, I will lie calmly on the sofa, blotting out the horror of it all as best I can.

There is a tap-tap at the door. I ignore it. Whoever it is will go away. Then there is a knock-knock, louder and more emphatic. Still I ignore it. So they ring the doorbell. I'd stay still, but they seem so insistent that I am alarmed that they may come round the back to knock on the patio door. I daren't risk having anyone in the garden. I imagine that black cat digging furiously by the garage. And whoever it is wandering across for a closer look.

I walk downstairs, checking myself over, imagining I am covered in blood and hair and skin. My clothes are clean enough, but I must look a sight. I straighten my hair, tucking loose strands behind my ears. There's no time for anything else. I open the door, ready to send a debt collector packing with sharp words. I go to say, "Gary Morris is not here," but stop as I see who it is. The creepy man from over the way.

He looks at me, this seedy little fifty-something man, making a click-click noise with his mouth, as though he is talking to a horse that needs persuading to do something. It is a repulsive sound. He introduces himself as Terry, and I reply, "Nina." I add, "In a hurry." He laughs as though I am being jolly and friendly. I'm not. I want him to go and leave me alone.

He gazes up and down, mentally undressing me, and then kind of jumps, startled, and stares into my eyes. I think he is trying to be funny, flirtatious even, but he repels me. Older men never seem to see themselves as younger women do. He is short and stocky, with greasy grey hair and a whiskery white beard. He's in a stained tee shirt and grimy jeans and looks like he hasn't washed for a few days. There are marks on the front of his jeans. I don't want to think about those.

"Well ..." I say, "I've got to be getting along." I smile at him vaguely and step back, going to shut the door. To my horror, he lifts his foot up – dirty old boot and all – and puts it inside the door frame. I stare at him, so, so fiercely, as I am tired and worried and really can do without any of this. I go to say, 'Move your foot,' but then he speaks, chilling me with his opening words.

"I've been watching you."

I swallow hard, wondering what he means by that. The extent of it.

He leers. "I've always liked you, Nina." I feel sick and confused, not knowing where he is going with this. "I saw your old man's van being taken away ... all his stuff on your lawn."

I nod, not sure how to reply.

"Thing is ..." he adds, nodding at me, as though choosing his words carefully, "I've not been working for a while, and I want to earn a bit of extra cash ... so I'd like to borrow that window-cleaning equipment."

I just stare at him, nonplussed.

"I'd make it worth your while." He looks at me and winks. I feel revolted by the implication of that wink. I shake my head, trying to shut the door two, three times, against his boot. I pull the door back, going to slam it, and he removes the boot quickly. He stands outside and shouts, "Think about it. I'll come back ... when you're feeling yourself." As he walks off, laughing horribly at his stupid innuendo, I stifle a sob, wondering what he has seen, watching me, and what it means going forward.

———

I HAVE to put all thoughts of the creepy man out of my head. After a sandwich and a glass of milk – I barely start, let alone finish, either – I have another shower and walk around the house again, feeling so low. I'm on a downwards spiral. I have to snap out of it somehow.

I lie on the sofa for a while, feeling shattered, and finally fall into an uneasy sleep. I fight it for as long as I can. My mind is always full of dreams, nightmares really. But I am so tired.

I awake, two hours or so later, still tired, but forcing myself to get up. I wash and change and put on fresh make-up and drive into town to get something for our tea. The creepy man is by a bedroom window as I leave and return. As he always is and will be forever. I ignore him waving at me.

Liam arrives just before six o'clock as I'm putting our teas – pie, peas and potatoes, a jug of orange squash and bananas and apples – on the table. I smile at him and gesture to go upstairs and wash his hands. I find comfort in routine and the minutiae of life. I cling to normality.

He comes down five minutes later in a fresh tee shirt and jeans, and we sit opposite each other at the table. Usually, he glances at me and smiles. Tonight, he seems to want to avoid my eyes, giving short nods and tight smiles in answer to my gentle questions. He does not look at me.

I ask if he has had a nice day, and he replies, "Yes," and that, "The weather was sunny." I could scream, wanting to know what he has been doing, where and with whom. I do not want to risk driving him away, so I bite my tongue, simply saying, as though a passing afterthought, "What did you do?"

He just responds, "You know, the pier ... amusements."

For eight hours? I let it go. Something is going on behind my back, though. Him and his new friends. Perhaps a would-be partner.

We eat and drink, Liam quickly and greedily, like he wants to be out again as soon as he can. I glance at him, catching his eye, and he gives me another tight little smile and pours orange squash from the jug into his glass tumbler. He eats more slowly. I pick at my food, having no appetite. I wash as much of it down as I can with mouthfuls of squash.

I try to be jolly, attempting conversations about the weather, maybe having a night in with a movie and popcorn, or even having a day out to Bury St Edmunds or Norwich. I offer to buy him some shoes, as he only ever seems to wear the same pair of trainers. Why do teenage boys all seem to wear white trainers? I don't know. I think he'll wear them until they fall off his feet. He mumbles and mutters, saying he is going out later – he does not say where or why or when, and I do not wish to ask. But he agrees to a movie and popcorn tomorrow night. It's a promise I hope he keeps.

I know, in my heart, that last night has changed every-thing between us. How could it not? But I want to somehow bring us close again. I think, in a way, we are bound together forever because of what happened. But I am not sure if Liam sees it like that, an unbreakable bond. Perhaps he feels trapped here, wanting to go back to his adoptive parents, but is frightened to, in case I reveal what happened to someone. Does he stay to keep guard? I don't know. Then, suddenly, he comes to life.

"What have you done today about ...?" He inclines his head towards the garden. He looks at me and then takes a mouthful of food, as though we're talking about nothing more than planting flowers and pulling weeds.

I go through what I have done. "I've cleaned everything again, just to be safe ... put some more of his clothes that were in my washing pile in the garage with his window-cleaning equipment." I don't mention the creepy man. I don't wish to think about him. "And a few in the two suitcases in the box room where you are ..."

I tail off and then decide to say the van has been repossessed. Liam looks at me, not understanding. So I say, "I don't think Gary was up to date with his payments, so they took it back. A stroke of luck."

He nods, seeming to agree. I'm not sure he knows what I mean. Do teenagers know much about leases and repossessions and all of that? I doubt it. I don't suppose it matters.

I go on, "We'll have to get rid of that bedroom carpet. We can leave it for now. We'll have to burn it along with the rucksack and clothes in the garage, sometime soon."

"The clothes and stuff in the suitcases in ... your room ... can sit there ... as we're expecting him to come back, aren't we? Once he's calmed down and come to his senses."

He laughs, more jovially than I would have expected. Then asks, as he swallows a mouthful of banana, a question. "Are you going to report him missing?"

The question troubles me, as though it is me who killed Gary and is responsible for all of this. "No." I shake my head. "He's left me. Why would I then file a report about it?"

He chews his food and shrugs. "Someone ... Chloe ... will come round. She won't believe he's just left and not contacted her. She'll report him missing if you don't." His words hang in the air ominously. "Might seem odd if you don't get in first."

"He's left me, so there's nothing to report. We'll ..." I hesitate, angry suddenly that all of this hell is down to me to resolve. "We'll ... cut the grass and the bushes and the trees in a day or two ... have a big old bonfire, with the carpet and his clothes at the bottom."

He nods as he finishes his banana, putting the skin and

his knife and fork together and then drinking the last mouthfuls of his orange squash. He asks the question I know that's coming: "What about the body?"

Before I can reply, he answers himself, "The two suit-cases in the bedroom ... burn whatever's in them, you can say he came back and took everything. We'll then get the body into the garage ..." He breathes deeply, then swallows hard, his eyes watering. "I'll get it into the suitcases, and we'll take them miles away, to woods, and burn the lot and bury what's left."

I gag involuntarily and then rush to the kitchen, where I am sick into the sink once, twice and then three times. Liam walks into the kitchen behind me, carrying his plate and glass tumbler, as though we just talked about getting rid of a dog mess on the pavement. "Okay?" he asks, and I nod, although I am not and will never be. But he is correct: it is the only way, our only chance of getting through this.

I turn to him, waiting, hoping, that he will step forward and take me in his arms and hug me long and hard, consoling me. But he does not. He loads his plate and cutlery and tumbler into the dishwasher and then turns to leave, to go to the pier or wherever, with whomever he is meeting. I follow him out.

There is one last thing. "His wallet ... cards ... his phone," Liam asks, "where are they? If he's left like you say, he'll have used his cards, to get cash out to live on. You'll need to start getting cash out somewhere as if it is him."

I nod, bewildered and alarmed that I had not thought of this. I wonder how long I will need to keep withdrawing cash. It feels like it's inviting trouble.

"And you'll have to destroy his phone. If he's reported

missing, that's the first thing they'll check. If it's here, they'll wonder why he never took it."

I nod, angry with myself, as it's another obvious thing I've missed, and I am also fearful that I have overlooked other, so many, giveaway signs of wrongdoing.

"It might be a good idea," Liam says as he stands by the front door, ready to leave. He puts on a jacket I bought him when he first arrived, that's now hanging on a hook in the hallway, and concludes, "if you sent yourself messages from his phone, as if he were writing them, telling you he'd gone up north to see an old friend. A woman? Then destroy the phone."

I nod in agreement. Then he is gone, leaving me more alarmed than calm.

I spend the evening in front of the television, a series of BBC programmes playing out with the volume so low I cannot hear any of them. No matter; my mind is in utter turmoil.

I go over everything I have done, racking my brains about anything I may have missed. I feel sick, with a strong sense I have overlooked something so blindingly obvious that it will be the end of me.

And I decide, as I go upstairs to bed, that I will, in the morning, dig out Gary's cards and phone from the pocket in his jacket in the rucksack in the garage. I hope that I can access them to start setting out a new story, with cash withdrawals and phone messages, that will fool the police if they come calling. No. When they come calling to arrest me.

I GOT THROUGH TODAY, one way or other, by being practical and staying focused on what needed to be done, one thing after another. At least, I tried my best. As I will do every day from now on.

At night, I sleep so badly, in fits and starts, my tormented mind going over whatever troubles me. Before I sleep tonight, I run through everything that might go wrong in the days and weeks ahead. I believe, in my heart, the police will come. I'm sure they will. I will end my days in prison.

Even as I fall asleep, through utter exhaustion, I fight it, knowing the nightmares will cram into my mind. As they do most nights, as my subconscious surfaces and punishes me. They were always about my sweet baby and Gary beating me. Now, I fear there are others waiting to force their way in as I begin nodding off.

It is night-time, and I am in the middle of a field. It is pitch-black. The sky is cloudy, so I cannot see the moon.

It is silent except for the sound of my laboured breathing. I try to hold my breath as I can hear something, somewhere, behind me. A scratching, scraping noise, coming closer.

I can't look back. I just can't. But I know there are trees, so many trees. It is a forest. And it lives and breathes. And something in there is coming for me.

I break into a run, across this field, towards a fence that I must climb over to get into the next field, where I will be safe. I just have to reach it.

But I cannot move swiftly. I'm stumbling and falling into the mud that sucks at my feet. I pull one foot out and then another. And I try to run again.

I trip and fall once more into the mud, and this time my hands and feet are stuck fast. I pull and pull and pull until I collapse with exhaustion.

I lie there and hear it, whatever it is, coming towards me from the forest. It will kill me, I know that. I struggle again to free myself. I cannot.

It – the monster – does not come hurtling towards me so that my death is quick and merciful. Instead, it creeps and slithers and stops and starts and crawls forward again until I am shaking with fear, waiting for the attack.

I try to turn onto my back so that I can see it, whatever it is, and try to fight it off. But I cannot move at all. It is about to strike.

Then, in front of me, between my body and the fence, there is movement, a shaking, a rumbling, and I watch as the mud churns and moves this way and that, into a shapeless blob.

For a moment, a split second, I think it is somehow going to save me from whatever is coming up behind to kill me. I watch as it rises up.

The mud is now a living, breathing thing, and I sense it is malevolent. It takes a form – a head and two arms appearing at the same instant. And then I recognise it – Gary's corpse – as it lunges towards me. And I scream and scream and scream helplessly.

I awake violently, my skin clammy, my mouth gasping for air, as I come back into the real world. It takes me a moment or two of agony to realise I am safe, at least physically.

I lie here, breathing heavily, listening to the silence all around me. Dawn should be a peaceful time, but it is not. I imagine people outside, hiding, waiting to come for me. The police.

These waking moments should be ones of relief, perhaps even relaxation, but they can never be. I do not know what the day might bring; sometime sooner than later, my shameful secret will be revealed, and my life as it has been will be over.

11

SATURDAY, 15 JULY, MID-MORNING

I am so edgy sitting at the table opposite Liam, because he just has his breakfast – a later one, today – and an evening meal and then goes out in between and after. I feel as though I'm running some sort of hotel.

I did not mind it before ... before what happened ... as I wanted him, encouraged him, to go and make friends, as I thought it might make staying here much more appealing. But now he's out almost all the time. And I resent it.

Especially now, after Gary has ... died. He did it, not me. I helped him, as any loving mother would do. But he should be here, supporting me, not just going off and leaving me to this. It's too much.

Liam seems to have an appetite this morning, asking for bacon and eggs and then porridge, which I made for him, and now sit watching him ploughing his way through everything. I don't know how he can.

The smell of the bacon makes me feel nauseous, and I have a split-second thought that it might be morning sickness. But I've not been intimate with Gary, at least not in that way, since I lost my baby, and I breathe a sigh of relief.

Even so, I struggle with my toast and honey, fiddling with it, nibbling the insides and leaving the crusts, like I am a little girl. I sip at my black coffee, putting the mug back heavily on the table between each mouthful.

I am struggling, in the face of Liam's indifference, with my temper. I can feel my anger rising, and think about what I might say to him. *Why do you go off every day and evening and leave this mess to me? Could you not stay and help just for once? I'm doing all of this for you!*

Then, suddenly, he looks up at me and says, quite simply, "What's the matter?" It's a kind look, not a dismissive one.

I go to say something sharp to him, but he carries on, sounding concerned and adding, "Mum." It makes me hesitate, feeling emotional. I wonder if he is manipulating me. An awful thought. I dismiss it straightaway.

Before I can reply, he says, as if he senses how I feel, "I'd stay here today, help you, but I want to go over to look at the university in Ipswich, just checking out the site."

My spirits soar at the thought, the implication, that he may stay here and not go to Oxford in the autumn. I can scarcely believe it – that he'd swap smarty-pants Oxford for dull-as-ditchwater Ipswich – but he must mean it if he says it; why would he otherwise?

I cannot help myself. I half-rise, leaning across the table to hug him awkwardly. He laughs and gently disentangles himself from my embrace. He then points to a smear of ketchup on my elbow, and he passes me a serviette. We laugh together, and I feel, suddenly, slightly better.

I realise that to stay here and turn down such a golden opportunity at Oxford, there must be more to it than being with me. He has met someone and wants to continue that relationship. Young man. Young woman. Whoever. I am so happy for him – and for me, too.

I go to ask him, hesitating, if he has met someone ... 'someone special' – from amongst the friends he's made at the seafront, but as I formulate the words, he seems to anticipate the question and is already getting to his feet.

I understand. No teenager wants to be grilled about their love life by their mother, at least not until they are ready to make introductions. I remember how I resented my mother when she first asked about Ryan. By the end, I hated her.

As he leaves, taking his plates and what have you into the kitchen, he turns and hugs me. For one moment, despite everything, it is all okay again. A moment of joy amongst the horror all around us. He reminds me what I need to do today – with Gary's phone and cards – and then finishes with the words I want to hear.

"Tonight, I promise, I'll stay in, and we can have a night together. Popcorn, a movie ... you've got Netflix? And we can chat about anything you want."

I tell him that would be lovely and go to kiss him on the cheek. He moves. And I kiss him accidentally, full on the lips. I pull a face. He laughs. All is well. At least for now.

AFTER LIAM HAS LEFT, I spend some time going from room to room, checking again to see if I have missed anything. I will never shake off this fear that's triggering my obsessive behaviour. I force myself to look forward, not back. We will, tomorrow I think, have to roll up the carpet and underlay and take them and the two suitcases and their contents to the garden for burning. And then deal with the body. I just cannot bear the thought of any of it right now. It overwhelms me.

I sit for a while on the edge of Liam's bed in the box room, just thinking about Gary and what we are doing. I feel such a sense of self-disgust. There must be other ways to conceal what has happened to him. What we have done. I think it might be easier to put concrete and slabs and a bench by the garage but realise that when, one day, police come here with sniffer dogs, they will still uncover the body. I don't know what to do. His body has to go.

I walk to the garage, rummaging through the rucksack for Gary's jacket, then into the pockets to take out his wallet full of cards and his mobile phone. I cannot believe I never thought of them before. A stupid mistake like this will be my downfall. I pack everything else back into the rucksack and sit there looking at the wallet and phone.

His wallet contains his driving licence, an RAC breakdown card, two discount cards for wholesalers in Ipswich, and two debit cards, one for his business and the other for his personal bank account. I put my fingers into nooks and crannies and find a folded-over £10 note and a small passport-sized photo, taken in a booth, of Gary and Gemma with Chloe as a smiley toddler in happier times.

Something – the photo – sets me off crying. It is more than that though, it is seeing Chloe's cherub face, such sweetness and happiness in sharp contrast to the damaged and angry teen she has become. And even more, I cry because her father has been taken from her, and she will be devastated that he is no longer here. And eventually, she will become suspicious. She will never believe he has left her behind without a word.

I look at Gary's phone, trying various numbers, his year of birth, Chloe's, even Gemma's, to get into it. I am thinking of sending a message to myself, in case the police get involved at some stage, *I've left you, Nina. Sorry. I've met someone else.* I think, suddenly, that this is such a foolish thing to do. He might have left me like that, but he would not ignore Chloe afterwards. That will be the telltale sign that something bad has happened. I should text Chloe as him, but cannot face the immediate consequences of dealing with her replies. Besides, I cannot even get into the phone.

A thought occurs to me. If my story were true, Gary would have left in a fury, driving away from it all to start a new life. He would maybe have hurled his phone from his car window as he sped along the A14 from Felixstowe to wherever he was going.

That is what I will do now – get in my car, drive and dump the phone in a layby somewhere on the A14 between Bury St Edmunds and Cambridge, fifty or sixty miles away. When it is discovered – if – by the police they will make that assumption. I wipe the phone over with the sleeve of my cardigan and slip it carefully into a pocket.

I will also find an ATM in a village close to Cambridge, perhaps attached to the local stores, where there won't be any CCTV cameras recording me taking out cash. If – when – the police check his bank account, they will note the withdrawal and assume he ran out of cash today and took some out to keep going until he gets where he is going.

I prepare to leave, going round and round checking the house again before eventually going to my car. The creepy man is at his bedroom window. I am tempted to stick my finger up. But it may make things worse. He could so easily turn nasty. I just ignore him.

It's warm and sunny, and the A14 out over the Orwell Bridge and on towards Cambridge has little traffic at this time of day. I keep the car in the inside lane at a steady sixty miles per hour, as if I'm just out for a pleasant drive.

I feel as though I am taking my driving test, so careful am I to do everything just so, as I do not want to draw attention to myself. I keep my distance and even do 'mirror, signal, manoeuvre' when overtaking an elderly man trundling along in his car at twenty miles an hour.

As I pass by Ipswich, Stowmarket and Bury St Edmunds, some forty minutes from home, I feel myself growing in confidence. If I can stage Gary's 'departure' successfully, it will help if or when the police turn up.

I slow the car on a long, rural stretch of road between Bury St Edmunds and Cambridge, a rare moment when there is no traffic behind or on the other side of the road coming towards me. I press a button to unwind the passenger window and hurl the phone out as hard as I can into bushes and trees.

Later, I come off the A14 before I get to Cambridge, driving slowly through village after village until I find an out-of-the-way ATM where I can withdraw cash. I try to take out £250, but it won't let me, as there are 'insufficient funds'. I take what there is, £180, and tuck it into my purse. I'm not sure what I will do with that. I cannot bring myself to spend it. I then park the car down the road and sit in it, cutting up the debit card with nail scissors from my handbag.

As I drive home, feeling relieved, I throw one half of the debit card out the window towards roadside ditches – when there are no cars in sight – and then the same again with the other, ten to twenty miles on. The police, if or when involved, will think Gary spent Thursday and Friday nights on a friend's sofa, then threw his phone away in anger and took out cash before heading off, towards an old lover, perhaps.

Approaching the Orwell Bridge, returning to Felixstowe at last, my mind begins to fill with doubts and fears. If Gary left in a rage, why did he spend a night or two on a friend's sofa and not just go? Why has he not texted me or Chloe or Gemma or someone, something? Why would he, with little or no money, throw his phone away? It makes no sense, none of it. I have been so rash today, opening up so many possible lines of enquiry.

By the time I approach the close, I am shaking with nerves. More and more questions flood my mind. Why didn't Gary take out cash the night he left, and why go so far off the main road to use an ATM in a village when most petrol stations on the A14 have one? These questions cannot be answered easily.

I feel agitated and so, so angry with myself. In trying to set up a story that sounds believable, I have raised even more questions. And the answers, truth be told, point to my guilt. I wonder, as I turn my car into the close, if I should do more or leave things as they are and just hope for the best.

As I approach my house, I gasp out loud, seeing someone going into my back garden, pulling the gate closed behind them. I don't see who it is, just the gate slamming shut. I feel fear rising in my throat.

———

I SIT in the car on the driveway, my mind scrambling through all the possibilities. It's not Liam, he comes in through the back gate, but it's too early for him. And Chloe,

Gemma with her most probably, would come to the front door.

I wonder if it's something or nothing. I fear the police, but they'd not sneak in round the back. There would be cars, officers and dogs everywhere. An Amazon delivery driver, then, tucking a parcel safely out of sight. But I've not ordered anything, and there isn't a van parked in the close.

I get out of the car, my heart thumping, my mouth drying, walking, hurrying to the back gate. I push it open carefully, unsure what I'll see. I feel a surge of relief and then anger – fury, really. It's the creepy man, pulling at the door of my garage, stepping inside out of sight.

Worse than that though, his Jack Russell is sniffing and pawing at the soil behind the garage; he's discovered the shallow grave.

"Hey! Hey!" I shout, running towards the dog, waving desperately at it with my hands to move away. "Shoo! Shoo!"

It does not. It has the scent of Gary's body and digs more frantically. The bin bags and brown tape will be uncovered in seconds, then torn apart just as the creepy man comes out of the garage, hearing the commotion.

I grab the dog by the collar and pull it backwards as it snaps and snarls, wanting to break free to resume its digging down to the body.

I struggle desperately, trying not to hurt the dog, but knowing I have to stop it returning to the shallow grave, no matter what. It twists and turns so much that I think my wrist will break.

I can see, in amongst the soil between the pots, ragged pieces of black plastic from the bin bag, Gary's body so close to being exposed. And the dog is about to wrench itself free from me.

Then the creepy man is coming out of the garage door, shouting at the dog and running across to pull it away from me. He cuffs the dog with the back of his hand, aiming a misplaced kick as the dog runs away.

I think the dog will dash into a far corner of the garden, cowering from the man, waiting to be led out and back to its own home. But it does not. It just runs round and round in a circle, faster and faster, getting ever more excited. Yap! Yap! Yap! Yap! Yap!

The dog then turns and races back to the shallow grave, the creepy man running towards it as it starts digging again. I pick up a garden spade that's leaning by the garage door. One of us must have left it there when … you know. Gary. I edge forwards. The man grabs the dog by the collar and drags it away. He turns, shouting, "No need for that!" He's assuming I was going to hit the dog. I wouldn't. I like dogs well enough. I was going to hit *him* if he looked down and saw Gary's body.

The creepy man lifts the dog and hurries out of the back gate with it. He shouts over his shoulder as he leaves. I do not catch what he says. But I believe he says he's coming back. I want to know what the hell he thinks he is doing, coming on to my property and going into my garage like that.

I hurry towards the shallow grave. The black and brown of the bin bags and tape are exposed in two places, and I use the side of my left shoe to scrape some of the soil back over them. I move the pots to cover the two places. Then I turn, hot and sweaty, towards the garden gate.

He comes back, apologising: "Sorry about that; he's always digging." I wonder if he will ask why the dog went to that patch – or, even worse, whether he will go over to look.

I'm not sure the two pots cover everything. I imagine him bending down, pulling at a loose piece of black plastic, crying 'What's this?' as I raise the spade above his head and bring it crashing down.

"What the hell do you think you're doing?" I snap, as much to distract him as to receive an answer. "Coming into my garden, bringing your dog, going into my garage? How dare you."

He looks hot and bothered, through his exertions with the dog, rather than awkward or embarrassed as I would have hoped. He laughs, an uncomfortable sound, and says, staring at me, "I came to look at your fellow's equipment ... make you an offer you can't refuse." He always makes everything he says sound salacious, as if licking his lips.

Steal it, more like, I think, but do not say. I am suddenly nervous, if not scared of him. We are out of sight of anyone. He is making a sexual remark towards me. He seems on edge. I suspect he's got a temper. I need to get him out of here. "It's not for sale," I reply firmly.

We look at each other, face-to-face, in something of a stand-off. I'd be happy to give him the equipment just to get him to go away. But that would seem odd and may encourage him in other ways. I could sell to him, but that too might seem odd down the line. "Why," a police officer might ask, "did you sell your partner's equipment when he might come back for it?"

I walk towards the gate, as though encouraging him to follow me. When I get there and stand waiting, he reluctantly comes towards me. He stands closer than he should. I can smell tobacco and alcohol on his breath. I think he is about to touch me – assault me – his hands on my breasts or pulling me towards him, his hand on my bottom. Instead, he speaks, and what he says is chilling.

He looks at the patch of dirt where Gary is buried and states, "I've some leftover pansies and whatnots ... I'll come back some time and plant them for you. We can have another chat about the window cleaning." He leers at me, and I can see stumps and spaces in amongst his yellowing teeth. He is repugnant. I say nothing but gesture him towards the gate. He winks and smirks, then leaves, and I shut the gate behind him. I don't know what he – or I – will do next.

After a glass of squash and a sit-down, I get our tea ready, sausages, chips and beans. I cannot be bothered to do much else; I am so tired and fed up. My mind should be running over all that I have done today – ticking off what's on my checklist – and going through what else there is to do. But my mind is constantly on the creepy man watching me and waiting for his next opportunity to come across and hassle me.

I don't have a bolt on the back gate, but think maybe I will get one and see if I can fix it on. The garage door has a key – two, originally, I think – but they both seem to have disappeared. Gary was always losing things, and I suspect he went out with them some time or other and dropped them. Or maybe they are in the garage, slipped down the side of the unit and accidentally kicked into the corner. I will look. The kitchen door is hard to lock and unlock, as the key is stiff to turn. I often leave the door unlocked. A bad habit. I must be more careful when I go out.

Liam returns a few minutes before six o'clock and goes upstairs to wash and change. He is back down and smiles when he sees his plate on the table; it's piled high with chips.

"We always used to have this every Saturday at the ..." I think he's going to say more, but he goes into the kitchen to cut himself some bread and butter. Chip sandwiches, I expect. Then he is back, and I ask if he is going to stay in tonight – I almost say, 'as you promised', but bite my lip. I don't want to pressure him. But he smiles and says, "Yes!"

12

SATURDAY, 16 JULY, SUNSET

After our early evening meal, Liam and I are sitting, in PJs and dressing gowns, side by side on the living room sofa, a bowl of popcorn between us, glasses of Coke Zero on side tables, watching a movie. *Fast & Furious* number something or other. His choice, not mine.

We sit here, if I am honest, rather awkwardly. We seem to have tacitly agreed not to talk about Gary anymore; what has happened has ripped the heart out of our relationship. It will take time to rebuild it to something close to what it was. We barely speak, just watching the movie and eating and drinking. It is a start, though. We can be happy again.

There is a tapping at the front door, a knuckle on the strip of frosted glass in the middle of it. I jump.

Liam looks startled, but his carefree expression – that mask of his – soon falls back into place. I wonder if he is ever as relaxed as he appears.

We gaze silently at each other, against a jangling, noisy backdrop of cars racing in the movie. He pulls a *No, don't answer it* face. I point to the television, suggesting, *Whoever it is, they know we're in.*

I use the remote control to turn down the sound on the television and then get to my feet. Liam is already standing up, seeming more nervous than I'd have expected. My mind wonders who it might be. Debt collectors? Too late at night. Neighbours, unlikely, given we keep our distance. Chloe and Gemma? Chloe has a key. Something and nothing, then? I feel sick and suspect I always will do whenever the doorbell rings.

I look at Liam, who's clearly tense and edgy, and wonder why. He obviously suspects whoever is at the door is a threat to us – to him, more likely. Perhaps it is his friend, who has come to say hello. I don't know why that should worry him. I do not know if this 'friend' is just that, someone to spend time with at the amusements. It may be more, a lover, male or female. It makes no difference to me. Maybe he thinks I won't approve.

Then it hits me, as there is a louder rat-a-tat-tat on the door – *I'm not leaving!* – that Liam may have said something to his friend, his lover even, foolishly sharing the secret with what he considers the love of his life. As young people often do when they fall so heavily for the first time. That friend, the lover, has gone to the police, and it is they who are now at the door. Liam swivels on his feet, towards the kitchen, perhaps to get a glass of water, possibly to make a run for it.

I go to the front door as Liam enters the kitchen. I sense him standing there, listening and waiting, ready to go either way.

There is a dark shape, a man, on the other side of the frosted glass. I take a deep breath, hardly able to believe what it is I am seeing – it is Ryan standing on the doorstep.

I open the door, for some reason laughing, harder and louder than I could ever have imagined. I feel a surge of utter relief. Perhaps more than that.

"Um," he says cheerfully, "am I interrupting something?" He looks to the side, to where Gary's white van used to be. It's almost a question.

"No. No," I reply and then add instinctively, "He's gone, Gary. My ... ex ... he's not coming back."

He smiles and laughs too, and we look at each other, and in that moment, we are teenagers again. And it is a glorious, uplifting feeling. 'I'm yours ... if you want me,' I think, but do not say.

So we stand there goofily, him on the doorstep, me inside the door, just staring, really. He looks as though he has just had a haircut and a fresh shave, and I can smell some sort of musky aftershave on him. He wears a plain black tee shirt and black trousers, jeans really, with black-and-brown boat shoes. He looks so nice and friendly. I wonder if he is here for me.

I reach for my hair, pushing a loose strand back up my forehead. I must look a sight without make-up and my hair, most of it, scraped back in an Alice band. I am in my pyjamas and a faded pink dressing gown that's seen far better days. I pull the edges of the dressing gown together, covering myself. I have, for some reason, Gary's old, brown-checked slippers on, which I have worn for so long. I don't know why. They are comfortable. Ryan looks me up and down, as men do with women, and seems to like what he sees.

The music in the background to all this staring at each other without speaking should really be some gloopy, romantic tune. But we have the sound of *Fast & Furious* something or other as our backdrop. Ryan appears to hear it suddenly, cocking his head at an angle, almost theatrically, and asking, "You're into, ah, high-speed car chases."

I laugh, unsure what to say, realising, in this moment, that I am going to have to introduce Ryan to Liam.

As I am about to reply, say something like, "You found me," Liam comes out of the kitchen, walks up behind me and heads back towards the sofa. He obviously just thinks it is a neighbour, and that I am getting rid of them as fast as I can. But Ryan, hearing the noise, leans to the side so he can see inside. He calls, "Hello!" and Liam stops, standing there.

I watch Ryan's face as he realises it is Liam. I see it change to one of shock and then sudden emotion. He struggles for several seconds before his neutral mask slips back into place.

Before either can speak, to give each other their name, I am inviting Ryan in, stepping back, forcing Liam to take a few paces backwards as well.

Ryan comes in through the hallway, smiles, hesitating, as he passes Liam and takes his place, where I indicate, at the far end of the sofa. I gesture to Liam to take the remote control and lower the sound. He clicks the television off. I turn automatically towards the kitchen to make a pot of tea, or to bring through another bottle of Coke Zero, but then stop, not wanting to leave the two of them alone, not even for a moment.

Ryan sits there, straight-backed, on the edge of the sofa. He cannot, in truth, take his eyes off Liam. I feel a sudden surge of emotion, whether anger or dismay, I'm not sure. I'd hoped Ryan was here for me. At least in part. Liam glances at Ryan, sees his expression, and then looks nervously towards me. I think, in that split second, Liam realises who Ryan is. Nothing needs to be said. I gesture Liam to sit down in an armchair, which he does. He seems ill at ease.

I look at both of them, and it strikes me, quite forcefully, that they do not look like each other, and that bothers me somehow. I think Liam has more of a look of me, facially, although it is hard to see yourself in close family members. I've been told I have my father's face, but my mother's body shape. I never saw either. Not that it matters.

As I sit down between them, on the other end of the sofa, Ryan smiles broadly at Liam, who smiles politely back, and then I say the words I never expected to speak out loud: "Ryan, this is Liam, your son. Liam, this is Ryan, your biological father." God knows how this will go.

THERE IS THE LONGEST SILENCE. I stare, tense and nervous, into the space between them, waiting for one of them to respond. I don't know what to add to the words I've just said.

I glance at Liam. He notices the tilt of my head and looks at me. There is anger across his face. I wonder if he recognises Ryan from our lunch at the quayside and believes I have blindsided him. Tricked him into this meeting, maybe.

I look at Ryan, and he is leaning forward, his face flushed with shock and delight. He is so thrilled; I can see it for sure. That makes me happy. He does not look at me, though.

"Ah." Ryan breathes out. "Ah. Ah. Um, Christ. Liam ..." I think he wants to come across and hug Liam. But Liam sits there, stiff and unwelcoming. Ryan turns to me, "Nina? I mean ... what ..." He stops and swallows hard.

I look again at both in turn and smile. I address Ryan, starting with a surprisingly strong voice. "Liam is our son ... biological son ... he traced me recently and ... well, here he is ..." My voice then tails away, seeing Liam's response.

He still has a face like thunder; I don't know why. I thought this would be what he wanted. But he looks like he feels trapped and is utterly furious about it.

I don't know what to do. I hesitate in the awkward silence. Ryan is kind of twisting and turning with so much suppressed emotion. Liam is all rigid and affronted. It's up to me to do something. I say I'll go and make tea and biscuits, thinking that these few minutes will give them – father and son – a chance to talk on their own. Whatever I say may make things worse.

I stand there in the kitchen, the kettle boiling, watching them through the half-open door. Ryan leans so close to Liam and starts talking. Liam leans forward too, listening. I cannot hear what's being said. But looking at them, it seems hopeful.

I fiddle with a tray and mugs and tea bags and milk and sugar and sweeteners and teaspoons, breaking open a packet of chocolate digestives and putting a dozen of them on a plate in two circles. I am being as slow as I can, giving them time to talk. I imagine Liam will say much as he said to me. Ryan will summarise his life as positively as he can.

Then I am back in the living room, my tray of tea and biscuits held high. Ryan gets to his feet and takes it from me, putting it on the coffee table. He looks fit to burst, just so happy. Liam looks calmer now, more at ease; at least that bland expression of his is back in place.

I sit down where I was before, and we all lean in to take a

mug of tea and a chocolate biscuit each. I gesture towards the three teaspoons, the tube of sweeteners, and a half bag of sugar I've put on the tray, saying, "Help yourselves." I smile to myself that, at this moment of high emotion, this life-changing time, I am worrying about such nonsense.

Ryan takes charge, sipping at his tea and talking, recapping what he said to Liam, perhaps for my benefit. It is much the same as he said to me at the waterfront. He sounds successful. I then add a little about myself, by and large, the same as I have said to Ryan and Liam before. I try to make it as upbeat as I can. Ryan teases all sorts of snippets of information from Liam about his childhood; silly stuff, really, walking to school, buying pick 'n' mix sweets on the way home. Liam makes it sound idyllic. I feel repeated jabs of jealousy whenever he mentions his 'parents'.

Then another silence and, seeing the clock on the fireplace is moving towards ten o'clock, Ryan gets reluctantly to his feet. "Well, I was just passing by ... I won't take up any more of your time; it's late. It's been lovely to see you both ... I must go ... leave you in peace." He takes business cards from his back pocket, reaches for a pen in a bowl of potpourri on the coffee table, and writes on the back of two of them before handing one to each of us. He's giving Liam his personal mobile phone number. Me too, although I have it already. Perhaps he has forgotten.

"We must have a proper meal one evening. I can't do tomorrow, and I work late, NHS stuff, on Monday and Tuesday, but another time, maybe?"

We both nod. I am about to say Wednesday – that's obviously what Ryan wants – but before I can respond, Liam speaks, suggesting next Saturday. I think Ryan and I are both disappointed, but we smile brightly enough. To be fair, it is a lot for Liam to take in, on top of what's happened with Gary, so he probably needs time to think things over.

Ryan then says, "Choose somewhere you both like ... and book a table for 8pm, next Saturday ... and let me know? It's on me." Ryan hesitates, then reaches out to shake Liam's hand. An old-fashioned gesture these days. They smile warmly at each other as Ryan turns to go. To my astonishment, Liam suddenly pats Ryan on the back, he turns round, and they hug each other.

I see Ryan to the front door. He says, "He looks like you, Nina, he does ... and ..." He chokes for a second or two. "I'm so pleased to see you again." He lunges forward, hugging me, and I can feel him struggling with his emotions. This professional man. He lets go, steps back, and I wonder if he is about to kiss me. A proper kiss. But he does not. He kind of waves, almost embarrassed, his hand in front of his face. I watch as he goes to his car, reverses and leaves. He does not look back, as he seems to be weeping. I wish he had kissed me. I wonder if he ever will.

I GO BACK INDOORS, a sense of hope, possible happiness again, inside me. I've not felt like this in years. Since I was with Ryan, really. So, so long ago. I wonder if I could feel this way again – and this time, forever. I think it might just be possible, somehow.

Liam has turned the television back on, using the remote control to work through to where we'd got to with the movie, the umpteenth noisy car chase. I thought he'd have headed off to bed. Instead, I think he wants to talk.

We sit back down on the sofa, in the same positions as

before. I link my arm through his, and as he does not resist or even tense, I lay my head on his shoulder. For a second, I hold my breath, expecting him to pull back. He does not. And so I relax. It is a marvellous feeling.

"What did you think of him ... Ryan?" I ask gently after a few minutes watching the movie, lifting my head off his shoulder, sitting upright next to him.

"Nice ... nice," he answers after a short pause to gather his thoughts. Then he adds, "I liked him."

"Me too," I reply. I think about saying how I saw Ryan at the waterfront, in case Liam raises the issue, wondering how Ryan otherwise just happened to turn up like this out of the blue. I know I have to say something.

"Ryan saw us at the quayside and put two and two together. Tracked me down online ... I'm probably still in the phone book ... easy to find, me ... Nina B ... and here we are!" My voice sounds squeaky. I'm thrilled that Ryan seems to have been accepted by Liam.

Liam nods, reaching for the remote control to lower the sound on the television. I expect him to confirm he saw me talking to Ryan at the waterfront, admonishing me in a way. Instead, his words surprise me.

"He likes you. A lot. I could tell."

I feel myself flush.

"He'd definitely ... you know." Liam laughs, and I do too. I'm not sure what he was going to say, but the comment makes me feel good.

"Well ... perhaps." I think maybe I should state that it's complicated, because he's divorced with two daughters, pre-teens I guess, and that will probably be a tangled mess. And in truth, I believe Ryan is more interested in Liam than me.

But I can dream, even if it's just for tonight. I know the

chances of happy-ever-after with Ryan are remote. He may still love his ex-wife. His daughters will be protective of their dad. And they might all react badly when they learn about Liam – who may have been his lifelong secret, too. Ryan could be forced to choose between his family and us. He might want Liam. He won't pick me.

And Liam will not be here forever; he will soon be heading back to his – I have to think the words – *parents* at the end of summer before going to university. I am not sure if Ryan would still want me when Liam has gone. At the waterfront, and tonight, almost all of Ryan's looks and glances were at Liam, not me, whatever Liam might have just said.

Then there is Gary – his ever-present body out there as a constant reminder of this appalling thing we have done. His body – *remains,* as it will become – will always be waiting to be uncovered. A long hot summer with flies buzzing around his shallow grave. A hard, cold winter with the soil sinking and revealing what's left of him. The bones, by then, I imagine.

But now, just tonight, as we watch the end of this movie, I will let myself enjoy my flights of fancy. How we will have a meal together, the three of us, somewhere nice next weekend. At the end, we will raise our glasses of wine, clinking them together and saying, 'To us!'

Ryan will start visiting regularly, and we will go to the cinema and for more meals, perhaps days out. And eventually, maybe, just maybe, this little family will become everything I have always wanted.

And Ryan and I will go out for candlelight suppers, and we will kiss and cuddle in his car afterwards. Then, one night, not so long after, he will stay here with me, and from there all my dreams will come true. Could it happen? I think so. I'd love it to be so more than anything.

Then, after our life-changing evening, Liam and I head to bed. My mind is everywhere. Good thoughts about Ryan. Liam, too. What might happen. I try to force the bad thoughts – Gary, all the things we need to do to cover our tracks, the fear of exposure – to the back of my mind. As I get into bed, the good thoughts dominate, and I feel uplifted. I don't know for how long.

———

I LIE IN BED, my mind flitting this way and that, filled with so many different, troubling thoughts. I hate the night.

During the day, I can just get on with things. At night-time, with nothing to do but try to sleep, my mind takes control. And it sends me on a twisty-turny journey to hell.

Each concern, every worry, is magnified one hundred times. A look, a word, whatever, is analysed every which way, filling me with fear. And then, eventually, I am falling asleep.

It is night-time, I am in woodland, and the only light is a the moon shining through the trees like a spotlight. I have to keep out of the light.

I stay still, standing behind a huge oak, in the shadows, being as small and as quiet as I can, trying to be invisible.

There are things – beasts and monsters – in the woods, and they are hunting me. They watch and wait for me to reveal myself.

All I can hear is my breathing, great big gulps of breath that give me away.

I try to breathe quietly, as shallow as I can, but my rising fear makes me breathe louder and louder.

I hear stirrings in the undergrowth as monsters creep carefully towards me, circling, ready to attack.

Then I am running as fast as I can, away from the monsters, and I hear my sobbing breaths and crackling footsteps turning into a cacophony of noise.

Behind me, the monsters are chasing, echoing my noises with their grunts and slobberings as they get ever closer, to attack, tearing me limb from limb.

So I stop, hardly able to stand and breathe, and turn towards them to fight to the last. As I do, they scatter so fast I cannot see them taking up their hiding places.

I stand there, in fearful silence, peering into the darkness to find where they are. There are so many of them, yet I cannot see any.

And I realise suddenly that I am standing in the light of the moon, alone and exposed, for all of them to see.

I can hear more and more beasts and monsters moving about out of sight until I am encircled by them. They are creeping closer.

I fall to my knees, crouching and covering my head with my hands. I know, somehow, that I deserve to die. I just don't know why.

I try to focus on being calm, accepting my fate. But I cannot. I am angry and defiant. I don't want to die. Not in this way.

And I am up on my feet, roaring, shouting as loud as I can, about to run in one direction, punching and kicking and pushing my way through to freedom.

Then I awake, drenched in sweat as I always am when I have this dream, or one much like it. It takes me a moment or two to realise I am safe, at least for now, but longer to restore a sense of calm.

I realise that this dream – this nightmare – is triggered by a mix of guilt and fear. That I covered up Gary's death, and one day, it will be uncovered.

What I do not know, as I always wake up in the same instant, is whether I could punch and kick and push my way out to safety in the nightmare. I doubt it. And I realise that it will be like this in real life. I won't be able to get away.

13

SUNDAY, 15 JULY, DAYBREAK

I am up early, heading downstairs, fussing about with tidying and vacuuming and getting the breakfast things out. I find myself putting the cereal packets next to each other in order of their size. And I wonder if perhaps I have a mild form of OCD. Then again, perhaps I just think too much.

As I sit here, looking out across the close, all quiet on a Sunday morning, I can put the horrors of the night behind me and try focusing on the positives of Ryan coming back. There are still things to be done before we are safe – Gary's body, his belongings and more – and I run through everything in my mind as a checklist.

Then Liam is down, and after the usual pleasantries, we start eating and drinking. I want to ask him if he might now spend the day here, that we could go out for lunch, maybe have a walk along the promenade. A nice Sunday afternoon. But he seems somehow out of sorts this morning. I can't tell why. I wait for him to say something. He does, eventually, about Ryan. After talking around what happened last night, he gets to the point, and my heart sinks.

"He's rich, isn't he? Ryan." He looks at me with an unpleasant expression on his face. Like he's someone else, a hard, calculating person.

I nod, keeping things pleasant, smiling as if to say, *Yes, I guess so.* I don't want to dwell on money.

"I thought you were rich, but he's something else. A private dentist. Did you see his Audi A3?"

I nod again, smiling a little tighter this time. Something about what he says is jarring. Beyond the crass words. I'm not sure what it is. This doesn't sound like him.

"He's divorced ... two daughters ... did he say?" I ask, a touch of vim in my voice. "He won't have much to spare for you ... if anything."

Liam nods, as if to respond, *That doesn't matter.* He stares out the window, and I don't know what to think. Perhaps it was just something to say.

I still have, after Ryan left, having hugged and come close to kissing me, the wild idea that the three of us might somehow end up together as a family. It would be the perfect, happy-ever-after ending. I was full of joy at one point, but it's all just been swept away in this moment.

Liam's response is not what I expected, nor wanted. He should be thrilled that he has found both of his birth parents, be rejoicing in that, not thinking about money. I wonder if that's why he came here, because he believes I have money. I'm not rich, although I do own my own home and have savings because of my parents' deaths. You'd have to be poor to consider me rich, though.

And beyond Liam's response, there is that one thing that would prevent us getting together as a family, at least here.

Gary's body. I have a sudden, appalling image of the three of us having a picnic in the back garden. There is a sudden noise. The sound of collapsing earth by the garage. Ryan wandering over, looking down, gasping in horror.

"We need to move Gary," I say, changing the subject, "before Ryan comes back. We can't take a chance."

He nods, my co-conspirator in perverting the course of justice, although both of us could well be charged with murder if or when Gary is uncovered.

"Yes," he answers slowly, "somewhere he'll never be found."

I nod, not sure what else to say. Part of me thinks he won't be discovered here, just so long as he's well covered and I stand guard for ever.

He then adds, "I saw this true crime programme once. This woman and her son killed an abusive husband and buried him in different places. Miles apart."

I feel sick at the thought of that. "Leave it for now. I need to think about it." I don't really. I can't face anything like that. I'd rather take my chances where he is.

Then we are getting up, and I still wish he'd spend the day here with me and we could work more on rebuilding our fractured relationship. But not today. He goes upstairs and returns wearing a silly bucket hat he must have bought recently. He comes into the kitchen, heading out the back.

"I'll book a table, shall I? For Saturday," he says, fiddling with his phone. "Somewhere expensive in Ipswich? Where we'll eat caviar and drink champagne ... and eat, what are they, quails' eggs?" He laughs at his own joke. But it is not a nice sound. He is still thinking about Ryan's money. I wonder if he wants some of it. "I'll text you the booking confirmation later," he adds.

I snap back, angrier than I mean it to sound, as he steps outside, "Is that why you're here? For money? I've not got enough, so you're going to move on to him?"

He looks at me, startled at what I've said and my snapping tone. He goes to say something, maybe conciliatory, but I pull the door to and turn away from him.

———

I AM STANDING by the window of the living room, looking out over the close, trying to calm my frayed nerves. I want to think about Liam, working through the morning's conversation in my head. But I am distracted by the sight of next-door Tony, my neighbour to my left, strolling up my path. We smile and say hello when we pass each other, and occasionally stop for a brief chat. He manages a vintage clothes shop up the town. I've never been in. But I've seen him out and about. He's nice enough.

I don't know why, but I imagine he's going out on this hot sunny day and wants me to take in an Amazon parcel that's going to be left on his doorstep for all to see. I don't mind doing that. Then I see he has a folder under his right arm, and I worry that might mean it is more significant, a will to witness or something. I step back instinctively, but he glances across at that moment, and I am sure he sees me through the half-open blinds.

He rings the doorbell, and after hesitating, I go to answer it. Tony is an older man, early sixties I'd guess, and his partner, Stephen, died many years ago. That's all I know. He's a quiet sort. I've seen a younger man, sandy-haired, maybe forty, going in and out lately, but he tends to look away if we cross paths – more shy than rude, I think. He has a sweet face.

I open the front door. Tony and I smile at each other. We exchange pleasantries and comments about the weather, and then we look at each other slightly awkwardly.

"I, uh, was wondering ..." He stops and looks around, back towards where Gary's van was. "If James, my partner, and I ... might come round in the week to talk to you, and ... and ..." He glances back at the driveway again. "About this."

He hands me the folder and gestures, almost nervously, that I should open it. I do, and, on top, is a photograph of a posh conservatory. Trying to appear interested, I flick through the other sheets of paper, just drawings and notes and forms.

I feel a sudden sharp stab of alarm as though my subconscious knows something bad is about to happen before I do. I smile as best I can and go to hand the file back to him. I try to appear non-committal. He does not take the file.

"James is moving in." His face kind of flutters joyfully for a second, and I smile encouragingly at him, even though my mind is racing ahead, filling full of horror. "And we want to add a sunroom. Well, an orangery, really. It's like a conservatory but with more ... well, anyway." He smiles again. I nod.

He continues, this nice but twitchy man. "James is speaking to a friend of a friend – of a friend! – who works at the council today, to see if we need planning permission, and I said I'd have a word with you. It's going to be noisy for a while, and ... I know you've not been well, and I wanted to see how you'd feel about that." He pauses, then adds almost breathlessly, "We'd be very strict with them!"

I laugh at this sweet man and his silly comments. I don't know how he knew about my baby. I did not tell anyone in the close, but I guess someone told somebody who told someone else who told him. That's what it's like here. It's a small place, Felixstowe.

"Fine, absolutely fine, do whatever! No need to come round." I hand the file back to him, and he takes it.

"Oh," he says suddenly, flapping his arms. "I wanted to ... the builder asked if he could put up a ... what do you call it ... um, like scaffolding. Just a frame and planks, so they can move around more easily ... up top. It will be a quicker that way ... save me a few pennies."

I look at him, feeling niggled that there will be work people up there, looking into my garden. More than that. It worries me. Yet there is nothing for them to see from there. I nod; I must act normally. "That's okay ... sure ... whatever's easiest for you."

But I see his face and know there is more. I feel my stomach sinking.

"He wants to know if he can put the, you know, the struts ... the support thingies ... on your side of the fence. By the garage." He looks at me brightly as I fight the sick feeling coming up from my stomach. I try to offer a neutral expression, but I need to hurry to the bathroom. I have to cut this conversation short. So I nod my agreement and smile and gesture inside, as though I have a pan on the boil, and kind of wave goodbye. He takes the hint, not really noticing my anguish, and just looks relieved as he turns to go. I think he thought he'd have to convince me.

I sit crouched over the toilet in the bathroom, bringing up what's in my stomach. I then continue gagging drool and spit into the bowl. Eventually, I wash my face and hands in the sink. I put the lid of the toilet down and sit on it, my head in my hands, working out what I have to do.

If I do nothing, just hold my nerve, workmen will come into my garden sometime soon, putting up scaffolding that will go into the ground where Gary is buried. I know I should have said no to the man next door, and perhaps I should go round there later and say I've changed my mind. But he will look at me, clearly thinking 'Why?' and I won't know how to answer.

I'M SITTING HERE, in the living room, have been all morning, since I spoke to next-door Tony. I am unable to relax, spending the time flicking through TV channels, reading old magazines, and fiddling repeatedly with my phone. News and nonsense. I think about all sorts of things, including the scaffolding, but my mind just keeps going back to Gary and the appalling thing Liam and I have done. I feel such remorse.

I try to focus my mind on the practicalities of how to keep this a secret forever. But increasingly, my emotions come to the surface. As they do now. Gary, I don't think, deep down, really liked Liam.

But Gary was the father of my lost baby. He would have been my husband. And we would have had children together. He was not a bad man. He had a difficult life. He was poor with money, useless, to be honest. He was not really a nasty man, more frustrated. I think now that all of the anger and aggression may have covered some sort of mental ill-health. Depression, possibly. I could have shown more empathy. I had feelings for him; they may have grown into love. Maybe.

Gary disliked Liam – perhaps even hated him – because

he was jealous of what Liam and I had together. An obvious closeness. A bond.

Perhaps he even suspected Liam was more than just a cousin. "Who are you? Who are you?" he cried. I wonder if he would have eventually realised that Liam was my son. No matter now; Liam was so fast to confess to it.

That confession tipped Gary over the edge, leading to that final, shocking fight and on to where we are now. One killing. Two ruined lives.

Some thought at the back of my mind is troubling me, though. I cannot work out what it is. It's to do with Gary and Liam. Something I'm missing. That I have forgotten. I rack my brains without success. No, it has gone. I replay the imagined confrontation between Gary and Liam again and again, trying to catch the thought. It comes to me at last.

Who are you? Who are you? My God. Gary was not asking that because he thought Liam was my son, but because he did not know who he was. It all comes rushing back at me. How Gary had looked on social media, and there was no trace of Liam, and how odd that is for someone of Liam's age. "He's not who he says he is!" Gary shouted angrily at me.

I sit back on the sofa, my mind all over the place. I had, with all the horrors, the murder, the cover-up, the visitors to my door, forgotten about Gary's furious claims. The mind plays tricks. Blotting things out. Perhaps mine was protecting me.

Until now. It strikes me that I need to know more, to check online about Liam, coming to my own conclusions. That's what I'll do all afternoon.

I flick through my phone, searching for 'Liam Riley' on Instagram, X and so on. There are so many Liam Rileys everywhere. I scroll through and through, looking at photos and descriptions, checking some more closely than others. It takes so long. I do not see 'my' Liam anywhere. I take a break for a cup of tea and then come back to my online research.

I Google 'Liam Riley', producing a never-ending task to trawl through millions and millions of results. I add more search terms, 'Springham', 'Chelmsford', 'Essex' and so on. Even then, there are more than one million results. I look, page after page after page, feeling utterly frustrated. Another break, to go to the bathroom, and I am back at it again.

I look more generally in the area for 'Riley, Liam', other 'Rileys', even 'Alex' and 'Alexander Riley'. I remember how he hesitated over his name when he came here, and I wonder if he's still legally Alex but just prefers the name Liam. At school, there was a boy in my class who was called Kevin, after his old father, but preferred the name Richie. Eventually, I create a list of possible places to check in Springham. All 'Riley' but different first names.

I go further, all sorts of random ideas going through my mind – looking at message boards about archaeology and Oxford University, even schools in and around Chelmsford. Hours later, I accept Gary was correct. I have not found a 'Liam Riley'. It is as if he does not exist.

Still I go on, doggedly searching 'Springham' and 'Essex'. I see, over and again, references to a children's home there. Something nags at me whenever I see one. A comment Liam made somewhere, some time. I can't recall it. That bothers me.

Then, suddenly, an intake of breath. A news story of a boy, a young man, Alex but a different surname, killed last year in Chelmsford, not far from Springham. A hit-and-run. A picture of elderly, grieving parents holding a photograph of their Alex, who looks a bit like Ryan. I sit back, stunned.

Thoughts, so many confusing ideas, swirl around my head. Is Liam, the Liam here in my home, really my son? There, I've thought it out loud at last.

If not, who is he – and is there a link between him and this hit-and-run from last year, or maybe even the children's home at Springham?

My imagination runs riot. I can scarcely believe where it is going. Is my mind turning odd comments and internet news stories into a fairy story? Or have I just stumbled on the shocking truth? I have to find out.

———

LIAM IS late for his tea, so I eat my tuna-filled baked potato and leafy green salad alone – worrying, if I am honest, about him. Not being late. Just him being him. Or not. Being someone else. And what that means about Alex. And for me. Thoughts race through my mind.

I replay so many conversations between us from when he first came here: about his adoptive parents, his childhood and Springham. He has mentioned the children's home there before, in passing, but enough times now for it to raise a flag with me. Like he's been scratching at a sore.

And I recall his conversation with Ryan, the two of them sitting there together, glancing across at me. There is something that worries me about that, but I can't quite work out what it is.

I finish my tea, going into the kitchen to fill the dishwasher and make myself a cup of tea. I wonder why Liam is so late, almost an hour. He has never been so late before.

I stand in the living room looking out, waiting, although he could come in the back way, over the fields, slipping in the back gate and through the kitchen door. He does that more and more now, I think. It's as though he does not want to be seen.

I take his plate of food and put it into the fridge. He can have it later if he fancies it. And then I sit in the living room with my mug of tea and start worrying again – this time that, after our tense conversation this morning, he may simply have upped and gone, leaving me with unanswered questions. And, of course, Gary's body.

The early evening moves into mid-evening as I sit here, deciding whether to keep on waiting or to give up and just have a bath and go to bed. As I move to get up and go, I hear Liam coming in through the kitchen door. He has been drinking. I can smell it on him. And smoking. I can smell that too. But not tobacco, something else, something more acrid-smelling. Weed.

I had hoped he would come back and have his tea, with me sitting opposite him, asking some gentle questions – his family, his childhood, that children's home – to get some answers. Even if he avoided my questions or gave vague replies, I would see his face and could come to my own conclusions.

But now, in his state, I think – I hope – that he is going to go straight up to bed. To sleep things off. I can talk to him, ask my careful questions, at breakfast tomorrow before I head down the A12. But then he sees me as he walks to the stairs, and he stops, and I doubt he'll be up at breakfast time the condition he's in.

I speak before he can. "I'm out for the day tomorrow, early on. I've got a couple of things to do ... work-wise," I add, although, of course, I intend to go to Springham to see what I can uncover. "I might leave before breakfast ... you can sort yourself out for once?" It sounds snappy, but I don't think he's noticed. I doubt he'll even remember this conversation.

He looks at me and smiles, a great big beatific smile, and kind of waves his hand in the air, a greeting or a goodbye, I cannot tell. It alarms me, seeing him like this. I fear he may talk about things to his friends at the pier, letting our secret slip.

He turns away from me and stumbles on the first step of the stairs. He giggles to himself and then stands upright, placing his left foot on the next step. He moves his right foot up after it. Then a sudden wobble, and he moves onto the next step.

"Who the hell are you?" I ask quietly, almost to myself. He does not respond, simply walking upstairs. And I am left wondering if he did not hear me because he is drunk or wasted – or, as likely, he simply did not know what to say. He won't remember either way. And I will find out the truth tomorrow anyway.

I SPEND HALF an hour in the bath, listening to Liam. There is a silence when I think he must have gone to bed. Then a burst of crashing about, drawers pulled out and pushed back, and, finally, an almighty thump followed by the longest, never-ending silence.

I think he's tried to get changed into the pyjamas I bought him, struggled to get them on and passed out on the bed. I wonder how and why he's got himself like this. Guilt? Shame? Fear? I hope he's not going to suddenly decide to confess.

Most likely, it's just him letting off steam with his friends, drinking and smoking weed, probably a regular Saturday night thing for teenagers in Felixstowe – everywhere, really, these days. No matter, I will try to get a good night's sleep before my journey to Springham in the morning.

I am facing the mirror in the bathroom a few minutes later, looking at my face and rubbing cream gently into my forehead, around my eyes, and so on.

A thought is nagging at me, at the back of my mind. On and on it goes, about Liam.

But I can't remember what it is. Or why it troubles me now. Something important, I know that. I just don't recall what it is.

I think back to when Liam met Ryan and I saw the two of them together. That's when it started bugging me. Whatever it is.

And then I look at my eyes, my brown eyes, and I know immediately what has been worrying away at my subconscious.

Ryan has brown eyes. I have brown eyes. Liam has blue eyes. I do not think two brown-eyed parents can have a blue-eyed child. It's as simple as that.

I hurry to get changed into my pyjamas and slippers and pick up my phone and go to my bedroom, closing the door behind me. I Google what I need to know. I read out loud the first thing that comes up. I don't know why.

"Both parents with brown eyes: 75 per cent chance of a baby with brown eyes, 18.8 per cent chance of a baby with green eyes, 6.3 per cent chance of a baby with blue eyes."

It's not 100 per cent definite, then. It would have been, if it had been the other way round. If Ryan and I both had blue eyes, then there is a 0 per cent chance of Liam having brown eyes. But it's still 93.7 per cent, and that's decisive enough for me. *Almost.* I must be sure.

I lie down on my bed, trying to make sense of it all. If Liam is not our son – mine and Ryan's – who is he? He's not Alex, or at least 93.7 per cent not our Alex. So, somehow, this boy, Liam, or whatever he is called, has found out about me and come here for only one thing. Money. I'm sure of it.

My visit to Springham in the morning now takes on huge significance. I will go first to the houses – the possible 'Riley' houses – and see what I can uncover there. Then, somehow, to visit the parents of the teen who died. Maybe that was our boy, Alex. Finally, I will visit the children's home.

And then what? The long drive back up the A12 from Colchester and along the A14 to Felixstowe, knowing now, beyond doubt, that this teenager in my home is not my son. "Who are you?" I will shout loudly at him, my hand around his whittling knife that I still keep in my pocket or close by at all times. I will unfold it carefully. "And what have you done with my son?"

14

MONDAY, 17 JULY, HIGH NOON

I'm in Springham. I sit in my car parked in a layby along the road from a big, detached house set well back from the pavement. It is a grand place, much as I imagined it from Liam's occasional comments, and I can see it clearly from here. I haven't seen any comings or goings. But there is a smart black BMW on the driveway. So someone is at home.

I glance down at the notes I've made in a booklet – seven possible addresses where Liam may live with what I think of as his adoptive parents. From what Liam has said, I am looking for an upmarket home that reeks of money. And then it hits me – if Liam comes from such a background, why has he come to me for money? It does not make sense. I will think about that later.

For now, I run through what I am going to say when one, perhaps both adoptive parents, opens the door. "Hello, I'm Nina, Liam's birth mother." That does not feel right, but I have to be sure he is who he says he is. I can't believe I am doing this. I feel so conflicted. But I must be 100 per cent certain.

I have been to three addresses so far without success. The first was a run-down bungalow, nothing like the place I've pictured from Liam's words. I drove straight on to the next.

The second one was a picture-perfect cottage, thatched roof, roses round the door – beautiful but tiny – and again, nothing like the place Liam has mentioned now and then.

Driving to the next address, I thought for an instant this was it – a huge house, almost a mansion, with a sweeping, gravelly drive. But the sign outside the house implied it had been divided up into so many apartments, ten, twelve maybe more. A home for well-off retirees. My spirits sank.

But this house, the fourth, ticks all of the boxes. I trawl my memory, through snippets of conversation, to form a checklist of things that Liam has said. Not much, truth be told. It's hard to get much out of teenage boys, I guess. The house was a 'big' one. 'Near the station'. A 'five-minute walk' from his school. There is a parade of shops between the house and the school where he'd sometimes stop to 'get sweets and a fizzy drink' on the way home.

Well, the house is certainly a big one, and it has a look of wealth about it – everything is immaculate and cared-for, no expense spared. The adoptive parents don't need to save up to do anything. They just do what they want when they want. There is a bronze sculpture on the lawn – two naked men entwined in an embrace – that must have cost thousands of pounds.

Looking at Google Maps, the school is a twelve-minute walk, the station twenty minutes. I cannot see a parade of shops between the school and this house – there are some shops about fifteen minutes away, but it would be a detour. Maybe I've remembered Liam's words incorrectly, or it could be that something's there that's not showing on Google Maps. There is a petrol station about halfway between; perhaps Liam stopped inside for his sweets.

I'm sure this is it. I feel suddenly nervous, as though intimidated by the wealth and luxury in front of me. Liam has never said much about the adoptive parents. He has been coy and protective. The man works for the government, clearly high-up and successful. The woman, Liam says, is a housewife, although I suspect her time is spent mostly on coffee mornings and visits to the spa. A comfortable, if not luxurious, life.

I change my mind about what I'm going to say. It has to be something less challenging. "Hi, is Liam in?" Like I'm a lovelorn teenager. I'll pretend to be someone from the school, a market researcher, whatever, I don't know. Someone of no importance.

They'll reply in one of two ways. Either, "Sorry, no, he's away at the moment." Or quite simply, "Who?" Whatever their reply, I'll have my answer and can make my excuses and leave.

If Liam does live here, and they acknowledge that, it's all I need to know. He is who he says he is. I've been worrying over nothing. I get out of my car, walk along the pavement and up the driveway to the front door.

As I approach, the door swings open, and two men, in their mid-thirties, in pink and yellow and black Lycra, come out, both wheeling racing bicycles from the hallway. They glance at me, as though I am of no importance. One points at a 'No Junk Mail' sticker by the doorbell. The other shakes his head dismissively.

"I'm looking for Liam," I blurt out, showing them a photo of Liam, taken slightly from the side, but recognisable to anyone who knows him. I was so sure this was the house.

"No Liam here, lovey," one says patronisingly.

"Now if you don't mind," the other adds, and I am sent on my way. I turn, crunching my way back along the drive-way, feeling bereft. I feel somehow that Liam, 'my' Liam, is not who he says. He is not my son. I sit in my car and weep quietly for a few minutes.

Three more addresses to visit, although I am so close to giving up. The fifth, an identikit box of a detached house on an estate, seems unlikely. I ring the doorbell anyway, just to be sure. A young woman in her early twenties with a crying toddler in tow comes to the door. I look at her irritated face, and I make my excuses: 'So sorry, wrong house,' and leave quickly.

I accelerate the car by the sixth – a beaten-up old semi on what was a former council estate – with a feeling of increasing despair. I know in my heart that I am not going to find what I've been looking for.

The seventh and final address, 76a something or other, turns out to be a semi-detached house divided into apart-ments. I see young people coming in and out at the same time and guess this is student accommodation, no more and no less.

That's that. My search is over.

A LITTLE LATER, I sit in my car in a supermarket car park, having been in to go to the toilet and to pick up a latte and a packet of shortbread biscuits. After I have drunk and eaten and calmed myself, I incline my chair and shut my eyes, thinking through what this means. I feel so bewildered and distressed.

Liam said he was my son and came from Springham. Was adopted by an older couple with the surname Riley. Lived in a big house. Near this. Close to that. Not far from the other. I have visited all seven addresses where people with that surname live. It ... they ... him ... do not exist. It is as simple as that. I have been conned. I just don't know why.

Whoever the 'Liam' is in my house, he is not my son, my Alexander, and I cannot comprehend what that now means for us. For me, really. I do not know who he can be. Or how he found me. Or knew my story. Nor why he is here. It makes no sense. None at all. I am not a particularly rich woman. I own my own house and have savings in the bank, enough for me to not have to work for a while, if I choose. I wonder if that is why this boy – this young man – is targeting me. To scam me out of my money. That's the 'why' of him being here. But I want to know the 'how' of it, too.

I can drive home now, confronting him, demanding to know who he is. But if I corner him, exposing his lies, proving that we are not mother and son, he may turn on me. He may do to me what he did to Gary. I sob at the thought. I can call the police and tell them what happened, the whole truth of it. But Liam may deny it, saying the killing was done by me. I certainly perverted the course of justice, and that will mean a long prison sentence. I don't know what to do.

I am crying now, partly because Liam is not my son and what that means for me. Prison at best, I think. But mostly, and I realise this with a sudden stab of pain, because it means I do not know what has happened to my Alexander. I wonder, as I have done so many times, if he is still out there somewhere, happy or sad. Or, as I finally flick through my booklet, at the notes I've made about the 'Alex' who was in that fatal car crash, if he is dead. I must find out, however horrifying the truth may be.

AN HOUR OR SO LATER, I am sitting in the sun lounge of a large dormer bungalow, sipping a cup of tea with a man, in his late fifties, opposite me. He looks older than his years, with his straggly hair and greying beard, and dressed in old-man cardigan and slippers. He has given up on life, everything, really. He has what looks like snot in his moustache.

This is a man with all the cares of the world on his shoulders. His wife, he says, is at the hospital for treatment. He does not say what it is, and I do not ask, but he adds that an ambulance picks her up and returns her, and he glances at a clock on the wall; she should be back soon.

He gets up and walks crookedly by me, as though he has something wrong with his legs. He says he is going to fetch a packet of biscuits from the kitchen. He touches me lightly on the shoulder as he passes, almost affectionately, and says he hopes I will stay to meet his wife, as she will be thrilled. I feel ashamed and such a fraud.

When I was in the car in the supermarket car park, I scrolled and reread the story of 'Alex Burton' who was killed in a hit-and-run accident. He was the same age as my Alex, had a look of Ryan about him from the lead photograph, and I convinced myself that he was 'my Alex', adopted and retaining the name I'd chosen for him.

The story, a double-page spread, was heart-breaking to read, with quotes from his parents, John and Elsa, about how kind and caring he was and photographs of the three of them in happy times. In a photograph just of the parents, one holding a favourite photo of Alex, the other a home-made card for his next birthday, I could see a sign behind them with the number of their house.

I tracked them down easily enough online and turned up on the doorstep, driven by my obsession, forty-five minutes later. He opened the door, and I gabbled some story about how I used to teach Alex years ago and had been abroad and just returned and heard what had happened. I was so shocked and sorry. What I said didn't really make much sense, but he smiled and seemed pleased and stepped back to invite me in. I followed him down a hallway with framed photographs of Alex on the walls, and through the living room to the sun lounge, as he called it.

And now the man is back, tugging at the side of a packet of Rich Tea biscuits. I take it from him, running a fingernail into the packaging to open it. I take a biscuit, offering the rest to him, but he shakes his head, so I put the packet on a wicker table next to me.

"Where, um, did you teach Alex?" he asks politely. "Was it his primary school?" He looks across, all watery-eyed, not a trace of suspicion on his face. His manner encourages me to speak more than I should.

"Yes, I was part-time. I came in and did arts and crafts with the children in the aft–" I was going to say the 'after-noons' and that 'Alex was very good at it'.

But he interrupts me, not rudely, just as though he has had a sudden thought and has to say it before he loses the thread. "What did you say your name was?" He's just curious.

"Mandy Barnes," I lie, giving the name of a girl I used to

know at school, and swallowing hard. I do not think he notices. If I give my real name, Nina Bolitho, he will, if this Alex is my Alex, become upset or angry that I have come here in this underhand way. I don't want to do that. I need to find out more subtly.

He shakes his head. "I'm sorry, that doesn't ring a bell. Elsa will know. When she gets back. She knew all his primary school teachers. Do you remember her?"

I feel myself sweating – this now feels claustrophobic somehow, as though everything is closing in on me. I don't know which way to answer.

"I remember Alex!" I respond finally as brightly as I can. My voice sounds fake and brittle. "He was so, so good at art." I leave it at that.

The man pulls a face, a look of doubt. "He was never very good at ... that sort of thing. He liked toy soldiers ... and my old train set." He pauses, shaking his head and adding, "Ah, well, maybe a bit, I suppose, with ..." He tails off, his voice wistful.

We sit there quietly, each drinking our tea, as though reminiscing to ourselves. I take another biscuit, thinking what to say to this sad man, to find out what I need to know without hurting him.

"Is that one of Alex's?" I ask, pointing to a home-made pottery jug on the windowsill, pens and pencils sticking out of it.

He shakes his head. "No, that's Elsa's. She made it at an evening class. She used to go to them regularly before ... you know." His voice fades away, and we sit there again, struggling to know what to say.

Then there are noises at the front door, and he says, "Ah, here she is now. She'll be pleased to see you again." He gets up and walks by me, painfully slowly this time. I wonder if his touch on my shoulder before was simply to steady himself. "Wait here."

I hear snatches of voices, his and hers, whispered and urgent, in the hallway, as he tells her they have a visitor, a teacher who knew Alex! Her voice, her reply, sounds jagged and angry, and I'm sure I hear her say, "Can't be doing with it."

She clump, clump, clumps down the hallway, through the living room, and then she is standing in the sun room. This short, stout woman with gingery-tinted curly hair and a dark raincoat despite the summer sunshine. I notice she has one ordinary-looking black heavy shoe and another built up for a shorter leg.

"Who are you?" she asks me, in a tired and short-tempered voice – all she really wants to do is to sit down and have a cup of tea. He's not in sight, and I think he's gone to the kitchen to make one for her.

I stand up, not sure whether to step forward to shake her hand. But she is bristling with irritation and has no time for me. I am flustered by this sudden turn of events. "I ... ah ... used to teach Alex ... and ... I wanted to pay my respects."

She looks me up and down dismissively. "I don't remember you ... and there's a book of remembrance at both the schools ... from last year." She pauses and adds, close to anger now, "What are you doing here?"

"I ... um ... just wanted to talk about Alex." I am torn between keeping up the pretence, or just saying who I am and asking her outright if Alex is their adopted child.

"What about Alex?" she says, still standing and clearly wanting me gone. I hear the man stumbling back through, and then he is behind her, holding a newspaper, the *Daily*

Mail, out for her. I hear the kettle boiling in the background.

They both stand there looking at me, him slightly bewildered, her just about keeping a lid on her temper.

"My maiden name was Bolitho," I say suddenly, looking at their faces for a reaction.

There is none, not as I was expecting, hoping for even. He smiles vaguely, almost encouraging me to go on. If they adopted my Alex – Alexander James Bolitho – he'd surely remember such a distinctive name and react in shock.

She reacts, but not as she would if she knew she was being confronted by the birth mother of her dead, adopted son. "I don't know who you are ... or what you're up to ... but I'm calling the police." She rummages in her pocket.

"I'm sorry. I'm sorry," I respond, close to tears, and I move to go by her. In my haste, my panic really, I bump into her, and she falls sideways against the door and on to the carpet. He leans forward, unsteady on his feet, trying to help her up.

I brush by him, into the living room and on to the hallway. I hear her cry out in pain, and I shout back again, "I'm sorry, really sorry."

I am at my car by the pavement, fumbling for my keys, getting in, revving the car, stalling it, and then, eventually, driving away. I look back in the mirror and see him on the doorstep watching me. I cannot see the expression on his face; bewildered, I suspect.

I park the car in a layby some distance along the road and just sit there fighting back more tears. I made such a mess of that meeting. I should not have gone. It was foolish. And cruel of me. A waste of time too. I think that the man will have noted my number plate and given it to her to call the police.

The thought that I might be somewhere on the police's radar fills me with dread. That the report might feed through to my local police force and an officer might come knocking, asking questions. Then, later, if or when Gary is reported missing, some bright spark might put two and two together and come back again with further questions.

I sit back, wishing I had never come here, but slowly realising that there is nothing I can do if the woman calls the police and makes a complaint about me. I will have to deal with the consequences. I must concoct some sort of story. I have no idea what it might be. The fact is, I am exhausted and heart-broken, and it is time to head for home, to have a confrontation with Liam, whoever he might be.

As I DRIVE SLOWLY along the road, breathing deeply to calm my mind, I see, up ahead on the left, a sign for a children's home, the one that Liam has mentioned two or three times. I wonder suddenly if this place might be of some significance.

I turn the car and head towards the home along twisty, woody lanes. I pull up in the car park and look at the big, forbidding Victorian building. It's like something out of a Charles Dickens novel.

Sitting for a little while, regaining my composure, I wonder what I am going to do. As my mind rushes about, I sense suddenly that Liam comes from here. Why else would he keep mentioning it? I must find out. I take the photo of Liam from my pocket, get out of the car, lock it and walk towards the building.

I have to ring a doorbell to gain entry, saying into the speakerphone, or whatever the stupid thing is called, that

I'm here with 'an enquiry'. I hold my breath, expecting to be turned away. But I am let in by a cleaner, an elderly woman with a wizened but friendly face, who smiles at me. I smile back. I think she probably should have retired years ago.

I'm not sure what to say to the officious-looking woman behind the desk in the grand, oak-panelled reception area. This is more like a health spa or a conference centre than a children's home. It is quiet and not the lively, perhaps even feral, place I'd have imagined. Perhaps the children are all somewhere out the back.

I simply say I have to come to speak to someone about a boy who used to live here. I sense the receptionist is about to send me away with carefully rehearsed sentences about data protection and so on. But she is distracted by a phone ringing next to her. She says she'll get someone to come to speak to me, gesturing towards a seating area where the elderly woman is now sweeping the floor with a soft brush and a dustpan. The receptionist then answers the phone.

Sitting in an old, leather Chesterfield sofa, from a bygone era, I rehearse what I am going to say. I'll show the photo of Liam to whoever comes out. "This is Liam, my son. He used to live here. Can you tell me about him, please?"

Whoever it is will say no. They'll have to. There are laws and regulations and protocols to follow. They cannot give out a child's details just because someone asks for them. That does not matter, though, not really.

I'll know – by giving the name, showing the photo, looking at the person's face – if Liam is from here. If not, they will say something like, 'Never seen him before'. But I suspect he is, and they will hide instantly behind the law. 'We're not allowed to say anything.' And that will be enough. I'll know. I will have my answer.

I hear the receptionist finish her call, see her glance up and over at me, and then press a button somewhere, saying something in a quiet voice. I sit, waiting.

The cleaner, huffing and puffing, drops a cloth on the wooden floor, groaning slightly as she bends over to pick it up. Back pain, I think. She smiles at me again, glancing at the photograph in my hand, and I smile, too. Still I wait.

After what seems an age, a young man, maybe late twenties, in an ill-fitting grey suit, crisp white shirt and a striped-red tie, comes out. He speaks to the receptionist and then turns towards me as she gestures in my direction. He is an administrative sort. A man in a suit.

The conversation goes much as I expected. I say what I have rehearsed. He looks at the photograph, swallows and twitches ever so slightly, and then summarises, with prepared words and sentences and intonations, why he cannot talk about anything. I can write in or fill out a form for Head Office. Blah. Blah. Blah.

I smile and thank him and say I understand, all in a sympathetic voice, as though I have wronged him in some way. And we look and smile insincerely at each other. Then I turn to leave, happy with what I have seen. That oh-so-slight swallow and that blink-and-you'd-miss-it twitch revealing that Liam does indeed come from here.

Walking to the door, I have what I need to know. The boy – young man – in my house is not my son. He is a chancer, a con artist, a malicious artful dodger. A young man who has somehow found out about Alex, tracking me down to con me out of my money somehow. To give him something each month to live on? To buy him an apartment? Who knows? He has killed Gary to do it, and incriminated me so that I cannot go to the police. And now, when I return, his plan will unfold further. I wonder, with horror, if he intends to kill me.

I shut the front door of the children's home behind me, smiling politely again at the elderly cleaner now sweeping the steps as I walk down them. She moves to the side and stops, gesturing towards the photograph still in my hand.

"Is he your boy?" she asks in a raspy, smoker's voice. I shake my head, suddenly unable to speak. I breathe in deeply to stop my emotions overwhelming me.

"I used to call them 'the Likely Lads'," she says.

I look at her, puzzled by the expression but intrigued, maybe even excited too. Before I can reply, she goes on.

"Him and his pal. The terrible twins. Inseparable, they were. Always getting into trouble. They were kind to me, though. They gave me chocolate bars one Christmas." She laughs, a joyful sound, at the memory.

I am stunned, realising suddenly that this is how Liam knew about Alex and me – because they were together in this children's home. I bring my hand to my mouth, stifling a sob at the thought that Alex is still alive somewhere. "Were they happy?" It's all I can think of to say.

Her face clouds over, and she looks as though she's not sure how to answer. She shakes her head slightly as if to respond, *No, not really.* Then she says, "They've been gone a year or more now. I've not seen them since."

"What were their names?" I ask. "Alex and Liam?"

She stops and shakes her head. She heard it before me: the front door is being opened, and I see the young man in the suit appear.

He gestures her back inside. "There's been a spillage, Yvonne. Can you clean it up, please." More of a statement than a question. I suspect he saw us talking and does not want the conversation to continue. The 'spillage', if there is one, was not an accident.

She glances at me as she picks up her brush and dustpan, smiles fleetingly and says, "Yes ... goodbye." And then she is gone, with him looking at me dismissively before following her and shutting the door behind him.

I walk back to my car, sitting in it and staring into space for some minutes. I believe her final 'yes' was an answer to my question, 'Alex and Liam?' That she said it so I would know before she was hurried back indoors.

So Alex, my Alex, and this Liam were both in this children's home. I cry at the thought that Alex spent his life in care rather than in a loving adopted home. Or perhaps he was a troubled soul, going from one set of foster parents to another until finally he ended up in this place.

Even so, my heart lifts at what the elderly cleaner said. Alex and Liam left here a year ago, I assume just after they passed eighteen years of age. I imagine they went to a life of benefits and bedsits and low-paid jobs. And then Liam, having found out about me somehow from Alex, made his way here. But then ... how could he be sure Alex wouldn't do the same thing, track me down, come find me?

Only one way.

I am crying again.

It hits me hard. Liam killed Alex, maybe three, six, twelve months ago. I choke on the thought. He buried my son in woods somewhere. I sob uncontrollably at my terrible imaginings.

He came to me, pretending to be my son. I feel myself close to retching. He killed Gary. I gag, bringing up drool. As 'Alex', he thinks he is my next of kin, at least on paper. I don't believe, as he was adopted, he has a legal right to my money, but suspect he does not realise it.

He will, at some stage, scam me from my money. Or worse, it suddenly hits me, if I do not give it to him, I will have an 'accident'.

Unless I kill him first ...

PART III

THE UNRAVELLING

15

MONDAY, 17 JULY, LATE AFTERNOON

I drive on to the A12 at Chelmsford and go steadily towards Colchester, at sixty miles per hour. I need to think. And I don't want to the attract the attentions of any passing police cars by speeding or going very slow.

I wonder what I will face when I arrive home, and how I will react. I need to be prepared for anything. Violence, most likely, if I confront him. I am ill-equipped for that.

Different scenarios play out in my mind. I am angry and frightened and cannot decide what I'll do. I want to do the right thing, but am not sure what that is, nor what it means for me.

I know what I should do. Pull over into the next layby, and call 999, asking for the police, and then telling them exactly what happened. That Liam, pretending to be my long-lost son, moved in to stay for the summer. He had an argument with my partner, Gary, and stabbed him to death. I came back and saw Gary lying there. And then a little white lie to save myself. Liam forced me to bury the body and stay quiet; otherwise he would kill me, too. I had no choice.

I would urge the police to go to my house, where Liam now is, and look in the back garden by the garage, where they will find the body. They should then arrest Liam. I will say I am in my car in a layby on the A12 between Chelmsford and Colchester and can wait here for the police, or I can drive to the nearest police station and hand myself in. I will tell the truth, the whole truth, and almost nothing but. I'll take what's coming to me.

Prison, almost certainly. I'll not walk free from this. At best, I'll be charged with 'aiding and abetting' or 'perverting the course of justice', whatever it is called. I'm not sure. I pull over into a layby, my mind in turmoil, and Google 'perverting the course of justice ... murder' and read, *those found guilty of this offence may face up to life in prison*. I recall reading somewhere, sometime, that a life sentence is eleven years in the UK. So long. But worse, I could be charged with murder and might be locked up even longer. I might not get out until I am in my fifties, the best years of my life behind me. My child-bearing years. 'You'll never have another baby' tap-tap-taps incessantly at the back of my mind.

I drive on and go by the junction for Colchester and am heading onwards towards the football stadium on my right and the McDonald's on my left.

I am torn between right and wrong. And saving myself – this, I think, dominates my thoughts. That and my chances of never being uncovered. It is a hellish balancing act.

I should stop properly at McDonald's, sit in the car park drinking a coffee, and gather my thoughts, telephoning the police from there.

But something stops me, a sense that the time for confession has already passed. I needed to do it on the night, or the next morning, at the latest. The police would ask, if I had been threatened with death, why I did not simply run out of the house at the first opportunity. The neighbours will say I've been seen coming and going as and when I wanted. My call now, days after the murder, will see me spend so many years in prison. Longer than it would have been had I done the right thing at the time.

I should kill Liam for what he has done. I do not doubt that Alex, my beautiful boy, had a heart-breaking life and spent many years in care. Liam drew him in and learned his story. Then they left the home together. Liam killed and buried Alex and stole his identity, coming here for my money. Whether I can prove that without involving the police, I don't know. I doubt it.

I imagine, as I accelerate steadily up to seventy miles an hour, a revenge killing. Me taking Liam's life. An eye for an eye. I could wait in my car somewhere until it is late, into the early hours, when he will be asleep in bed. Waking up as he feels me sitting astride his body, the blade of the whittling knife or a bigger, sharper kitchen knife pressed against his throat, cutting into his flesh. "Tell me what happened," I'd demand. "Tell me the truth about Alex ... or else I'll kill you."

But I know in my heart, I could not kill anyone in cold blood, even Liam, the murderer of my son. I could defend myself if I were attacked, maybe even stabbing or slashing with a knife. In self-defence. But not premeditated murder. If I held a knife to his throat, it would be a bluff. I don't know what I'd do if – when – he refused to answer. I'd hesitate, and he'd push back, wrestling the knife from me and holding it to my own throat. He's killed before. Twice. He'd kill again. Then disappear into the night.

I reach the Copdock interchange and turn on to the A14,

taking me to Felixstowe. Just fifteen minutes or so from home now.

I have to finally decide what I am going to do, something in between the two extremes of going to the police and killing Liam. Neither, truth be told, are realistic possibilities.

I have to take charge of what is happening, though, being active rather than reactive. I must set out a course of action and follow through.

I want to know all about my darling boy, Alex. How he looked. The cleaning lady called Alex and Liam twins. What he liked and disliked. Did we share anything in common? What he was good at and not so good at? Did he take after me or Ryan – or both of us? How did he end up in the home? It would break my heart, knowing that. But the only way I can uncover the truth is to say to Liam that I know he is not Alex. And then what would he do?

And I want to move Gary's body somewhere far away, where it will never be found. That might bring some sort of peace. Liam will eventually leave, perhaps after he has taken some money from me. And I can begin rebuilding my life. I have always yearned for two things: a loving husband and children. At heart, I am an old-fashioned woman. Nothing wrong with that. It's what makes me happy. I am not ashamed of it. I think I still have a chance of that happy-ever-after.

Perhaps with Ryan, my first love. The man I have dreamed of – along with Alex – all of my life. I suspect my dream is some way from reality; he has never come for me riding a white charger over the years. And it nags at me that his ex-wife and daughters will be more important to him than I could ever be. Even if he is more interested in Liam, he can still have thoughts for me. I would like to try to see what might happen between us. It might be my last chance of happiness.

As I come off at the Trimley St Martin – Trimley St Mary roundabout, my mind is made up. I'll hold my tongue for now and see what happens.

Move Gary's body. Wait for Liam to leave, perhaps at the end of summer, if I give him some money. Then encourage Ryan and see where that goes. I also have to know about Alex, somehow. That troubles me more than I can say. I will bide my time with that. What else can I do?

I pull off the road, turning into the estate and then finally the close and my home. I look up, slamming on my brakes, horrified by what I see.

THE WHOLE HOUSE is lit up, lights shining from every window. I can hear music, some sort of trance music, thumping through the wide-open front door. Boom. Boom. Boom.

Liam stands there, his body blocking the entrance, his arms and legs pressed against the door frame as though he is guarding it. Gemma and Chloe are on the doorstep, shouting at him. Like 'two fishwives', as my mother would have put it.

Gemma's car is on the driveway, one door open, the headlights on full beam and aimed at Liam. Beyond that, neighbours are watching at windows. The creepy man has his window open, a premium view in the front row of the dress circle at the theatre. Tony and James from next door take turns peeking through a crack in their curtains. I imagine other curtains are twitching as well.

I park my car a little way along the close, pick up my

handbag, and walk with as much dignity as I can muster towards my house.

The creepy man calls out to me. Some ribald remark. I can't quite hear his words. I ignore him anyway, and everyone else, too.

As I walk up the path, Liam glances and sees me approaching. He looks fearful and relieved, too. Gemma and Chloe follow his gaze, turning towards me.

"Where's Gary?" Gemma demands. She looks blazing mad. She gestures towards the ill-at-ease Liam and adds, "He says he's left you. That right?" A sudden smirk.

Both Gemma and Chloe move forward, towards Liam, obviously expecting to be allowed into the house to discuss the matter now that I have arrived. That's not happening.

I stand tall, on the driveway, suddenly full of strength. I can do without this. "He's gone. His van was repossessed. Then he went ... he's left me for someone else." I almost add a less decisive 'I think', but stop myself.

Gemma shakes her head, nonplussed. "I don't believe it," she says, not in an *I don't believe what you are saying* kind of way – more as *I don't believe this is happening.* Then she thrusts a handful of opened envelopes and folded-over letters at me and adds, "More of these fucking things. Give them to him ... there's one from the taxman ... they actually came to my house ... he owes thousands ... and tell him he owes me money for Chloe's keep first."

I don't take the envelopes and letters, keeping my hands by my sides. She jabs them at me again. Still I refuse to take them. She looks as though she is going to hit me.

"He's gone, I told you. I don't want them," I reply, turning to Liam. He swallows and looks guilty. I wonder what he said to them before I arrived. Something contradictory maybe.

"Who's he anyway? Mr High-And-Fucking-Mighty?" Gemma asks. We answer at the same time.

"Lodger," Liam says.

"Cousin," I reply.

Gemma looks from Liam to me and laughs nastily. "Make your fucking minds up."

There is a moment's pause. None of us seem to know what to say or do next.

Then Gemma presses on. "Chloe needs some things ... from her bedroom." She points to Liam. "Shit-For-Brains won't let her in. She fucking lives here."

Chloe steps forward, towards Liam, expecting him to move to one side. He does not. "Well ...?" she says, almost squaring up to Liam. He seems nervous, glancing again at me, not sure what to do.

I nod, and he steps aside so Chloe can push by, spitting the c-word obscenity at him. I hate these people. The hostility. The swearing. The aggression. I incline my head, indicating to Liam that he should follow her upstairs, just in case. He does.

Gemma then turns towards me, so we are standing face-to-face. I imagine her lunging forwards, digging her claws into my cheeks, knocking me over, brawling for all to see. I stare her down, ignoring the creepy man shouting out more words of encouragement, mostly lost in the wind. He thinks it's funny.

"I'm not surprised he left you." She looks me up and down. "I don't know what he saw in you in the first place."

I don't take the bait. I know I'm no great beauty. Neither is she. Beneath the cemented-on make-up, she has a hard face. She looks like a horse, all pink gums and tombstone teeth. A knackered old nag.

"Free board and lodgings, I suppose," she carries on. "And he likes his home comforts." She looks pointedly at my lower half. She knows I lost my baby. I wait for her to make a vicious dig. I will fight the urge to react. But she seems to pull back suddenly, eventually just saying, "He'll come crawling when he's had his fill elsewhere. He has before, not that I let him back in my bed."

I think she is about to add something else, perhaps even placatory, as though we are two women both wronged by the same unfaithful, good-for-nothing man. But she falls silent. As do I. And we wait for Chloe to come back down and leave. I am close to breathing a sigh of relief. I've got away with it.

But then there is a commotion upstairs. Sounds of an argument. I hear Chloe shouting, louder than she needs to, wanting to be heard. "Get off me! Don't touch me! Fuck off, leave me alone." And she is hurrying downstairs, a bag full of clothes and other belongings over her shoulder. Liam is following her, a few steps behind.

She stares at me, full of teenage fury. "Who the fuck does he think he is ... fucking bodyguard." She looks back up the stairs where Liam is standing, making sure he has heard her.

Then she stares around the close, looking at the creepy man and two or three other neighbours watching from between curtains at various houses over the way. I think she is going to shout at them. Instead, she raises the middle finger of her right hand and holds it up towards them.

I do not respond to any of this teenage angst, knowing I am so close to the two of them going, the whole 'what-happened-to-Gary' issue believed and resolved. And, as a bonus, Chloe is clearly now going to stay with Gemma permanently.

But then everything turns, with Chloe's next words to me. "You said his van was repossessed and he left." She laughs sourly. "How did he leave with all his things without his van?"

I hesitate, not sure what to say, beyond a shrug and a shake of my head. I am formulating an answer about a young woman picking him up in a sports car, but Chloe continues.

"And he hasn't texted me at all. At all," she repeats for emphasis. "Not since Thursday ... and we text all the time. And I've called him over the weekend, and his phone goes straight to voicemail. And I texted him today with my birthday list, and he's not replied to that." She hesitates and adds, almost plaintively, "He wouldn't just ignore me. Not my dad."

And. And. And. And. And. I don't know what to say, nor how to answer her questions. I stand here, Chloe and Gemma both watching me, unable to speak. Then, as Chloe turns to storm off and Gemma follows, she says the fateful words: "Something's happened to him. I'm calling the police."

———

LIAM AND I NOW STAND, a few minutes later, in the living room, looking at each other, neither of us knowing what to say. We are both stunned by Chloe's final words.

"I didn't want to let them in," Liam says eventually. "In case ... you know ... I shouldn't have answered the door. But ..."

"Chloe has a key," I interrupt. "She could have just come in any time she wanted."

"She said she'd left it at home ... at her mother's."

I nod, wondering how we can be having such a pointless conversation when the police could be on their way at any moment. "What do we do now? The police?" I ask as he turns and walks to the kitchen, taking a glass tumbler from the draining board and filling it with water. I go into the kitchen, watching him drinking, waiting to hear what he has to say. He thinks for simply ages.

"Nothing," he replies at last, then rinses the tumbler under the tap and puts it back on the draining board. "Just keep to what we agreed to say."

He looks at me, seeing the expression of disbelief on my face. I cannot now bear the idea of sitting here waiting for the police to arrive and uncover everything. It was always a possibility. Now it is a reality.

He carries on: "If we move the body tonight, or try to, we'll be seen. The neighbours are all awake and watching. It's too risky in daylight ... carrying the body from the back gate to the car. It was a real struggle to move him last time, and someone's bound to see. There are always people about. That cut-through to the field for dog-walkers."

I swallow, imagining the creepy man and his dog seeing us. But I am far from convinced that leaving the body – Gary, I must think of him as Gary – where he is can be the best thing to do. But what Liam says about tonight and tomorrow is true. Besides, I cannot bear the thought of digging him up.

Liam then says, "Even if she reports him missing, it's not going to be a priority, is it? He's not a child. Or a vulnerable teenager. Or someone with mental health issues. Or a celebrity. He's just a middle-aged man having a mid-life crisis who's run off with someone else."

I nod, agreeing with what Liam is saying. At most, the

police will send a couple of community officers round to ask a few questions. We just stick to the story. It will get put on file somewhere and soon be forgotten.

Liam's next words echo my thoughts. "She'll fill out a form online. It will get read in a week, and someone will visit her a week later. By the time anyone comes here ... if they do ... it will just be a routine matter."

I smile as best I can, clicking on the kettle to make a mug of tea before we go to bed. Liam seems matter-of-fact about it all, as ever. I gesture towards the kettle but he shakes his head. "Must be going up."

Then, in an extraordinary, unexpected moment, he leans towards me and hugs me. I let him, but then turn my head away in case he goes to kiss me, fussing about as if mugs and tea bags and sweeteners and milk are oh so important.

And then he is gone, taking the stairs two at a time, going into the bathroom, running the tap to clean his teeth and then standing by the toilet, lifting the lid up to pee into it. For some reason, distracted, I stand and listen to him from the kitchen.

I make my mug of tea, taking it through into the living room. I pull back the curtains. The creepy man is no longer by his window. But dog-walkers, an old man and an old woman both wearing Panama hats, go by with a wire terrier off its lead, and they glance across as I pull the curtains together. I feel like an animal in a zoo.

I sit here, trapped and waiting. One day soon, police officers will come, and I, and Liam if he is still here, will say what happened. Our made-up story. They may or may not have picked up on the cash withdrawal or discovered the phone in the layby. I don't know what to say about those anyway, if they have.

And they will, before they leave, almost certainly say, 'Mind if we take a look around?' There are those suitcases upstairs. And the things in the garage. I can weave them into the fictionalised account of what took place. But the blood-soaked carpet in the bedroom will be the giveaway. We must do something with it, and quickly, first thing in the morning before anyone arrives.

Even then, in my heart, I know I am doomed eventually. Chloe is correct. Gary would not simply go off and vanish without trace, never contacting her again. She will report him missing. And chase the police. Go to the local newspapers and radio and online news sources. It will be all over everywhere. And she will never give up until she has found him. One day, when all the other options are exhausted, and there is only one possibility left, she'll stand in front of me and yell, "Oh. My. God. You killed my dad, didn't you?"

A FEW MINUTES LATER, I am standing by the box room door, listening. I want to knock, getting Liam up and out and helping me to do something with the carpet straightaway.

We will cut out the bloodied part of the carpet and underlay. That will have to be burned somehow in the garden in the morning. The rest can be rolled up and taken to the dump. I'll then get new carpet and underlay fitted by a local shop this week.

I knock on the box room door, calling softly, "Liam. Liam?" I wait a moment or two, wondering if he could be asleep. I can see a faint light under the door and suspect he's on his phone, tapping and texting away. I wait, hesitating for such a while. Then finally, reluctantly, I go to bed to snatch a few hours' troubled sleep.

I am in the attic of a Victorian mansion, old and abandoned, with moonlight streaming through holes in the roof, casting shadows into the corners of this long, thin room.

I stand still, surrounded by creaking floorboards and dust hanging like a fog in the air. Then I turn around. Facing the other way. Then turn back. Facing the way I was.

Whichever way I go, there is always something behind me, just out of sight, in the corner of my eye. It is watching and waiting, expecting me to run. And I want to run fast, getting out of here. But it will chase and kill me the moment I move.

And then I am somehow creeping, step by step, down an old wooden staircase, going round and round, as though this is a lighthouse. The light above me is getting brighter.

I have escaped from whatever it is up in the attic. I sense, somehow, that I am safe, that it will stay there, whatever it is, just as long as I don't go back or even look upwards. Even so, there is something down below, too.

As my weight goes onto each step, it groans, alerting whatever it is downstairs that I am coming. I cannot turn round, so I have to keep going.

I am now on the ground floor of the Victorian mansion, with all the walls of the rooms rotting away, leaving just the doors intact. I have to go through one of them to be safe. I don't know which.

Again, the floor is full of dust and shadows, with light streaming through from the roof and somehow shining on the doors.

I walk slowly to each, in turn, listening carefully to what's on the other side. I hear scratchings on the wood at every one. I recoil, knowing I am trapped as the clawing grows ever louder.

Then I am running, in fear and panic and hope, along the corridor, unopened doors to either side, towards the front door, which is ever so slightly open. I see the brightest light there, on the other side.

I push, and it opens wide, and I run through, into the blazing sunlight. Blinded, I fall to my knees, weeping with relief.

And I look up, my eyes adjusting to the light, and I start seeing the shapes of police cars and officers and arc lights facing my house. And I hear someone bellowing, "Arms up. Hands in the air. You're under arrest."

I awake, coming out of my nightmare and back into reality. I lie here in my bed for a few minutes, calming myself with long, deep breaths. I feel as though I have been under physical attack. I still do, really, one way or another.

I turn my head towards the illuminated clock on my bedside cabinet. I have been asleep for seventeen minutes. The nightmare felt as if it lasted for hours. My life is a living hell. Even at night, I get no peace. My nightmares are so vivid, frightening and exhausting me.

I lie in bed, now unable to sleep, just waiting for sunrise. As soon as we can after that, I need to work with Liam to do what we have to do before the police come calling. To make our story as watertight as we can. Somehow, no matter what we do, I don't think it will be enough. I am done for, I know it.

16

TUESDAY, 18 JULY, THE MORNING

I pull open my bedroom curtains as the sun comes up, and stand there, exhausted by another night's restless sleep. I look out across the close. There are no signs of life yet. I do this sometimes, the sight of the sun and the coming warmth lifting my spirits. I find it hard to find comfort this morning, though.

Checking my phone, I note it is going to be increasingly hot today, moving close to thirty degrees. Last year, if I had been off work, I would have lain in the garden, sunbathing in the morning, coming inside in the midday heat. Now, all I can think about is Gary's body rotting in the heat of the sun and the stench of it.

I have to stifle the sense of panic I feel down inside, and rising fast. I want to busy myself with urgency, sorting the carpet and the suitcases and the other belongings in the garage now. I force myself to stay calm, doing my breathing exercises, waiting until Liam and I have had breakfast.

At breakfast, I am filled with a sense of melancholy

mixed with the now ever-present feeling of impending doom. Head down, I eat and drink, barely speaking a word beyond courtesies. I am so restless to get on with things.

Liam is much the same, and he fiddles with his phone more and more now, hardly looking at me. I don't doubt he is texting someone he has met at the pier, a special friend, a lover. I don't ask. Fact is, I really don't care anymore.

Close to finishing, we both look up at the same moment. A car – I wonder whether it is an unmarked police car – pulls up outside the house. It blocks my car on the driveway. I wonder if that is to stop me driving off, escaping.

Liam looks at me and then downwards, tapping something quickly into his phone. This angers me. Like this car arriving is so unimportant. I expected him to say something supportive, not text his stupid friend from the pier.

I watch as a woman of about my age, dressed in something close to black combat gear, gets out of the car. She looks, from here, hard-faced and purposeful, although that may be my imagination. She walks briskly up the path.

I look at Liam again for help, even a word of encouragement, but his head is still down, and he is texting. He's too busy for me. "It's the police," I say. "Already ... what shall I do?" I can hear my voice shaking.

He finishes texting and gives me his attention at last. "Answer it," he replies abruptly, picking up his bowl and plate and mug and heading for the kitchen. He stops by the hallway and slips on his trainers.

I hear the doorbell ringing as he enters the kitchen and pushes the door to, as though he is going to wash up his things. I know why he has his trainers on. If it is the police, he will dash out the back, making a run for it.

And so, knowing the game may be up, with other police officers possibly coming round the back to block an escape route, I open the door. What else can I do? They'll only storm in if not. I have to keep up the pretence of normality as long as I can. Try to somehow bluff my way out of this horrifying moment.

The woman stands there, head-to-toe in black, and holds out an official-looking card towards me. I swallow, looking down, peering at it, and I breathe a sigh of relief. I'm not sure how to pronounce her Eastern-European sounding name, but her job title, '*HM Revenue & Customs Field Officer*', shows she is not from the police, and for me. She's here for Gary and his unpaid, mounting debts. I wonder if she is the same officer who went to Gemma's house.

She asks if Gary Morris is in, and moves slightly forward as though she expects to be invited indoors. "No," I reply, my mind distracted by sounds from the kitchen as Liam creaks the door open to listen to what's being said. "He doesn't live here anymore. He left me last week."

We have a brief conversation, all matter-of fact. She is guarded, not wanting to give anything away, only that she wants to talk to Gary 'as a matter of urgency'. She does not look happy. I imagine Gemma told her to eff off. I knock her back too, stonewalling, saying I don't know where he is. I mention Gemma and offer her address to the woman, not that I know it exactly. Not the postcode, anyway. "Chantry," I say. "Up that way." But the woman confirms she has been there and was sent on here.

There is a silence for a moment, a sense of a stalemate. Then she is putting her hand in her pocket, taking out a card with her name, job title and a phone number on it. She hands it to me as though it is ever so important, and I thank her for it. I don't know why. I don't want it. Then she is walking away. I watch as she does a three-point turn in her car and is gone, not even glancing my way. Hopefully, that's that.

Liam opens the kitchen door fully, comes through, seeming bright and breezy. I look at him and smile, something of a fake smile, as he's only looking like that because he realises it is not the police. Otherwise, she'd have come in, for a proper conversation and a look around. And as she did, he'd have been out the back, running away.

He asks, almost casually, who it is was at the door – like he does not know – and I say it was someone from the tax office looking for Gary. He pulls a face, as if we are both long-suffering, and says he's going upstairs to change. I nod, watching him go, ready to follow him to start disposing of the bloodied part of the bedroom carpet.

And suddenly, it occurs to me how, when the carpet and everything has been sorted, I can send him on his way. I can tell him I've had a call from the police and that they are coming to interview me under caution. He's nineteen. And not worldly-wise. He will believe it. And he will panic. It may be enough to get him gone.

I'd still want to know about Alex, though. Somehow. That's what troubles me most. If I mention Alex – that I know he is not Alex – he may kill me. What else can he do? If I do not, I'll spend my life in torment, never knowing. It was unbearable before – now it will be even worse, imagining Alex out there somewhere, buried in woodland.

ASTER CHANGING OUR CLOTHES, we are now working through the rest of the morning in a fast and purposeful manner. I have drawn up a checklist; I will destroy the piece of paper after I've ticked off everything.

We are so close, working away, almost touching at times. I try to act natural, although I feel repulsed by him. What he might have done to Alex, my boy. I want to scream, *Tell me about Alex! My darling boy. Tell me!* I loathe him.

But self-preservation kicks in. I dare not raise any suspicions about him, fearing his response. I'm keeping the folded-over whittling knife tucked inside a pocket of my cardigan. I want to come through this and maybe have a chance of love with Ryan, somehow.

We use kitchen knives and scissors and then a Stanley knife from Gary's toolbox to tear and pull the bloodstained part of the carpet and underlay into strips. I put them into a large black bin bag and take it down to the concrete slabs of the patio.

Liam reads up online how to build a bonfire. It sounds simple enough from what he says. We cut some branches of the trees at the bottom of the garden to act as kindling. Put in newspaper and Sunday supplement magazines amongst the strips of carpet. Douse it all with petrol from a half-empty can next to the lawnmower in the garage.

We use a weed-burner I have for the mossy cracks between the patio slabs to set it alight. It is quickly out of control, the wind sending burning newspaper everywhere, and I unravel the garden hose quickly from the wall-mounted reel below the kitchen window, putting out the fires. This was a foolish thing to do.

The carpet strips are barely burned. Searching Google, I

learn carpet is hard to burn and creates a black, acrid smoke for everyone around us to see and smell. It's a good job we stopped. I imagine next-door Tony coming round to complain politely in his mannered tones, seeing we are burning carpet and asking, "Why?" It would seem so odd. What would I say? I can't take a chance. Not wanting to take them to the dump, where the still-obvious bloodstains would raise the alarm, we bury them as deep as we can between the conifers at the back of the garden. It will have to do – I should have thought more carefully before we started this.

We cut the rest of the carpet into three pieces, so it is less obvious that part of it has been cut out, and put it and the pieces of underlay in my car, back seats down, ready to take to the dump. They just look like leftovers from a big roll for a main room and would not attract attention.

I don't want anyone round from a carpet shop, measuring and fitting and spotting a streak of blood I've overlooked. So I go online and order new carpet and underlay from a site that delivers to the door. It is, in truth, a smallish room and almost a perfect square. The carpet should be easy to put down and cut into place. I'll have a go at it myself.

We sit for a moment, Liam and I, on the landing, a kind of no-man's land in the house. We are both tired and edgy. But we know we need to get these tasks done to protect ourselves.

I suggest he go to his room, get down the two suitcases full of Gary's clothes and put them on the patio. I will get Gary's belongings from the garage and put them on the slabs, too. We will then decide what to do next.

As he heads to the box room, my phone beeps as a text

message comes in. I rarely get texts or phone calls or emails – the odd one from work, asking me when I'm coming back, that's all. I look down, expecting it to be from my line manager, Adam, with opening words of faux sympathy. But it is from Gemma. Translating it from text-speak and correcting the spelling mistakes, including 'Ninna', it reads:

'Nina, it's Gemma. Can I come and talk to you about Gary. I've an idea. I want your help. Are you about at 5.30?'

It's odd – so weird – that she's contacting me like this. As if we are friends! She must want something important from me, and really badly.

I um and ah and decide I will engage with her so that I will at least know what they are doing with the police. I have to, really. 'Forewarned is forearmed', as the saying goes. But I don't want her in the house, asking to use the bathroom, sneaking about on the way there and back. Seeing things. It would make me too uneasy. I keep feeling I've missed something so obvious that she would notice.

So I text her: *'Meet me in the Alex – bar on Felixstowe seafront – 5.30?'*

Within seconds, she texts back, *'Yes.'*

A few minutes later, Liam and I stand on the patio, suit-cases and belongings at our feet on the slabs. We cannot be seen from neighbouring houses. I reach a decision quickly – that I am going to pack everything up and take all the bin bags to the recycling centre now rather than keeping them a while and then burning them, as I had first intended. I am spooked by the thoughts of smoke blowing about and next-door Tony coming round to see me burning Gary's clothes. Less odd than burning carpet, but still weird.

Our story was that I'd keep these clothes and belongings until Gary, supposedly, might come back for them. But I think it's just as likely that, as a woman scorned, I would be so angry that I'd get rid of them straightaway. The clothes, at least. So that's what I am going to do. I take them in bin bags, loading them into the boot of the car.

I come back to find Liam has gone into the kitchen, returned with some wipes and is now cleaning the handles and the outsides of the suitcases, where his hands and fingers have been. It seems odd to me, but then he asks, "Are these going to the dump, too?"

I hesitate, thinking it might seem strange to dump two perfectly good suitcases, so I shake my head and tell him to keep cleaning and then put them back where they came from. He wraps wipes around the handles before carrying them upstairs. The gesture troubles me.

I go on my phone to book a slot at the dump – 'the recycling centre', as it's more grandly known – and get one for fifteen minutes' time. I then turn and look at what's left on the patio. Gary's window-cleaning equipment. I decide, and am surprised I had not thought of it before, to kill two birds with one stone, as they say, to just give the items to the creepy man. It will get rid of them and stop him coming over again and again. Perhaps my mind is now working properly; it seems the obvious thing to do.

Liam is still upstairs, doing whatever he is doing, going to the toilet most likely, so rather than wait, I take the window-cleaning equipment piece by piece to the creepy man's house and leave them on his driveway. I tear off the bottom half of my checklist page, write 'All Yours' on it and tuck it under a brush.

I come back for the last item, the ladder, and see Liam is standing on the patio, not sure what to do. I say, "Nearly done ... just help me with the ladder over the road." He hesitates so long that I almost shout at him, *Come on!* and he does help me take it to the creepy man's house. Liam looks out of sorts, and I have to break into a trot as he walks briskly back to the back garden gate and then the patio.

"The dump, then," I say, and he shakes his head to imply, *Not me.* And I turn to go, and it occurs to me suddenly that he is in some way attempting to distance himself from me. I am not sure if that is a good or bad thing, or of no relevance at all – just my overactive imagination seeing plotting and schemes when it's all just random.

"I've seen two slabs at the back of the garage, left over from when you did the patio?"

I nod, assuming they've been there since the house was built. I've never noticed them. I must look puzzled as Liam carries on, "Underneath the shelf, by the bag of cement."

I nod again, more confident now. He adds, "I'm going to put them down over ... you know ... whilst you're gone."

I smile at last – I think, with the carpet and underlay and clothes and belongings gone, and the extra slabs on top of the body – Gary – we've done all we can possibly do. It gives us a chance, anyway. I head to the car and then to the dump at the far end of town, close to the docks, and my heart and mind start to feel, if not happy, at least moving some way towards a sense of peace. Hope, that's what I mean. A sense of hope.

———

As I arrive home, I see the back gate is open, and wonder what that means. Nothing, most probably, just Liam or I having left it off the latch without noticing. My mind sees danger where none exists.

But then, as I turn off the engine and get out of the car, I see the creepy man coming out of the back gate, pulling it closed behind him. I try to swallow, a feeling of sickness rising in my throat.

I imagine all sorts of horrors, the dog digging up Gary, and the creepy man coming out to call the police. Liam running off. Leaving it all to me. But then I see the creepy man's face, and it's something neither here nor there. Better still, he doesn't have the dog with him, which is a relief.

He saunters across, and I realise he's just going to thank me for the window-cleaning equipment. He'll no doubt make some patronising comment that I changed my mind 'as a woman ... a lady ... is entitled to do'. And I will bite my tongue. The longer I'm quiet, the sooner he will be gone. I stand to the right of the car, him on the left, and as he moves one way, towards me, I instinctively move the other, as though I want to keep the car between us – as much distance as I can.

He laughs, thinking I am being funny, even flirting with him, and he kind of hops, skips and jumps around and towards me as though he's trying to be funny, too. This horrible man. I stand still, smiling vaguely, hoping he does not get too near.

He stands in front of me, closer than I'd like, looking as creepy as ever. He wears blue corduroy trousers – incongruous in this heat – with his flies undone. I imagine blue nylon Y-fronts underneath, unchanged for days. I raise my glance to his smiling face and gummy smile. It looks as though he has eaten a whole packet of digestive biscuits.

"I came over to thank you," he says, looking me up and down as ever. "But there was no answer. So I went round the back – I didn't bring Benny! – and knocked on your back door. I was just coming out."

He's an odd man and seems ever creepier. He'd have known I was out – probably saw me driving off or at least could see the car was not there. But still he came round. I wonder if this is more than a simple 'thank you'.

I think – hope – Liam heard him at the front door, then went out the back, off to the pier as usual, locking the kitchen door behind him. The creepy man would have peered through, tugged at the door handle, and then gone.

"Do you have any other equipment?" he asks. "I don't think it's everything."

I sigh, partly from relief, as that explains why he's come back sneaking about, but also from irritation. That this man isn't happy with what he's got, for free, and wants more.

"Come on," I reply, a snapping tone in my voice. I lead the way, gesturing to him to follow me through the gate and into the garage. Frankly, he may have been here already. But we can do it again.

We stand in the garage, both of us looking about, taking it all in. I feel my confidence rising; there is nothing for him to see here. I can be bullish.

"There, see, nothing. You've got everything, the whole lot. Nothing more to give you, I'm afraid." He looks crestfallen. To avoid a long, drawn-out conversation, I walk to the door, into the garden and out the front, shutting the gate behind me.

He follows me here, this hopeless man who lives with his mother and has never worked, so far as I know, living on benefits and waiting for his mother to die, when he'll do God knows what. And I realise, suddenly, that it's all nonsense, that he does not really want to go out and be a window cleaner, earning money, living a normal life. That this is just an excuse.

"Tell you what," I say angrily. "There's nothing else. Do you want it or not?"

He stands there sheepishly, not meeting my eye, his head down, not saying anything.

"Fine, I'll take it all back." I know this man has mental health issues, but I don't have time to coax him out of his sad situation.

And so I am across to his front lawn, picking up this and that and carrying it back across and putting it in my garage. He stands, watching me, looking awkward, as I go back and forth. Then, with just the ladder left and with me holding one end and looking at him, he jumps into life, coming across and helping me.

With everything in the garage, I lead him back to the gate, indicating he should leave. He stands there, looking pathetic, mumbling, "I only asked ..." And I am so angry that I just gesture *go, get out of here*. Still he stands there, so I snap at him.

"It's done. Someone else can have it. I'm just ... look, I really don't want to see you again." It sounds like I'm breaking up with a lover, so I hurry on. "Just leave me be, alright? Stop watching me from your window, shouting out, coming round. Keep hassling me and I'll call the police, okay?"

He shuffles and squirms, pulls a face as though he's mortally offended, and then, finally, he goes. I could almost bloody cheer as I go back inside. I note that Liam has vanished, as I had assumed.

Still feeling furious, I book another visit to the dump, taking much of Gary's window-cleaning equipment there.

When I get back, I look long and hard at the ladder, an old wooden one, and decide I will just leave it laid out against the wall of the garage. I don't need to worry about that. I go back indoors and decide I'll have a lazy afternoon, watching TV and listening to music. For once, I'm feeling good about myself.

17

TUESDAY, 18 JULY, THE AFTERNOON

The Alex is a café-bar-restaurant on the seafront at Felixstowe midway between the Spa Pavilion theatre and the pier. It's a nice place. Quite posh. Posh for Felixstowe, anyway.

It's busy, as it often is at this time of day. I'm sitting at a raised table with two tall bar stools some way towards the back, waiting for Gemma. I have two glasses of Pepsi Max in front of me and am facing the entrance. I am desperate to know, to ask, about the police, what Chloe has said and done. But I will not rush at this, which would seem odd; rather, I'll wait for it to come up naturally in conversation.

Then she's coming in, hair up, full warpaint, shiny dress, handbag and shoes, like she's out on the prowl for the night. She looks around as though she's weighing up every man (and the size of his wallet) in the place, and then sees me, pulls her horsey-faced smile and comes across.

"Been waiting long?" she asks. Not that she'd be troubled if I'd been here for hours.

She sits on the bar stool opposite me as I smile and gesture towards the two drinks in front of us.

She lifts her glass, no word of thanks, and sips at it, pulling a face as though she's thinking, *There's no alcohol in this.*

"Would you like something to eat?" I ask, being polite, but she shakes her head. To be honest, I am relieved. The sooner I'm gone, the better. After another look around, to see if any men are checking her out, we're down to business.

"Gary," she says and looks at me. I gaze back with a non-committal expression, then sip my drink and repeat, "Gary," back to her, as in *Gary, what about him?* I'm not committing myself one way or the other until I've heard what she has to say.

She laughs and then says, "What a useless fucking bastard."

I laugh too, nodding in agreement. I don't add anything, though. I'm still cagey.

But, for once, just in this moment, we are in agreement with each other.

"The things I could tell you about him. He won £25,000 on a scratch card once; did he tell you?" I shake my head as she continues, "Worst thing that happened to him ... us. He thought he'd become an investor, live off his investments – crypto something and arbitrage, is it?"

I shake my head, not sure.

"He lost the lot. Obviously."

"So he went back to window cleaning, which he's always hated, and ..." She stops for a moment, realising that her high-pitched, grating voice is rather loud. She lowers it. "He tried to gamble to get another £25,000 ... and he's utterly hopeless, but you can't say anything ... else he gets so angry."

She looks at me and clenches a fist slightly. "Did he? With you?"

I shake my head, even though he came close and was oh so controlling.

"And he couldn't keep his dick in his trousers. You should see who he's been with ... really rough, some of them were ..." I look at her and stifle a response. Hard to imagine anyone rougher than Gemma. I must look incredulous, as she adds, "Karen Frankenstein, I called her ... anyway, he gave me a dose, and that was it. I sent him packing."

She pauses, drinking almost half of her drink quickly. I feel as if I should say something here. Not too much, just enough to get her fully on my side. And to reveal the reason why we're meeting like this.

"I don't blame you," I say agreeably. I'm not sure what to add. I don't want to compare notes about Gary and that side of things. He wasn't anything special, that's for sure, and he would always keep his holey socks on at all times, no matter what.

I take a mouthful of my drink and then look to her to get to the point, the reason why we are here. I just say, "So ...?" But she carries on talking regardless.

"I couldn't believe it when he got together with you." She looks at me, realising for a split second that her words might be offensive. "Not being funny or anything ... you're not ... his type. You're ... well, not posh, but ..." She looks round conspiratorially. "He once said you were the only woman he'd been with who wore a slip under her skirt." She does her stupid laugh, and I smile at her through gritted teeth.

"I thought he wanted your money. He said, you know, about ..."

I nod at the reference to my parents and my owned

home and my savings and feel slightly sour that he told her all my business. I had not told him not to, but just assumed he would keep all of that between us. No matter now, I suppose.

She goes on, "Anyway, no doubt he's off somewhere else ... someone richer.

"I'm sorry, you know ... about your baby." She is thoughtless and senseless, as always. I struggle to keep my face neutral, angry again that he has probably told her just about everything about me, and, even worse, that she feels entitled to raise whatever she wants in conversation. I'm thinking of something smart and snappy to say, but then she surprises me. "Honestly, I am ... I had two miscarriages myself." I did not know that. There is a moment's silence, and she reaches out her hand and puts it on top of mine. Like we're besties, as she'd put it.

"What is it, Gemma, that you want from me?" I keep my voice as plain as I can.

I leave my hand where it is, neither embracing hers or withdrawing mine. The moment is in the balance.

"Well ..." She looks around again, but this time to see if anyone can overhear. "Thing is, Nina, I want you to help me get rid of Gary." She makes it sound like she's asking me to kill him.

I BURST OUT LAUGHING. I can't help myself, bringing my half-full glass of Pepsi Max down on the table with a crashing noise. Loud, like the glass may crack in two.

People in the bar are turning, looking, and one wag, a Jack-the-Lad type, shouts, "She's starting early!" He'd need little encouragement to come strutting across groin first, but I ignore him, dipping my head.

Gemma, who's the sort who'd be the first to shout back, *Who's buying?* seems embarrassed. She shifts in her seat, away from everyone and closer towards me. "Not kill him or anything. I just ... I don't want him in our lives any more. Me and Chloe."

I look blankly at her.

She sighs – like I'm the stupid one – and shakes her head, pauses a while, and then she explains, "My fella, Glenn ... well, he's a good man, kind, and he loves me and adores Chloe." I glance at her, and she must see my dubious expression. "Nothing funny, nothing like that, he's just a decent bloke. Best I'll ever get."

"He wants us to be a proper family, you know, and I think this is ..." She stops, as though she is about to share an intimate secret with me. "My best chance of happiness, our best chance, me and Chloe. He'd be a good husband and a proper dad to Chloe ... it's what I've always wanted ... what we've always wanted."

I nod, about to ask her what she wants me to do, but she carries on, "She's had it tough with Gary. He comes and goes, is always in debt, doesn't treat people, women, properly. He's a shit. And a loser. He'll never make anything of himself. I don't want him in our lives anymore."

I lean forward and ask her, "Okay, so what do you want me to do about it?" It comes out harsher than it was meant to sound, but Gemma does not seem to notice.

She rummages in her bag, pulls out a phone and pushes it across the table to me. "Turn it on."

So I do, not sure what it is I'm supposed to be looking at.

"I've got this phone and a SIM thing, and, anyway ... I'd

like you to have it and send some texts to Chloe as if you are Gary ... and then, you know ..."

Thing is, I don't – so I put the phone on the table between us.

I try not to raise my voice as I respond, "You want me to send texts to Chloe, pretending I'm Gary, so her feelings aren't hurt. And then, what, you want me to let her down gently, saying he doesn't want to have anything to do with her anymore? That's just so ... stupid, honestly. Even if she just texts back – what if she calls him, expecting him to answer? What do I do? Text back as Gary, saying I've lost my voice? Seriously?"

I realise, of course, that Gemma thinks Gary is out there somewhere, so I have to add one more sentence: "And what if Gary texts her? Or phones her from a different mobile ... turns up in a week or two?" One last thing: "And why me? Why don't you do it?"

She leans back, grabbing the phone and putting it back in her bag. She's angry, partly with me, I think, but also with herself, because she realises the idea is just plain stupid. "Because ..." she answers, her voice shaking slightly, "... if I did it, I'd have to hide the phone. She's always in my things, my bag, my make-up, and she'd find it ... want to borrow it. And ... I thought you would do it, you know."

I don't know, actually.

She looks at me. I don't respond, just taking a final mouthful of my drink.

"I'm hoping he won't come back if he's found someone with more money who's a bit more generous with it." We look at each other. She pulls a 'sorry' face. "He's missed birthdays and stuff before. He might come crawling back eventually, but by then ..."

Her final comment suddenly fills me with joy and hope.

"I'll be honest with you, Nina. Glenn is selling his business ... and he's got a nest egg from his grandparents. We're going to go to Florida, early next year hopefully ... a fresh start. Open a nail bar or something. I like nails." She holds out her hands with her sparkly nine-year-old's nails, and I make an admiring noise. "Chloe doesn't know yet; we're going to tell her after her exam results. She'll love it. And I don't want Gary coming back between now and then and turning her head ... filling it with nonsense ... she'll soon forget about him once we're out there."

"She's not gone to the police yet, then?" I ask, trying to keep my voice as casual as I possibly can. This is why I am here. To get the answer to my question. I need to know so I can be well prepared.

She shakes her head. "No, I've put her off that for now. We don't want the police round ours, snooping about, poking their noses in where they're not wanted." She doesn't look at me, and I do not press. I don't doubt her 'fella' is dodgy in some way.

It occurs to me, there and then, that if I can keep Chloe happy until the lot of them go off to Florida and disappear forever, forgetting about Gary, my troubles – the police turning up – may be over. I smile at long last and say, "Okay, I'll do it. I'll text Chloe for you."

Gemma takes the phone out of her bag and passes it to me.

I wonder if this might be a life-changing moment. It might just be my 'get out of jail free card'.

WE SIT THERE, on our bar stools, having another fizzy drink and a bowl of nachos each, talking things through. On and on we go, agreeing what I'm going to text and when.

I can see where Gemma is coming from with this. I imagine many ex-wives would love to have nothing to do with their former husbands ever again. And she wants to protect Chloe. And frankly, it works for me too.

I don't understand why she is asking me, although I don't press her. She isn't the sort to have close friends. Not that I can talk. I guess it's because I'm just piggy in the middle between her, Chloe and Gary. Or maybe, if Chloe finds out, she can try to blame me.

"The first text," she says, "has to be to say he's gone away for work ... some sort of offer ... and this is the first chance he's had to get in touch."

"And," I add, "he's not going to be able to text very often, or talk. Um ..." We both look at each other, baffled about what to put.

"Years ago," she says, "he had this friend Baz, who got a job on the oil rigs ... away for ages ... hard to contact. So he said to his wife, anyway. Might that work?" She looks back at me.

I don't know what to say to that. It seems an unlikely scenario. I suddenly don't want to be doing this. The whole thing just feels really off.

But if I do nothing, Chloe may, at some stage, go the police. Sending a text, with Chloe showing it to Gemma, who will back up what I've written, will give me the chance to come through this.

So I pick up the phone and start typing a message, which I can show to Gemma, who, if she agrees, can then enter Chloe's number and press 'send'.

'Chloe, it's Dad, new phone. I'm so sorry. I've been offered a job on an oil rig. Flying out tonight.'

I go on, making it up, hoping it will sound believable to a sixteen-year-old.

'Three months in the North Sea. Out of touch. Sorry!'

Then the final touches: *'I couldn't stand Nina anymore. Job came up. Had to go. I love you. Dad x'*

I push the phone across the table to Gemma, who reads the message and inclines her head side to side as if saying, *yes, maybe.*

"Put Chlo, not Chloe," she instructs me. "He called her Chlo. And put 'sick of the fridge'. He called you that sometimes, 'the fridge'."

I go to say something – a retort, all the things he's called her – but she presses on.

"Oh, let me do it, for fuck's sake. Nobody writes like that anymore, Granny. He didn't." She deletes and adds and changes her mind, then tweaks a bit more, and then finally pushes the phone back across to me: "Okay?"

It's basically the same message, but full of abbreviations and emojis, most of which I don't recognise, other than the rather obvious ones of a fridge and a vomiting face. And a row of hearts at the end.

But she's correct: it is the way that Gary would text, and it won't arouse suspicions in the way mine would have done.

I nod my agreement, and Gemma takes back the phone and adds Chloe's number. "Send?" she asks, and I nod once more. She presses the button, and off it goes.

Gemma turns the phone off and hands it back to me. "Keep it switched off. Don't start texting back with your English essays – remember, you're on an oil rig, out of touch."

"You could have done that. You didn't need me. Why ask me?" I respond. I'm slightly ratty because of her comments about my writing. It's true. I'm out of touch. Never been in touch, really. Old before my time.

She shrugs. "We're both paid-up members of the Gary Morris Ex-Wives' Club ..." She pauses, and I can see her thinking that I was not a wife but a lover, and I expect her to make a fridge joke, but she does not.

"When I get home, some time tonight, she'll be in my bag ... for a tampon ... to see what sweets I've got ... or to borrow it to listen to Spotify, as her battery is dead. She'll see two phones and ... anyway ... are we done?" She finishes her drink and pushes her plate away. "I hate that green dip ... tastes like bogies."

As we get up to go, she says, "Chloe will show me the message tonight, and I'll tell her not to get her hopes up if he's out at sea. Hearing from him. You won't have to keep texting. Wait until her birthday."

She thinks for a minute as I hold open the door for her to go through to the pavement. "You'll have to text on her birthday, the seventh of September. I'll maybe try to get some money switched to her account. After that, she'll be so excited about Florida, she'll not think of him."

As I turn to go towards the pier where my car is parked, she opens her arms wide as if inviting a hug. Like we're now best friends forever. I hug her, keeping up the pretence, and breathe in the scent of her perfume. I'd expect it to be something cheap and nasty, but it's really rather nice. Then, with "Mwa, mwa" air-kissing noises and, "Talk soon!" (not too soon, hopefully), she is gone. As I head for my car and home, I feel so positive.

18

TUESDAY, 18 JULY, THE EVENING

I sit in my car on the driveway outside my home, bubbling over with hard-to-contain excitement. Relief, really. The carpet, Gary's clothes and belongings and his equipment have all gone. A new carpet is arriving next week.

The body – Gary – is beneath slabs, and I will put down shrubs and bushes in front of them in the autumn, as soon as the summer weather has cooled. I am going to put a note through next-door Tony's door saying I wish him well, but I don't want scaffolding in my garden. I'm about to have land-scaping done, or a pond or something – anything! I will do that soon.

And now, with Gemma's texting plan and her Florida move, the police will not be involved, will not call round, as long as Chloe never contacts them. And if I am careful, Gary can rest in peace in the garden forever. I'll not be able to move, but no matter. I love my home, even though the thought of Gary – no, I must stop thinking about him as

Gary – will always be at the back of my mind. Everything is perfect. Almost perfect.

I have, for years, longed for Ryan, daydreamed about him, desired him ... but when I have seen him out and about, my nerve has always failed me.

I should have gone up to him on one of those occasions, chatted, maybe, sometime down the line, hinted at how I felt about him.

But I always feared rejection, another heartbreak – and of course, that would probably have been the case when he was with his wife and daughters.

Now, though, things are different – he is alone, estranged from his wife and possibly his daughters too.

And he has been over, mainly to see Liam, maybe, but perhaps for me too. It's understandable that his focus is on Liam, the surprise and joy of it.

He may want me now if I gave him some encouragement. It would, once Liam has gone, be the perfect ending to my story. That happy-ever-after. Who'd have thought? It's there for me now. In front of me. It is. It truly is.

I still worry that, even if Liam leaves, he will forever be out there somewhere, waiting to return if times get tougher for him. But I will take my chances on that. He has as much to lose as me.

And Gary, the body in the garden. I can never leave here whilst he is there. Maybe, sometime, when he is no more than bones – I retch at the thought – I can move his remains and scatter them far and wide in woodlands and forests.

Alex, my beautiful boy, will always be a constant presence in my life. I want to go to the police, get justice for what Liam did. But how can I? My carefully built house of cards will all come tumbling down.

I rally my spirits, looking around the close, and it is still quiet and peaceful. A young girl, early-teens teenager, and her younger brother, maybe eight to ten, walk a golden retriever towards the fields. A puppy, really, and so much excitement about it from the children.

Liam will be indoors, wondering where I am, itching to have his tea and then be off with his friends on the pier and in the amusements. He has settled in so easily, as teenagers often do.

I pluck up my courage – it's now or never – and take out my phone, searching for Ryan's number. I find it and sit there for a while deciding what to put. A simple message, I think, without abbreviations or emojis.

'Ryan, hi, I was wondering if you'd like to go the cinema one night.'

I hesitate, but then add, *'Like we used to do.'* And finally, *'Love Nina x'*

I stare at it for an age, deciding if the wording is just so; I think it seems so old-fashioned and wordy. But that's just who I am, I guess. I fiddle a little, making the message snappier.

'How about cinema/meal on Wednesday? You and me. Like we used to do. Nina.'

I stare at that for ever such a while, add an emoji heart, and, before my courage fails me, I press 'send'.

I hold my breath, waiting, hoping, for an immediate reply, a breathless *Yes!* or a dismissive comment *No, Lol* or, most likely, no response at all, leaving me to draw my own conclusions. A kinder rejection, though.

I glance up and see, in my rear-view mirror, an older woman from over the way coming across. I don't know her name. We've smiled, but never spoken. She seems pleasant.

I wonder what she wants, and get ready to open my car door. I must look odd, sitting here like this for so long. I'll go indoors to avoid the conversation. But suddenly, she is veering off, towards next-door Tony's. I can't imagine why.

And so I look down, back at my phone, not expecting a reply. But there it is, staring me in the face.

'Love to. What's on?'

And – my heart bursts with joy – an emoji heart for me as well.

I am close to crying now. The heart, that silly little emoji, is the proof that he wants me too. That he feels the same. That this will be the first date of many.

I know I should pause, think, pick the words for my reply carefully, but all of a sudden my spirit surges and flies, and I am that lovestruck teenage girl once again. We keep texting.

'No idea! Shall we eat first and then see what's on?'

An almost immediate reply:

'OK. The pizza place you went with Liam? 6.00. Weds?'

'Love to!'

I then add five, six, seven, eight heart emojis, think better of it, and cut them back to three and then two and then one, and press 'send'. I don't want to seem too keen!

One last message from Ryan, and I am overwhelmed by its simplicity:

'It's a date.'

And a heart emoji. It's everything I could have hoped for.

I am up and out of the car, going into the house, almost jigging with joy. Liam comes out of the kitchen and looks taken aback by my jollity. He's been making something for our tea, I can smell the spices.

"It's Ryan," I gush, like a silly schoolgirl. I can't help myself; I'm so excited. "We've been texting." And then I do that thing that teenagers do, putting my fingers and thumbs together to form a heart.

He looks at me strangely, almost as though he is jealous in some way, but I ignore him as I dash upstairs to wash and change for tea, the happiest I have been for a long while, perhaps for ever.

As we sit down at the table, ready to eat Liam's curry – actually, two microwave meals from the back of the fridge-freezer – there is a polite tap-tap-tapping at the front door.

Liam, again, makes his excuses and heads for the kitchen, mumbling something about getting 'a glass of squash' even though there is an almost-full bottle of Coca-Cola and a jug of water on the table. It's as if he doesn't want anyone to see him.

It occurs to me suddenly that he has always been like this since he moved in, or soon after, coming and going through the back gate of the garden. Slipping and sneaking about. I never really noticed before. If anyone had seen him, they would think he were going for a walk over to the fields. Now I know why.

I don't have time to think about that now, as I am already calculating, click-click-click, who it might be at the front door. A debt collector, most likely, although I will send them packing easily enough. I have done it with that HM Revenue & Customs' field officer, so I can do it with anyone.

I open the door, and next-door Tony and his partner, James, are standing there, one holding a file, the other a bottle of Prosecco. They look excited, expecting to be invited in to discuss their extension.

Some wild part of me considers letting them in, just so I can see how Liam will react, whether he will stay in the kitchen or come out, either to be part of the conversation or to run upstairs. I think he will remain hidden. And it will be awkward, as they will see the two full plates of food. And of course, I'm about to disappoint them, too.

So I smile at them and say, before they can speak, as cheerfully as I can, "Hi, Tony, James ... I'd love to invite you in, but I've just sat down to have something to eat."

They go to say something, probably, *That's alright, but can we just ask if we can put up scaffolding in your garden this week?* So I press on as quickly and as kindly as I can.

"Um, look, I'm really sorry I've been meaning to tell you ... I'm having some landscaping done shortly in the garden, so I'm so sorry, I'm not going to be able to let you put your scaffolding up this side. Sorry," I add again for good measure.

I look at them both. I'm being strong and decisive and assertive, as I am entitled to be, and I can see disappointment on Tony's face, anger on James's. I wonder if they think I am lying about having landscaping done.

But their faces brighten at the same moment, in a false but jolly way. There are smiles and pleasant comments and fake bonhomie, 'Don't worry', 'No matter' and 'It's no trouble'. Then they are turning and walking away up the path and back to next door. I know they are both upset. More, I suspect, by my dismissiveness than anything else. I think they wanted to be friends. They brought that bottle of Prosecco. I imagine them drinking it sadly.

I think, as I shut the front door, that I am sorry I upset them. Next-door Tony is a sweet man. I do not know James, and his look of anger had a touch of nastiness, perhaps petulance, about it, but I would not wish to upset him, either. I think maybe, tomorrow, I might take a bunch of flowers round.

I mull it over as I go back and sit at the table, but then decide against it. My gesture may get their hopes up, dashed again as I have to explain, once more, that they cannot put up scaffolding on my side. There may be sourness and snide comments, perhaps a voices-raised argument, and I don't want any bad blood between us. I will leave the matter as it is and let time put things right.

I sit here, waiting for Liam to come back in from the kitchen. And I am so tempted, as he reappears with a full glass of orange squash, to ask him, *Why do you do that? Hide away? Not being seen with me in the close?*

But I don't say that. I daren't. And I don't ask him why he is here. *Money, isn't it?* I'm scared of him, that's why.

Nor do I ask him about Alex. *My son, you killed him, didn't you?* Because Liam has killed before and is capable of doing so again. My self-protection instinct kicks in. My survival depends on it. And I want to live.

After I explain who was at the door and what they wanted, we put our heads down and eat. I decide there and then: in the morning, I will check my funds and what I can withdraw and when, how much notice is needed, and so on. I will tell Liam I have had a call from the police, and that they want me to go into the station over at Martlesham, for an interview under caution.

That, I am sure, will be enough for him to be gone by the time I get back from this supposed meeting. But to be certain, absolutely one hundred per cent, I will offer him some money, too – transferring funds into the secret account for which he has a card, and letting him see the balance. A

huge sum to a teenager, but I can afford it. And then I will be
rid of him and can start my new life with Ryan.

———

WE CHAT about this and that – nothing much really, the heat,
the cooling breeze on the seafront, the busy beach, as we eat
what will be our last meal together. I should hate him for
everything – why he's here, Alex, the fact I am paying him off
– but somehow, all I can think about now is Ryan.

The fact is, in this moment, Ryan is all that matters to
me. I've waited almost twenty years for this – to begin our
lives together – and I cannot contain my feelings anymore.

As our general conversation grinds to a halt, I decide I
will tell Liam about what's happened to me today. Not the
meeting with Gemma and texting Chloe, but my messages to
and from Ryan. A part of me, deep down inside, wants Liam
to know that I love and am loved by Ryan.

"Ryan and I texted today," I say, plain and simple.

"Yes?" he replies, meaning, *What did he say?*

I hesitate, knowing he expects me to answer that Ryan
just wants to check the details for Saturday night or perhaps
to come round for his tea tomorrow. To see Liam, really.

I let the silence draw out, taking pleasure in knowing
that Liam wants to know, but is working hard pretending
not to.

Liam thinks, hopes, Ryan is here just for him and that, as
a rich private dentist, some money might be coming Liam's
way some time.

"Guess!" I say, in a cheery voice.

He shrugs. "I don't know." It comes out more like, *Uh,
dunno.*

"Go on, guess!" I repeat myself in a louder, even more jolly voice. "You must!"

He scrapes the last of his curry into the middle of his plate and then shovels it onto his fork with his finger and into his mouth.

He does all this without comment, looking almost surly.

"A date," I say, sounding almost triumphant.

He glances at me this time, then sharply away. His glance is not a nice look. He doesn't like the idea, that's for sure. He thought Liam was only here for him.

I take my phone from my pocket and go through it, showing Liam the last text from Ryan, with the emoji heart at the end of it. Ha!

He turns his head away, almost dismissively, and I feel a surge of pleasure and, more, a steely determination to press on with this.

"Yes," I say, "We're going out on Wednesday for a meal." I think, but do not say, *Long after you've gone for good.* Instead, I add, "Then we're going to see a film at Cineworld."

He swallows the last mouthful of his orange squash, keen to be gone, out of here, to play the slot machines with his stupid friends on the pier. Maybe his lover.

As he gets up, I send him on his way with a raucous, "After that, we might come back here!" It's not like me, this, but I have the devil inside me and want to feel as though I've got one over him at the end.

And I have. He is out the kitchen door, pulling at his phone, and through the back gate before I can even add my final, parting shot: *You might want to be asleep when we get back.* I so want to feel I've beaten him in some way.

I put the plates and what have you in the dishwasher. Then clean and tidy round. Have a bath and a hair wash.

Blow-dry my hair. Sit in the living room for a while, rereading the texts between Ryan and me. I am tempted to send him one more message before I go to bed. One emoji heart.

So I do. And wait. And a few minutes later, I get a message back: three emoji hearts.

And so I go, at last, to bed. It has been the longest day, but the best of days. All my troubles are, with a little luck, now behind me. Tomorrow morning, I will put paid to Liam and his stupid plans. He will be gone. And he will stay gone. And then I will get ready for Wednesday – a meal, a film and, perhaps, our first night together. One of many until the day we die ...

I LIE IN MY BED, exhausted from all that has happened today, but relieved, thinking that, at last, this will be the first good night's sleep I've had for a long time. I have such a sense of hope – no, more than that, certainty, that I will make it out to the other side of this hellish journey.

My mind click, click, clicks again through a checklist, ticking off everything that needed to be done to make me feel safe. The creepy man. The next-door neighbour. The debt collectors. Chloe and Gemma. The body in the garden. All ticks now rather than crosses.

All I need to do in the morning is to deal with Liam. And then I will be safe. He cannot talk without incriminating himself. I am more than safe. I shut my eyes, imagining my life with Ryan until I fall asleep.

I am in a maze, on a hot summer's day, the sun high in the sky, the hedges green and spiky and rising up all around me.

Somehow, I know where I am. I have been here before. A vague childhood memory. Hampton Court Palace. Leeds Castle. No matter which. I know where I am going.

The maze is crowded, full of families with young children. I push by, calling over my shoulder, 'Sorry, sorry.' There are good-natured comments and jolly enough shouts back at me.

I am going to the centre of the maze. I turn this way. Then that. And this way again. I know instinctively when to go left or right.

I do not know what is waiting for me in the middle of the maze. But I am excited as I hurry on. There is no pressure, no sense that it may be gone if I do not get there in time. Just a delicious sense of anticipation. An utter thrill.

As I get closer, I find I am on my own, the hubbub of young families and children still around me, but not close, out there now on the edges of the maze. I feel at peace as I turn left, one last time, and go into the middle.

A man stands there, lit in sunlight, his back to me. I hesitate, my eyes adjusting to the sunshine. The man's body shimmers. Eventually, my eyes clear, and I see that it is Ryan, my first love. My true love.

He is singing something softly to himself. I cannot make out the tune or the words. But it is sweet and gentle. I stand watching and listening, transfixed by the beauty of the moment.

Then he turns, and I see he is holding a baby in his arms, cradling and singing sweet nothings to her. I don't know why, but I can tell she is a beautiful little girl. Our daughter. Sophie, my favourite name.

I move forward, two, three, four steps, and wrap my arms around Ryan and our baby, my head tucked into the space between Ryan's chin and the baby's face.

I feel Ryan leaning forward, kissing my hair as I breathe in the soft scent of our baby's skin. And we are as one. Ryan. Our baby. Me. We are together, as we will always be from now on.

We stand there like this, in our loving embrace, for ages, on and on, the sun warming us with its glow. We could stay this way for ever and a day.

Eventually, we turn towards the exit, ready to make our way back out of the maze. To our home. I can see it in my mind's eye. A cottage nestling at the foot of a grassy hill stretching to a sunny sky. A babbling brook nearby. Deer in the woods. Everything I have ever wanted.

As we walk, everyone moves to one side, smiling and waving and laughing joyfully for us. We smile back, showing off our gorgeous baby girl. And we laugh together, kissing and hugging each other time and again. It is bliss.

As we get to the exit, I find myself a step or two ahead of Ryan and our baby. I move through, about to turn to embrace them again. Then I hear a terrible roaring sound, and I scream and scream and scream.

Liam is in my room, pulling back the duvet, grabbing my arms and wrenching me to my feet. As I scream, he knocks me back with his forearm, and I tumble onto the carpet. I am dazed.

He is at me again, pushing his clenched fist hard against my mouth, shouting, "Don't scream, don't scream." He yanks me to my feet and drags me, him walking backwards, me stumbling forward, out of the room. "I'm sorry," he says, over and again, nonsensically. "I have to do this. It's the only way."

Then we are in the back bedroom where he killed Gary, and I see the window is wide open and realise the cold, hard slabs of the patio are below it. I come to my senses as he spins me round and half-pushes, half-lifts me towards it to throw me out. Dear God, I am about to die.

19

TUESDAY, 18 JULY, CLOSE TO MIDNIGHT

"**W**hy?" I yell, ramming my feet, my heels, into the floorboards to slow him down. All of a sudden, I know why.

He's going to make this look like a suicide. My supposed guilt over killing Gary. He'll then have access to my cards and my money.

He does not say a word, just grunts as he struggles to lift me up off the floor and carry me towards the window.

There's no way he's going to get me through that window. I'll move my arms and legs to the sides of the window frame. Hanging on grimly to life.

Then scream endlessly into the silence of the night. No suicide, this.

As he lifts me off the floor, I push back hard, and he tumbles over, with me landing on top of him.

He puts his hands around my head, trying to clamp my mouth shut, but I bite his fingers as hard as I can.

Then I roll over, on top of him now, struggling to pin his arms and hands to the floorboards. We are evenly matched.

"Why?" I shout again. "Why are you doing this?" I move my hands quickly, banging his head on the floor, two, three, four times.

"I have to. I have to," he repeats, looking close to tears. There is an instant when I think he will sink back, give up, but he rallies furiously, struggling desperately to free himself.

"No!" I shout, pulling back and up and away from him. We stand there, face-to-face, both breathing heavily, the room lit only by moonlight.

"I know your plan," I say. "I've worked it out. You throw me out the window and leave me bleeding to death. Then take over my house and savings, everything."

He says something. *Not exactly,* I think, but I rage on, shouting him down, all the anger and pain pouring out of me. "That's so stupid! How the hell do you think you'll get away with that? Your DNA's over everything. Gary. There are witnesses to say you were here. Neighbours. People have seen you. You're in it up to your neck."

Then I slow and stop and say what I should have said already. "You're not my son ... you bastard, you're not Alex!"

He does not look surprised.

"I've been to that home where you and Alex lived. I know all about the two of you. And you killed him and came here, stealing his identity, wanting my money. I suppose Gary complicated things. Got in the way. But you soon got rid of him. You then just wanted to fake my suicide at the right moment. I guess this is it. Well, it isn't."

He stands there, looking distressed, as though he suddenly regrets everything he has done, is about to try to do. Kill me.

I lower my voice, speaking as calmly as I can. "You don't

need to do this. We can find a way through." My voice crackles with tension. "You didn't have to do any of it." I press on. "You could have had everything I have. I loved you. As a son. You still could, if ..."

My voice ebbs away. He seems to be in such torment, his head tipped back as though he is about to howl in the night.

"I didn't want to." He speaks quietly, quickly, close to sobbing. "Any of it. It's just ... what we ... you're such a nice person. But I have to." He looks at me, steeling himself. This is my last chance.

I take a step towards him. He looks frightened. Another step. He seems so confused. I go to embrace him. And then I stop. His phone is beeping. *Beep. Beep. Beep.* An incoming call or message.

He glances at the message. I see his face change, hardening, becoming determined. He reaches into his back pocket. Pulls out a knife he's got from the rack in the kitchen. He fumbles it, and I somehow lurch forward, knocking it to the floor.

I reach it first, turning and stabbing him hard in the chest. He steps back, making a gulping, gasping sound. I pull out the knife as he stands there. About to come at me. But then he collapses down onto the floor.

I crouch over him. His eyes seem to be looking at a point beyond my shoulder. Then they focus on mine, and I lean forward as he tries to say something through laboured, heavy breathing.

"I love Alex," he manages to say, half-smiling, half-grimacing towards me. His head turns slightly, and he gives me something close to a sickly-sweet grin.

I wait, watching him, hoping that my blow is enough – I

cannot face stabbing him again and again. I will if I have to, though. Eventually, his eyes close. I sob with relief.

And then I am spent. I roll over, lying next to Liam's body, the knife still in his chest, as it gurgles and whirrs its way to death and, finally, silence.

I LIE HERE, in this eternity of silence. The house is still. No sounds from the close. There is not even a hum of traffic from the A14 on the edge of the estate. The wind must be blowing the other way.

I try to work out, in my mind, which way that means the wind is blowing. North, I think. Or west. I laugh at my silly, nonsensical thoughts. My stunned mind going this way and that, desperately seeking normality.

Then I am crying. Not for Liam, but for myself – that I let this monstrous situation develop and unfold in the way it has. So that I am here now with one dead body next to me and the other buried down in the garden. I cry for Gary, as well. And even Chloe.

Finally, I sit up, tears and snot running down my face, and I wipe my lips and cheeks with the back of my hands. Then my hands, on my pyjama top.

I look over at Liam and am repulsed by his wide staring eyes and hanging-open mouth. I get unsteadily to my feet and walk, hesitantly, holding the banister rail, to the top of the stairs.

I sit here, my head in my hands, reliving every minute of all that has happened. Realising I should have done something different at every stage.

I should have asked Liam for ID when he arrived.

Demanded a DNA test early on.

That would have avoided all of this, everything.

When he turned up that first night, mugged, or so he said, I should have taken him back to his bed and breakfast. His scheme unravelling there and then.

If only I had listened to Gary's doubts, and we had confronted Liam together. Gary would be alive today.

When Liam killed Gary – and I believe now that was a premeditated murder to get him out the way – I should have gone straight to the police.

When I uncovered the truth about Liam at the children's home, I should have called the police.

Handed myself in. Taken what's coming to me.

I should not have come back home, trying to find my way through to happiness with Ryan.

But now, at last, I have come to a decision. The right one. The only one. I go and fetch my phone from the bedside cabinet in my room, slip on my dressing gown, and then walk slowly downstairs to call the police. I will tell the truth.

I cannot live my life as a lie. Liam dragged down, if I could, to the garage and left there, rotting. Gary under the soil, another ever-present reminder. The fear of exposure always there. Every minute of the day and night.

I will explain everything that happened, and hope that the police, the jury and the judge will be merciful. I may perhaps be found 'not guilty' of murder. If not, I will take what's coming to me and serve my sentence. Then walk free and start a new life. With Ryan, maybe.

I sit there, on the carpet in the living room, for a while, thinking of the words and sentences to say. Then I click into my phone and see that I have had three calls from Ryan. In the past fifteen minutes. I did not hear them, as I mute the sound at night.

And there is also a message – not from Ryan but *to* Ryan, from my phone. Sent, I guess, from my bedside cabinet by Liam before he attacked me, dragging me from my bed. It reads:

'I'm sorry, Ryan. I killed Gary. I can't live with myself anymore. I love you. Nina.'

So I was right about Liam. All of it. I sob with relief, knowing, from the three missed calls, that Ryan is coming for me.

I sit here, crying to myself for five, ten, fifteen minutes. And then, suddenly, I hear noises at the front door, someone rattling the handle as if wanting to come in. Ryan!

I rally, feeling my strength inside. Yes, I will tell the whole truth of what happened. If the police, the courts, whoever, decide this was all down to Liam, I may just walk free and into the waiting arms of Ryan. I still have a chance of lifelong happiness.

RYAN IS COMING round the back. I hear the gate being opened, footsteps on the patio and, finally, the kitchen door being pulled open. He's in the house.

I take a step towards the kitchen to greet him. The nightmare is over. I stand there, smiling at the figure in the kitchen doorway.

The smile is wiped from my face as I stagger back, my hand to my mouth, stunned into silence. My mind, my thoughts, my feelings, shatter into a million pieces.

"Hello, Mummy." He – the young man – says it in a

mocking, sing-song voice. He looks at me with contempt, hatred even.

I stand there, stunned. This is not my son. It is not. It cannot be. I don't want it to be.

But it is. The shock of brown hair. My forehead. My eyes. Ryan's nose. His chin. An unmistakeable merging of Ryan and me. It is the real Alex. Not dead. Alive.

I shake my head, unable to speak.

I open my mouth, wanting to say something. I don't know what.

I shake my head again, wondering what this means. All the times Liam was going out to see friends at the pier – he was meeting Alex.

He moves like he is dancing, a step this side, a step that, into the room, towards me.

Angles his head, looking at me, assessing, reaching his conclusions.

He smirks and then giggles, an incongruous sound, at his thoughts, whatever they are.

"You're meant to be dead," he says. He crooks his head at an angle. "Why aren't you dead?"

I shrug, stuttering, "I-I don't know."

"Where's Liam?" he demands, in a harsher voice. "He's not picking up his phone."

The tone of his voice – the threat in it – spurs me into speech, to save myself. "He's gone out ... to find you, I guess." If I tell the truth, that Liam's dead, he will kill me here and now.

He pulls out his phone, pressing buttons, stopping, listening. He pulls a face and puts the phone back in his pocket.

I can see the anger rising within him. His face is flushed,

and the whole shape of his body seems to change. He is ready to attack.

"I guess he bottled it," he says quickly. "Couldn't bring himself to do it. I'll have to."

I reply, buying myself time, "He's gone looking for you, telling him what to do next."

"You worked it out, then?" he asks. "Our plan?"

I shake my head. Then nod. And say, sounding calmer than I feel, "I think so. Tell me about it." I go on, "I know you and Liam were in that home together. Were friends. I found out that much."

He looks back at me. "He's the love of my life."

I swallow and nod – that makes sense – and say, "You found out about me. Liam came here to scam me out of my money. Gary was in the –"

He interrupts, his voice rising. "We were both in and out of foster care ... children's homes ... paedos, most of them ... and we ended up together at Springham. We fell in love."

He hesitates, then continues, "Me and Liam were both abandoned at birth by scum like you. *Mothers* is too good a word for you all."

I go to say something, to tell the truth of how I've felt all these years – the love I have for him – but he just raises his voice and keeps talking.

"When we were eighteen, we traced our birth mothers. We were going to kill you both. Have you seen that film *Strangers On A Train?*"

"The Hitchcock one, where they swap murders so they won't get caught? Yes, I know it." I feel a sense of horror.

"But you have money, lots of money, so we changed our plan. Liam was going to see how much he could screw out of you. You're so stupid."

I nod, breathing deeply, not sure how to respond. Even now, I want to say *I love you*. To stop this horror. But the words stick in my throat.

"Then your stupid boyfriend got in the way. But we got rid of him. We thought we'd get even more out of you."

We are beyond *I love you* now. There is no turning back. I don't know how this will end.

"And now, tonight, you've been talking about this Ryan and how you're going to marry him and live happily ever after. So we're not going to get your money. He will." He makes a derisive, snorting sound.

I move my hands from my sides to my dressing gown pockets and feel the whittling knife by my right hand. I unfold it slowly.

"So," he says, "we changed the plan again. You commit suicide. Liam vanishes. I turn up in a week or two's time, having read about it in the newspapers. Mummy's dead! I inherit everything!" He laughs out loud. On and on. Like he's mad.

I turn the knife in my right-hand pocket round ever so slowly so that my fingers are on the handle.

"I hate you so much," he says. His voice cracks, even though he's trying to sound matter-of-fact.

He takes a step forward. I know what he wants to do. Drag me upstairs and throw me out the window.

Then go back and search for Liam at the pier, the amusements, wherever he thinks he might be.

But, of course, Liam lies dead in that back bedroom with the wide-open window.

And I am not going to be dragged back upstairs. I won't be murdered by this evil boy.

I still want to say, to tell him, *I love you. I have always loved you more than anything.*

But I don't. It is too late. There is only one ending now. It's him or me. I can manipulate how it goes. I grasp the knife tightly. And I prepare the words I am going to say.

"I killed Liam," I tell him carefully. "He's up there now. Dead on the floor in the back bedroom. Where he tried to kill me. Go on ... go and see."

I expect Alex to rush towards me, shoving me to one side, sobbing as he runs up the stairs to his dead lover.

And I will have a choice. I can go out of the front door into the close, running away. Or, as Alex goes by me, I can stab him in the neck, an artery, and watch him fall at my feet. I know the ending I will choose.

But it does not happen like that. I watch as his face twists and turns in a mix of disbelief and then anger and, finally, heartbreak. And then he runs at me, pulling something from his pocket.

I try to tug the knife from mine, but it gets caught in the fabric of my dressing gown. I have a second or two to think I can yank it out in time and defend myself with it.

But I feel the savage stab of a knife in my chest, see the malevolence in his face so close to mine, and then I am falling to the floor. I am still conscious and am terrified now, fearing the agony of dying. I hope it will be as swift and as painless as possible.

I scream in pain as he pulls the knife out. And then I see him crouching down and raising the knife, plunging it into my chest again and again. I remember the first. And the second. Then, finally, he strikes the third devastating blow.

EPILOGUE

The young man with a shock of brown hair stands on the pavement, looking up at the big, detached house set well back from the road. The house is decorated lavishly with flickering Christmas figures of Santa and a snowman up high on the walls, and fairy lights down below and all around the surrounding bushes. A new 4x4 is parked on the gravel driveway.

The young man tips back his head and takes a deep breath. *This place reeks of money,* he thinks, not for the first time, and then breaks into laughter.

He's been living nearby for a while now, in a bedsit, and working in a pizza takeaway in the town centre, half a mile up the road. Biding his time.

He has been by this house on many occasions over the past few months, watching the woman and waiting for this moment. He has delivered pizzas on a putt-putt moped to neighbours.

Not so long ago, he got into the conversation with an

elderly man, in a too-big-for-him house over the road, and discovered what he needed to know.

The woman is a widower, her older husband dying of a heart attack at just forty-seven a year ago. A few days before Christmas. The anniversary today.

"She's been so brave," the elderly man said. "But she's so independent. She won't let anyone help her. We've all tried."

"And the house is so big," the elderly man went on, desperate for someone to talk to. "And all that money. She won't know what to do with it."

The young man has been here, within sight of the house, all morning, turning aside as the woman drove by in her big smart car. On the way to the cemetery, with flowers, to pay her respects, he assumed.

He has been to the cemetery several times, finding the grave and the headstone easily. A shiny black monstrosity with gold lettering: 'Michael James Cartwright – A Good Old Essex Boy' on it. Stood there for hours, smiling to himself.

Then she came back, roaring her car by him, up the road, his back to her, turning as he watched the car go up the driveway to that big, expensive house.

And so he now walks up the driveway, his boots crunch, crunch, crunching on the gravel, and he rehearses what he's going to say in his head. He does not really need to – he knows it by heart.

He steps into the porch, two six-foot Christmas trees to either side of the ornate front door. More wealth and riches. He gazes at the hand-made wreath on the door, and it reminds him of the one they had at the children's home in Springham. Not that there was any happiness there.

He raises his hand to the doorbell, then stops, listening to the sounds of laughter inside. The noises trouble him, but only for an instant. He hesitates for a second or two, then presses the doorbell.

He hears footsteps running down the staircase, more giggling and happy shrieks, and the door is opened. The woman stands before him. Face-to-face for the first time. She is in her late thirties, but looks older. Her face is lined and strained. She stares at him.

"Rachel Cartwright?" he asks. A strange expression crosses her face as she nods a reply. *She knows,* he thinks. *She knows.* And he delights in the moment.

"I'm Liam ... your son," he says, unable to stifle a snigger as he watches her stepping back, stumbling and falling to the floor. He does not move forward to help her.

Instead, he walks over her into the hallway and looks around at the opulent furniture and decorations. *This,* he thinks, *will soon be mine.*

There are two pretty little girls, twins, maybe three or four years old, standing at the foot of the stairs. They watch, unable to move, until eventually, one reaches out to hold the hand of the other.

"Hello, poppets!" The young man smiles as he walks towards them, going down on his knees and putting his arms around them. He pulls them close to him.

As the woman sits up, dazed and struggling to clear her mind, she sees the young man with the shock of brown hair – Alexander James Bolitho – hugging her frightened children. "Mummy!" he says, smiling brightly at her. "I'm home."

ABOUT THE AUTHOR

Did you enjoy *The New Son*? If you could spend a moment to write an honest review on Amazon, no matter how short, we would be extremely grateful. They really do help readers discover new authors.

Iain Maitland is the author of three previous psych thrillers for Inkubator Books: *The Soulmate, The Perfect Husband* and *The Girl Downstairs*.

Iain is also the author of two memoirs, *Dear Michael, Love Dad*, a book of letters written to his eldest son who experienced depression and anorexia, and (co-authored with Michael) *Out Of The Madhouse*.

He has also written a semi-autobiographical novel, *The Old Man, His Dog & Their Longest Journey*.

He is an Ambassador for Stem4, the teenage mental health charity. He talks regularly about mental health issues in schools and colleges and workplaces.

You can find Iain on his website:
www.iainmaitland.net

ACKNOWLEDGMENTS

Bringing a book from an author's mind to readers' hands is always a team effort, and I am very pleased and grateful that a terrific team has worked on *The New Son* with me.

Thank you Brian at Inkubator Books for commissioning *The New Son* off the back of my rambling thoughts about the set-up of the story and my incoherent ideas about where it might go.

I believe every author needs an excellent editor to produce story notes and line edits, stating 'more of this', 'less of that' and 'no-oo-oo'. Alice, you did a brilliant job.

Lizzie and Nebojsa – a fab cover is so important and you delivered it – the best yet!

Thanks again to Brian for writing the blurb – as important as the cover and another cracker.

Thanks too to Jodi for your copyediting services.

Pauline – as ever, thank you for your proofreading expertise.

Thank you as well, Claire, for seeing it through formatting.

Best of all, the Inkubator Books team is professional and calm and friendly whilst I just bounce off the walls and the floor and the ceiling – thank you, everyone, and I hope we will all be back again for my next psych thriller, provisionally titled *You're All Mine*.

PS. And finally, thank you as always Barbara for your cover quote – our next lunch is on me.

AUTHOR'S NOTES

When I am close to finishing writing a pysch, I have a zoom meeting with Brian at Inkubator Books where I pitch three outlines and we choose the story I will write next. So, after *The Soulmate*, we agreed I would write this psych, *The New Son*.

I'm not sure how other authors pitch outlines, but, hand on heart, I'm not terribly good at it. I rather suspect my fellow authors have everything planned out: chapter headings, key twists and turns and the ending. Not me.

I have the initial set-up – the new son at the front door – and the characters, Nina, Liam, Gary, etc. But I have no idea where I'm going with them nor the ending. So I kind of babble away to Brian about how this might happen, or that, and, um, anyway. Fortunately, Brian said to give this one a go.

The fact is, I really don't know where the characters and story will take me. Those of you who write will know that, as you get into a story, the characters kind of take over and lead you where they want to go. If you don't write, that probably sounds bonkers. Maybe it is.

I really try to create a strong cast – Nina and Liam to start with – and a compelling idea: her long-lost son arriving after nineteen years. That gives me a sense of where I am going – happy ever after? Well, perhaps not in a psych thriller.

I then mix in more troubling characters – Gary, Chloe, Gemma – who will get in the way of that happy ending. By the time I've got into the first part of the book – the happy part – the characters come to life and they're taking the story forwards.

I've now had my next zoom with Brian at Inkubator Books, pitching three more ideas, and we've agreed the next one I write will be *You're All Mine*.

Sophie has everything in her life except a baby. Her best friend, Lucy, offers to have a baby for her. And Sophie wants a baby more than anything in the whole, wide world …

I've just started writing this, and all being well, it will be out later this year. If you're looking for other titles to read in the meantime, please do check out *The Soulmate*, *The Perfect Husband* and *The Girl Downstairs*, by me, and all from Inkubator Books.

All for now, see you soon.

Best Wishes

Iain Maitland
18 January 2024

PS. I should have said – I usually set my pyschs in real places, usually Felixstowe, my home town. I've done the same this time with one exception.

Springham in Essex is not a real place. There's a Springfield, but it's not that, nor is my Springham based on Springfield. It's just a similar-sounding name.

And, of course, the book is a work of fiction – the characters, the story, the ending, all of it just comes from my mind.

ALSO BY IAIN MAITLAND

The Girl Downstairs

The Perfect Husband

The Soulmate

The New Son

Printed in Great Britain
by Amazon

39752724R00152